Tell Me One Thing

Tell Me One Thing

 STORIES

DEENA GOLDSTONE

 Nan A. Talese | DOUBLEDAY

NEW YORK LONDON TORONTO SYDNEY AUCKLAND

GOLDSTONE, D.

Copyright © 2014 by Deena Goldstone

All rights reserved. Published in the United States by Nan A. Talese/Doubleday, a division of Random House LLC, New York, and in Canada by Random House of Canada Limited, Toronto, Penguin Random House companies.

www.nanatalese.com

DOUBLEDAY is a registered trademark of Random House LLC. Nan A. Talese and the colophon are trademarks of Random House LLC.

Book design by Pei Loi Koay
Jacket design by Emily Mahon
Jacket photograph © Jan Stromme / The Image Bank / Getty Images

LIBRARY OF CONGRESS CATALOGING-IN-PUBLICATION DATA
Goldstone, Deena.
[Short stories. Selections]
Tell Me One Thing : Stories / Deena Goldstone. —
First Edition
pages   cm
I. Title.
PS3607.O48595A6 2014
813'.6—dc23   2013029513

ISBN 978-0-385-53875-6 (hardcover)
ISBN 978-0-385-53876-3 (eBook)

MANUFACTURED IN THE UNITED STATES OF AMERICA

10 9 8 7 6 5 4 3 2 1

First Edition

To Marty, for his steadfast belief

and

To Eva, for the gift of her spirit

Contents

Tell Me One Thing

Get Your Dead Man's Clothes

SITTING IN ST. TIMOTHY'S CATHEDRAL DUR-
ing his father's funeral Mass, Jamie has no idea how the rest of his
brothers and sisters feel about their father's death, but he knows
what he is feeling—nothing. Of that he is sure. Over the forty-two
years of his life he has cultivated nothingness when it comes to
his father, assiduously. Number seven in the line of eight children,
Jamie had ample opportunity to observe the wrong way to deal
with Hugh Casey O'Connor Sr.

His oldest brother, Hugh Jr., had taken his father on—matched
his screaming rants with his own screaming assaults. Their
fighting filled up the house with accusations and hateful words
and sometimes whacks and punches. Years later, all that rancor
seemed to drain away as soon as the two sat down over an open
bottle.

The next brother in the line, Kevin, sidestepped the arguments
but not the need for his father's attention. He played football in
the autumn, basketball in the winter, and ran track in the spring,
a star in all three, never happier than when his father showed up

to watch. And unfailingly sullen and disappointed on the far more frequent occasions when Hugh didn't. Jamie could see that it mattered far too much to Kevin what the old man thought.

Drew was born next, and he carved out a niche as his father's toady. He narrowed his sight to the public persona—the Hugh who went out of his way to help a neighbor build a back porch or the Hugh who drove old Mrs. Brennan to the doctor when her daughter couldn't get away from work. Drew refused to be disillusioned by the private Hugh who never lifted a finger at home and spent most of the weekends hurling criticisms at his various sons. The heart sees what the heart needs to see, so wherever their father was, Drew was by his side, frequently yelled at for some transgression never spelled out. Whatever the behavior of the old man, it only bonded Drew more closely to him.

Three girls came next—Moira, Kate, and Ellen—and they didn't count, Jamie thinks, because his father treated them so differently. Hugh left the girls to their mother to discipline and raise. What did he know about girls, Hugh always said. He allowed them leeway he'd never have allowed his sons, who were, after all, reflections on his own self.

By the time Jamie came along eleven months after Ellen, there was a whole diorama of behaviors in front of him, all instructive of how not to deal with Hugh Sr.'s temper and drinking and wily charm and basic, underlying need to humiliate his sons lest they get too big for their britches or, more likely, upstage the old man.

When Marianne was born ten years after Jamie, all bets were off. She was the baby, long after anyone thought there would be more children, and she got the best of everything.

HIS MOTHER, SITTING BESIDE HIM in St. Timothy's now, latches onto his hand. She doesn't turn in her seat or look at him, just grabs his hand for comfort. Somehow he has always known that he is his mother's favorite. Maybe it is because he was the only one who would sit glued to her side, eyes wide, on those rare occasions when she read to them. Even as a toddler, he would bring her well-worn picture books with loops of Crayola marks over most of the pages and ask to be read to. Sometimes, when she could, his mother would stop whatever she was doing, find an armchair, let him climb into her lap, and spend five minutes reading the book to him. It was only when Jamie was much older that he understood that she cherished these small respites in her day as much as he.

Jamie can see that she is destroyed by the old man's death, but it makes no sense to him. Hugh had had little use for women, unless they were young and pretty, and Carrie O'Connor had never been either as far as he could tell. His parents' wedding picture, sitting in a tarnished frame on top of the bookcase, provides ample evidence. What Jamie sees when he looks at that picture—and he finds himself staring at it more often than he thinks reasonable—is a thin woman wearing a navy blue suit, her sharp features scowling into the camera, her dark hair pulled away from her narrow face, and looking well older than her twenty-two years. Whatever was she thinking? he often wondered but never asked.

Today his mother is weeping, a creased handkerchief pressed to her lips. He glances over at his eldest sister, Moira, sitting on the other side of Carrie, holding her other hand. She is the sensible one of the bunch. Never a beauty, taking after their father with her sturdy frame and unruly auburn hair, she married a neighborhood boy who's in the trades, an electrician, and had her five kids quickly. It has always been Moira who checks in daily with their mother. She'll be the one to make sure Carrie gets on with things once their father is in the ground. Jamie is grateful to her but never says so. In their family there's little talk of anything that has to do with gratitude or vulnerability.

Moira seems fine. She long ago figured out the old man was a bullshit artist. But Ellen, sitting farther down the pew, looks like she's going to faint. Something has happened to her in the years she's been away. All the flesh seems to have melted off her, and the skin that is left is stretched too tightly across her face and large bones. Her collarbone looks naked. Her wrists are too large. The bones of her pelvis push through her black skirt in a painful thrust.

Jamie knows Ellen left the United States to be away from their father. Hugh Sr. had cast too large a shadow over every decision Ellen tried to make. In an act of desperation, she fled to Europe, settling in Malaga, a small town in Spain. Jamie doesn't know much of what she does there. "She's made a life for herself," his mother always says. Jamie has no idea what that means. But he figures she must speak Spanish by now, and that is more than the other seven of them have managed to do.

The woman sitting on the other side of Ellen, who came with her from Spain, looks straight ahead, her fingers busy on a rosary. She is small and older than Ellen and has a faint mustache above her lipsticked mouth. She seems to speak no English, so no one in the family has managed to figure out who she is to Ellen. There is speculation, but no one has asked directly. Contrary to what he guesses his brothers and sisters think, Jamie has the weird idea she is some kind of nurse or caretaker. It's the way she keeps Ellen in her proprietary sights and whispers to her from time to time. If he can get Ellen alone later, Jamie thinks, he may be able to ask her, but the chance of some quiet in his mother's house isn't likely.

AT THE CEMETERY, THE BROTHERS AND SISTERS stand in a line at the north side of the grave. No one suggested it, they just fell into the old order—Hugh, Kevin, Drew, Moira, Kate, Ellen, Jamie, and Marianne, the boys dark and sharp featured like their mother, the girls ruddy and large boned like their father. Only Marianne is truly lovely.

Hugh Sr. would line all eight of his children up in that very same order every Sunday to make sure the boys' ties were straight, that there were no smart-alecky attitudes evident, and that the girls had combed each other's hair. Then they'd pile into the family car, a sensible station wagon that came off the assembly line in Detroit, and drive the five minutes to St. Timothy's for Sunday Mass. Even today Jamie remembers that stuffy, crowded car where his brothers surreptitiously elbowed and punched each other in a vain attempt to get more space, an inch more breathing room, and his father screamed at them to shut up. As an adult he understands that car ride to be the perfect metaphor for his whole childhood.

Carrie wouldn't come to the cemetery. She said there was no way she could watch her husband of fifty-four years lowered into the ground. Her children would have to bear witness at their father's burial. It was her sister, Norah, who took her back to the house—the same narrow house they all grew up in—to help her lay out the food and wait for the children's return.

As the oldest son, it falls to Hugh Jr. to pick up the shovel. Jamie can tell he's barely sober enough to do it. Stumbling a bit, Hugh hefts a mound of damp earth and dumps it into the open grave. The sound of the clods hitting the wooden casket is star-tlingly loud. Jamie looks around—it's the stillness of the air in the cemetery that accentuates the sound. They are the only family there. No one else is being buried on this April day, so he can hear the rustle of Kate's silk dress as she shifts her weight onto her other leg, impatient. She wants this all to be over, bored and rest-less as she always is.

It's warmer than it has a right to be this time of year. The air is lovely and expectant before the grand rush of spring. The breeze only a whisper through the leafless trees, certainly not strong enough to cool the air, and the grandchildren, scattered around the other sides of the open grave, are already shedding sweaters and jackets.

Drew clears his throat and Jamie looks over quickly to see that Drew is trying hard not to cry. Jamie can't believe it, after all the grief the old man gave his brother.

When do you stop loving a parent? Jamie wonders. How much can a child take before that stubborn flame of necessary love sputters and dies? Moira would know the answer to that, he thinks, because she's busy whispering to her teenage son, Sean, and doesn't seem to take much notice of the dark brown casket lying just below her feet.

What happens to you, his train of thought goes, *if you never let that feeling in?* He can't remember a time he ever felt anything but fear toward his father. Fear and a desire to get away from him. Even on those nights when Hugh had had just enough to drink so that he was expansive and not so much to drink that he was dangerous, even then Jamie kept his distance. He knew the line could be crossed with lightning speed, well before anyone else could figure out where it was, and that his father would reach out and grab him, force him to stand in front of his blustery, perspiring face as he shook him and yelled accusations that made no sense to a seven-year-old.

What did it matter that the next morning while his father was drinking his coffee and reading the sports section that he would reach over and ruffle Jamie's hair with some sort of all-purpose, one-size-fits-all endearment? "There's my boy" was about as far as Hugh Sr. would go, and even at seven Jamie was sure his father didn't know which son he was talking to, head in the paper, his attention on the box scores from the day before.

And then, as the boys grew and their transgressions pro-

gressed into teenage rebellion, their father's punishments escalated accordingly. Hugh Sr. thought nothing of beating his sons
until his arm or the belt gave out, or kicking them down the stairs,
or even, one time when Jamie was fourteen, chasing him around
the house with a butcher knife grabbed from the kitchen counter
in a rage.

"He'd had too much to drink" was his mother's attempt at an
explanation the next morning. "You know how he gets."

"I know and so do you," Jamie's voice rising in pitch. "So why
do you put up with it?"

"Ahhh, Jamie, you wouldn't understand" was his mother's only
answer.

"Would you have let him kill me?" burst out of him before he
could think about it. "That's what he was yelling—that it was my
time to die!"

"You're making too much of it." Carrie turned away, packing
lunch boxes in the small kitchen.

"He had a knife!" Jamie fairly screamed.

"Did he not apologize this morning?"

"What difference does that make?! He'll only do it again."

And then Marianne came into the kitchen with her hairbrush
and two ribbons for Carrie to make her braids and their mother
turned gratefully away from Jamie's accusations, stated and
implied. *Where were you,* he wanted to ask, *why didn't you protect
me?* But he didn't, because he understood finally, clear as day, that
nothing was going to change in his parents' house. He shut up
about it and began to plot his escape. He set his sights on college
as his savior, a goal so far from his father's world that it felt safe.

Hugh Jr. wasn't interested in college at all. To no one's surprise, he joined his father in the small plumbing business the
old man had been running for more than twenty years. That way
their ongoing battles could continue. Now they argued about the

quality of copper piping or the need for low-flow toilets instead of about grades or curfew, but it didn't matter—the battles were what they wanted, the particulars were as changeable as the weather.

Kevin won an athletic scholarship to Holy Cross but never managed to distinguish himself in any sport once he was there. Jamie wasn't surprised when he got a coaching job at St. Sebastian Prep, not twenty minutes from the house they all grew up in.

Drew never managed to settle himself into any work. He took over the third-floor dormitory where all four boys were once housed, a ghost now, who came and went without explanation. Carrie shrugged her shoulders when one or another of the children would ask about Drew. "He's finding himself," she'd say and change the subject.

Jamie knew from the night of the kitchen knife attack that he was putting as much distance between himself and his father as he could. He applied only to colleges on the West Coast, those in Oregon, Washington, and California. When he chose San Diego State, where he reasoned the weather would be warm and the academic demands would be manageable, his father flatly refused to give him a dime, not for a school in California that wasn't even a Catholic college. That was his explanation, but Jamie suspected he just didn't want to spend any money on him.

Jamie went anyway. His first semester was paid for by money carefully saved from working summers all through high school, and still he had to work two jobs to make it through. Each semester after that was touch and go. Sometimes he managed the tuition, sometimes he had to drop out and work for a while to be able to reenroll. It took him longer than most to get his degree, but he accomplished it as well as another year of graduate work, which gave him his teaching credential. Now he taught English to middle schoolers at a charter school in San Diego and managed to never go home to visit. His father's funeral was the exception. He thought about skipping it, had talked to Moira about the fallout if he did, but allowed himself to be persuaded. "You need to do this for her," she had said, "not for the old bastard. I can't imagine how she'd get through it without you there." And Jamie didn't argue. He knew he had to go.

AT THE BRICK HOUSE ON CROSSLEY LANE where they all grew up, cars start arriving, one after another of his brothers and sisters and their families. Everyone parks on the street out of habit. It was a pet peeve of their father's—finding somebody's car in the driveway when he wanted to put his car into or take it out of the garage. So the edict—anyone parking in the driveway would be in serious trouble. What that trouble might be was never spelled out, but it didn't matter—the driveway remained bare.

As Jamie turns left onto Crossley Lane after his father's burial, he heads straight for the empty driveway and parks his rental car halfway up, just by the kitchen door.

Already the house is filling up with noise and far too many people. There is Moira, talking nonstop, bossy as always, ushering her five children into the house with an admonition here and there to watch their manners, her husband, Robbie, bringing up the rear, his preferred place.

Then Hugh Jr.'s family spills out of their SUV parked at the curb. Tina, his long-suffering wife, having assessed her husband's condition, is at the wheel. Hugh stumbles out of the passenger's side as their four adult children make their desultory way up the front path, doing their best to ignore their embarrassing father.

Kevin and Loretta are already inside. Jamie can hear her chirpy voice exclaiming how beautiful the service was, how the words of Father Malachi lifted her soul, and the day, did you ever see a more beautiful April day?! *God,* Jamie thinks, *doesn't she ever get tired of being so relentlessly upbeat?* Maybe that's why Kevin has mastered his consistently negative take on almost everything—to have some breathing room of his own. They have three children, all boys, all athletes, one even in the minor league system of some major league baseball team. He's the only one Kevin talks about, worrying constantly that Mark might suffer a career-ending injury and then what will he do?

Kate arrives with her two equally bored, but well-dressed, children. When Kate married up and moved to Atlanta, she shed her working-class identity as fast as she could say "I do." Her husband refused to fly into Buffalo for the funeral. "Buffalo?" he said. "Why would I want to go to Buffalo?" And Kate was relieved. She didn't want to spend the whole three days making excuses for the ways of her family.

Through the leaded glass windows of the dining room, Jamie can see Marianne bent over the heavy wooden table that served as the dinnertime battleground every night of their lives. She holds her youngest in one arm and rearranges platters with the other. *She's the only one who married smart,* Jamie thinks. Everyone loves her husband, Kent, unassuming but solid, generous and slyly funny. They have a set of twins and two younger children, all under six.

As Jamie enters the crowded kitchen, he stands for a minute and takes stock of his extended family. Five married, but only one married well. Three single—Drew, Ellen, and himself. *Is that about average for a large family,* he wonders, *one happy marriage out of eight?* Are most members of large families victims of the same kind of train wreck that he now understands his family to have been? It's possible that many families, large or small, are train wrecks, but he doesn't know. Never close to forming a family of his own, never attaching himself as a surrogate member to any other family, he has had little to compare the O'Connors to. He knows only what he felt growing up in this cramped, chaotic house they all congregate in now. And he knows only because he has been away, because the perspective of the West Coast has let him see his early years with fresh eyes.

He believes he sees more than his brothers and sisters, but he doesn't know what to do with this sight. Like everything else, he files it away and presents to the world a slightly bland facade, polite but not very approachable, competent but never impressive. It's almost as if he used up all his intensity growing up and now lives in the narrow band of emotions that's left over.

He can't say the same for the rest of his siblings. Already, Hugh Jr.'s voice carries over the scores of others packed in the small kitchen, loud and insistent and more than a little drunk.

"You're not listening to me!" he yells at Moira, who yells right back at him.

"Because you're drunk and you're not making any sense!"

"Who the hell are you to criticize me?!" Hugh yells before Tina is at his side, talking softly to him, trying to ease him out of the kitchen, but he's having none of it.

"You can barely stand up—I thought you were going to topple into the open grave when you hefted that shovel! That's what you wanted, isn't it, locked in with Dad for all eternity?!"

"Shut up!" is yelled even louder than Moira's elevated voice. This is from Drew, who has been leaning against the kitchen counter, downing beer after beer. "Don't talk about Dad like that!"

"Why not?" And this is from Kate, who has dropped her bored and superior attitude and descended into the maddening, loud muddle that is the O'Connor clan arguing. Apparently, the urge to participate is irresistible. "You think he's so powerful he can hear us from the grave?! You do, don't you? You've never seen him for the small man he really was!"

"Who told you to come home?!" Drew screams at her as Jamie eases himself out of the hot and claustrophobic space and into the dining room.

Unbothered by the opera that's taking place in the kitchen, the grandchildren are helping themselves to food—ham slices and a variety of precut cheeses, potato salad, a roast turkey that one of his sisters brought, probably Moira.

"The old man deserves some respect, this day of all days!" Jamie can hear Drew scream above the din and the answering hawking laugh from Moira.

And then Ellen is at his elbow. "Mom's lying down. She asked for you," she says quietly.

"Okay." But he stops her before she can slip away, a hand on her brittle arm. Just eleven months between them and a shared tenderness for each other that couldn't be expressed anywhere else in their chaotic house, Jamie and Ellen relied on each other. "Did you want to come back for this?" he asks her now.

She looks at him sharply. "It's not a matter of want, is it?"

"Ellen, are things all right with you?"

"I don't know yet."

"Who's the woman with you?"

"Estella."

"Come on, Ellen."

And she knows exactly what he means—*I didn't ask her name, I need to know who she is to you*—but Ellen shakes her head at him. "Someone I need right now" is all she says, is all she can say. Then, "Go on in to Mom. She's waiting."

INSIDE HIS PARENTS' BEDROOM, the heavy drapes are drawn against the late afternoon light. Their old wooden bed, bought with Hugh's first paycheck as a married man, is positioned against the far wall. When Jamie opens the door he immediately sees his mother lying on top of the spread, feet crossed at the ankles, her good shoes still on, a wrist over her closed eyes as if she has a headache. Even as Jamie closes the door, he can still hear the kitchen debate escalate further as Hugh gets drunker and Drew gets louder and Moira won't let the boys bulldoze her.

Jamie sits beside his mother gently on the bed. "Do you have a headache?"

"I never believed this day would come."

"What? You thought Dad was immortal?" Jamie says it with as much lightness in his voice as he can muster.

Carrie opens her eyes and looks at her best-loved son. "No, I was sure I would go before he did."

"I'm glad you didn't."

She shakes her head back and forth—she doesn't agree with him. Today her grief is too large to encompass.

"I need you to do something for me."

"Anything, Mom."

"Take his clothes. Take them out of here. Now. I can't look at them hanging there while your father is in the ground."

"All right, I will. Just tell me what you want me to do with—"

"Take them to St. Timothy's," she says as she rolls onto her side, away from him, away from what she knows will happen next. She can't watch it. "They'll give them to people in need."

Jamie nods, but she can't see him. He opens the closet door and stares at what's in front of him. If someone didn't know his father, he'd be able to guess a great deal from the clothes hanging there. All day long, for over fifty years, Hugh Sr. wore overalls and T-shirts for his work as a plumber, but when he dressed in his own clothes they had to be expensive and finely made. The clothes hanging in front of Jamie's eyes seem fit for a man well above the station Hugh Sr. occupied in life. It was a startling aspect of

his father—that he outfitted himself in such splendor and that
he was so fastidious about his personal care. Jamie has memories
of his father coming in from work and cleaning his hands in the
mudroom sink, meticulously washing them over and over with his
special soap and cleaning his nails with a brush he kept there just
for that purpose.

Carrie thought it was a kindness that Hugh performed each
night—to wash away the day's filth. Jamie always saw it as one
more aspect of his father's narcissism, a sort of preening. And to
Jamie, the clothes say that, too. Silk shirts in soft colors—ocher,
beige, dove gray—and cashmere sweaters in rich, dark tones.
Hand-tailored shoes of supple Italian leather. Each item carefully
bought and meant to last forever. That way, slowly, Hugh had
accumulated a wardrobe of beautiful things. No one would know
that he spent his days mucking out blocked toilets or flat on his
back in the crawl space of a house wrestling with corroded pipes.
No one would know that he screamed at his wife or beat his kids.
No, here was a man who bought only the finest, who deserved
only the best.

Jamie grabs an armful of the shirts and makes his way out of
the bedroom. His brothers and sisters are too busy arguing in the
kitchen to pay him much mind. He knows if he asked for help
the job would go more quickly, but he doesn't. He just makes the
many trips he has to make from the bedroom to the open trunk of
his car quietly, wanting the singular satisfaction of taking out of
the house all this personal evidence of his father's life.

Back in the bedroom, the closet now empty, he opens the top
drawer of his father's bureau and contemplates the neatly folded
pajama sets. Hugh made Carrie iron his pajamas, and each set is
pristine and wrinkle free. As Jamie reaches into the drawer, he
uncovers a very old pair, washed and ironed so many times that
the images of horses on them have faded to shadows of their for-
mer selves. The reds have become faded browns and the blues are

all but violet, and yet, immediately, the sight of the pajamas floods him with a moment in his childhood long forgotten.

There is his father, in those very pajamas, brightly colored then, sprawled in front of the television, in the middle of the night, his legs straight in front of him, his bony feet bare and splayed, his arms hanging off the side of the easy chair he had always claimed as his own. Of course, there's a bottle of beer in his right hand, the empties scattered on the rug—Jamie can see the image as if it's a movie scene playing in his head. The television is flickering with some middle-of-the-night black-and-white movie, and there he is, maybe three years old, running into the room, terrified, he remembers now. He even remembers the nightmare that propelled him out of bed and down the two flights of stairs, something big and clawlike coming through the bedroom window. And in his memory he watches his three-year-old self crying, hiccuping really, his heart beating far too fast as he scrambles into his father's lap, whimpering, "Daddy, Daddy!" *Don't do it,* he wants to say, in a vain attempt to stave off what he knows is coming. He understands now, of course, that asking for comfort from his father was the wrong thing to do.

Hugh Sr. sputters awake, still drunk, and pushes his son's small body off of him before he even knows what he's doing. But it's the words Jamie remembers now, so many years later, words he would hear again and again—"You little shit, get out of my sight!"

Such a small moment, but it has Jamie bent over the dresser, forehead resting on the top, grieving for that small, frightened boy. *This is why I don't come home,* he tells himself, *the past is too present here.*

As if his mother is reading his thoughts, she says to him now, without turning over, her face to the wall, "He loved you children, Jamie, you know that."

And he feels it—a surge of anger, like a lit match, roaring

through him. It snaps his body straight. *Love?! What is she talking about?! What grotesque universe does she live in that she can call what his father gave him, love? Dead and buried and she's still defending him. At the expense of the truth ... at the expense of her children.*

Jamie scoops up the contents of the drawer and leaves the room; his mother's body stretched out on the bed, doesn't move.

Outside, he flings the pajamas on top of all the other clothes in his car trunk, starts to slam the lid closed, and then—an inspiration. He stops. Slowly now, with the calm that deeply embedded anger can bring, Jamie grabs one of his father's very expensive suit jackets and holds it up.

"Dead man's clothes!" he yells. "Get your dead man's clothes!"

One of the nephews, kicking a soccer ball back and forth on the front lawn, hears him and comes up the driveway.

"Hey, what's going on, Uncle Jamie?"

Jamie throws the jacket at him. "Take it," Jamie says, "and a shirt to go with it." He grabs one at random and tosses it also. "How 'bout a tie, or two—all silk, looks good with the shirt."

He shoves the ties into his nephew's arms. "Cool" is all the teenager says, but then there are more nephews there, grabbing clothes from the open trunk. Sweaters are pulled over heads, a silk dressing gown is grabbed by one of his nieces, shoes are slipped onto feet. And through it all, Jamie is shouting, "Dead man's clothes, come and get 'em!"

The back door opens and some of his brothers and sisters are there. Drew is outraged but Moira is laughing and grabs something, anything now, it doesn't matter, putting it on, parading down the driveway. Bits and pieces of Hugh Sr. thrown around from child to child, cousin to cousin, put on, exchanged, traded with another cousin, scraps of Hugh's dignity walking across the front lawn. Hugh Jr. wants the hats—fine, gray fedoras that he claims for his own. The pajamas go, armfuls of them, and even his father's underwear is grabbed by someone.

"Put 'em on, take 'em off. Trade 'em. Sell 'em. Whatever you want, but get 'em now—your dead man's clothes!" Jamie yells.

And it's then that he looks up and sees his mother standing in the open kitchen doorway, ashen, horrified at the blasphemy of what he's doing. Her eyes hold his and Jamie doesn't flinch, doesn't look away. There is no guilt in him. He wants her to know that he's doing this with pleasure, with gusto, with revenge. "Get your dead man's clothes!"

 *Irish Twins*

VERY EARLY ON A SUNDAY MORNING, BEFORE the sun is even up, on the one-year anniversary of their father's death, Ellen O'Connor arrives on her brother's doorstep and rings the bell. Despite having lived in San Diego for the past thirteen years, Jamie O'Connor can think of no one he would be glad to see at 5:17 a.m. He assumes someone's made a mistake, turns over, and goes back to sleep.

Standing in front of the third door in an identical line of weathered gray doors of the Casa Nuevo Villa, condo units that didn't even look "nuevo" when they were built in the eighties, Ellen checks her cell phone for Jamie's address. She's exhausted; maybe she's made a mistake. Having flown all night from Spain, where she has exiled herself for the past seven years, Ellen's not sure she's at the right unit. She is. She rings the bell again.

Jaime groans in his bed. *It's Sunday,* he wants to shout. *Can't they*—an undefined, amorphous "they" that encompasses almost the whole world—*leave me alone?!* Then he hears "Jamie?" and the familiarity of the voice pulls him out of bed.

From his second-floor bedroom window he can look down on his front doorstep, and there she is, his sister Ellen, standing at the door, one small duffel bag in hand. *Well, at least she's alive* is his first thought. The last time he saw her he wouldn't have made a bet on that possibility.

He opens the window, sticks his head out, "Ellen," and she steps back so she can see him and then gives him that smile he remembers so well from their childhood, the one that promised something slightly naughty.

"Surprise," she says. And he just nods. "What are the chances of you letting me in?"

"Slim to none," he says as he reaches for his jeans and whatever T-shirt he had thrown on the floor the night before.

When he swings open the front door, he is relieved to see that she looks so much better. A year ago, as the eight O'Connor children gathered in Buffalo to bury their father, something had been seriously wrong, but she wouldn't speak about it. She had reminded him of pictures he had seen of hollow-eyed people, dying of malnutrition. And then there was that strange woman who arrived with Ellen, spoke only Spanish, and never left his sister's side.

Now he can see she's gained back some weight, not a lot, but enough so she doesn't look like she belongs in Darfur. And he can see that her expression is more animated, there's the promise of some fun in her eyes that reassures him she's much closer to the Ellen he had grown up with, the Ellen he had relied on to get him through. It wasn't just the scant eleven months that separated them that made them so close. It was their unspoken pact that they both saw the same thing—the perpetual calamity that was the O'Connor family.

Once Jamie left Buffalo and had some distance, he often wondered if all large families shared the O'Connors' habit of carelessness and neglect. Was it just that there were too many children for any two parents to really ride herd on? In his family, the struggle was to get through each day with everyone dressed, the older kids off to school, and with some kind of food on the table at dinnertime. Figuring out which child needed what specific attention or taking the emotional temperature of any one of them was way beyond the scope of either his mother or father. Hugh Sr. was too busy drinking and his mother, Carrie, was too busy, period, simply tending to the maintenance of so many bodies.

But there was more, and Jamie came to understand this only as an adult. There was his father's narcissism and casual cruelty. How he got pleasure from calling his sons "you little shits." How, in the privacy of his own house, the words were hurled with scorn and derision, often accompanied with a back-of-the-hand slap, almost an afterthought, that always landed across a cheek or tender lip. How, in public, he'd announce with a broad smile and sometimes a hand clapped across a listener's shoulder, "I've got so many of these little shits running around, I can't remember all their names." There'd be laughter. A joke, Hugh was always ready with a joke. Nobody minded that in one sentence he'd managed to label his sons as worthless *and* obliterate their identities. Nobody, that is, except his sons.

What it took Jamie much longer to understand was his mother's complicity, her complete denial of the raucous damage inflicted on each of them by her husband. Jamie's childhood battles were all with his father, but as an adult now, at the beginning of his forties, he's come to realize that it is his mother who never, not once, stepped in to protect him against his father's assaults. He's certain now that Carrie O'Connor's crime was the greater one.

Jamie has figured these things out for himself. Moving across the country to the West Coast helped. Knowing people who had been analyzed and therapy-ed gave him some language, but he has never discussed his conclusions with any of his siblings— about their childhood, the damage done, the most culpable parent. It's not that the children of the O'Connor clan don't talk to one another. They do. They shout, they argue, they discuss people they know, but they never delve beneath the surface. They skirt "judgment" as ungenerous. And any discussion of another's behavior is labeled judgment. So all eight of the O'Connor siblings have their own version of what life was like growing up in that narrow brick house in Buffalo, but no one has compared notes. Until now. Ellen has come halfway around the world for just that purpose.

"What if I wasn't home?" Jamie says to her as he opens the door wider and ushers her in.

"Where would you be at five thirty in the morning? You have no life."

"How would you know that, Ellen? I haven't spoken to you in a year."

"Jaime, you wear your singleness like a sign." But Ellen is taking stock of his living situation and not looking at her brother at all. "Holy mother," she says as she scans the living room/dining room space, "this is goddamn depressing. Could you have decorated a little bit at least? Put a picture on the wall. A bowl of fruit on the table. It's like nobody lives here."

"And I'm happy to see you, too."

Ellen drops her small bag on the couch. "Can you make us some coffee? I've been flying all night."

Jamie moves into the tidy kitchen and Ellen takes one of the two barstools at the breakfast bar so she can watch her brother and talk while he gets the coffeemaker going.

"You know what today is, don't you?" She speaks to his back as he grinds the beans, measures the coffee carefully into the machine.

"Liberation day plus one year."

"That's one way to look at it." And Ellen takes a pack of cigarettes out of her purse, a lighter.

"Not in here," Jaime says.

"When did you get to be such an old lady?" But Ellen puts the pack away.

Water gurgling now and seeping into the filter, Jamie turns his full attention to his sister. He leans against the counter and studies her. All the girls take after their father, large boned and rangy, with unruly ginger hair and the kind of skin that flushes with temperature changes or emotion. His mother contributed most of her genes to the boys. They all turned out dark like Carrie, with narrow faces, sharp chins, and a slightly haunted look. "I'm Black Irish," Carrie would always say with a hint of apology.

"What?" Ellen says now, challenging Jamie's scrutiny.

"I thought you were dying the last time I saw you."

"Oh, that . . ." Ellen waves her hand in the air, dismissing his concern with one airy gesture. "Nope. Just a bad patch."

Jamie wants to ask her what "a bad patch" means, but doesn't. "You seem better" is all he says, quietly.

Ellen shrugs. "Can I at least smoke on your microscopic patio?"

"If you don't leave your butts around."

"Jesus, Jamie." But she goes out through the living room's sliding glass door and makes sure to close it tightly behind her.

On the front patio she smokes and paces, back and forth, back and forth, as if she's working off some punishment. Thirty paces without cease. Jamie watches her and waits. He feels something within him stir, something buried under years of living alone. He loves this sister more than the others, more than the brothers who preceded him.

They were the perfect "Irish twins," who were treated as a team, a unit. Jamie knows that without Ellen he might not have survived at all. She was his protector, his guide, his interpreter of signs and storm warnings. All he could give her in return was his love, and he did. His adoration of Ellen knew no limits. At least until they hit adolescence, they were inseparable.

Ellen finishes her cigarette, resists the urge to flip the butt into the sparse shrubbery, and watches her brother find two mugs, pour the coffee into them, open the refrigerator, and rummage for milk. *He looks like an old man* leaps into her mind. It's the constrained movements—precise and miserly. The lack of energy. She shakes herself—this isn't the Jamie she knew. What's happened in the seven years she's been away?

Jamie was always the angriest of them all and the bravest, taking their father on when everyone else would scatter into rooms with locked doors, waiting out the "Hugh storm" as they called it. Too often Jamie's anger, his outrage over the injustice of Hugh's cruelty, would propel him into battles he could never win. And the punishments were severe. There were beatings with a belt or a fist well beyond any humane limit. There were times, and she doesn't like to remember them, when she feared for her brother's safety— the combination of Hugh's drunkenness and Jamie's righteous fury a recipe for disaster.

It's like someone has removed all his blood, Ellen thinks as she opens the sliding glass door and steps back into the living room. "Do you believe in vampires?" she asks him.

And he grins, a wide, wholesome grin, which is what she had hoped for. This grinning Jamie she recognizes.

"As in 'I vant to suck your blood'? Or are we speaking metaphorically here? Because metaphorically, yes, I do believe in vampires."

"Metaphorically?" she teases him. "No one would know you're an English teacher."

He pours her coffee and puts it on the breakfast bar and she climbs aboard a stool and they each sip their coffee and are silent. He wants to ask her what she's doing here. She wants to ask him the same question—*What are you doing here, Jamie? What's happened to you since I left the States?* But neither does. The admonition from their childhood to avoid intrusive questions—to mind your own business—still censors their speech.

"Do you want to sleep for a while?" Jamie asks instead.

"Sleep? I just got here. Take me somewhere, show me something, introduce me to someone. Feed me!" Ellen suddenly remembers she's ravenous.

"Okay." He grins again. Ellen can't get enough of that grin. "I can do the last. There's somewhere we can go for breakfast you'll like."

"Perfect!"

JAMIE AND ELLEN WALK SLOWLY into Hillcrest, a part of San Diego Jamie likes. It feels a little offbeat to him, not dangerously so, but not bland or modern or touristy as some of his adopted city can be. It's only a few minutes past seven and the staff at Sweet & Savory is just setting out the bright blue metal tables that occupy a thin strip of sidewalk.

Inside the shop, Ellen is instantly delighted. "Oh, look!" she tells Jamie as she surveys the large, open, high-ceilinged room, mostly taken up by enormous ovens and bread-making tables.

"I know," he tells her, amused at her exuberance, "I'm here all the time."

Behind tall panels of glass, customers can watch the various breads being mixed and kneaded, baked, and taken out of the ovens before being loaded onto cooling racks where they are displayed for sale.

"Oh, the smell!" Ellen says.

"And they have pastries." Jamie shows her the bulbous bakery case with its shelves upon shelves of flaky and sweet enticements. "There are scones or muffins, croissants, tarts, slices of frittata . . ."

"One of each!" she says instantly.

He grins at her, shaking his head.

"What?" she asks him. "I have appetites."

"Go get us a table outside," Jamie says, "and I'll bring the food and cappuccinos." He's still smiling. The expression on his face makes Ellen happy.

AT THE SMALL ROUND TABLE, just big enough for two people, a Shasta daisy resting in the center bud vase, white and fresh against the vivid blue, Ellen heaves a sigh as she sits down. She's made it here. She loves her brother. Everything will be all right. At this moment, she's certain of it. Checking to make sure Jamie is still engaged in pointing out their breakfast, she lights a quick cigarette.

She tells herself to calm down, that she must take things slowly. They will have to find their way back to that old intimacy that made them both feel some measure of safety. Maybe then he'll be able to hear her. *Small steps,* she cautions herself, although her blood is rushing with the urgency of disclosure.

"It's not one of everything, but it's a sampling," Jamie says as he unloads a tray holding several plates of various muffins—blueberry, corn with poppy seeds, banana nut—scones, and two croissants. There's a small bowl of clotted cream, another of jam, and one of sliced strawberries. He knows it's too much, but Ellen revels in excess. "The coffees are coming," he says as he sits down.

Ellen takes the chocolate croissant and watches a wisp of steam rise into the damp morning air as she opens it. "Oh, heaven," she says, "warm from the oven." She attends to adding jam, making sure to avoid her brother's eyes as she volunteers, "We should call Mom today." She knows what Jamie's going to say, and he says it—"What for?"

"Because today must be a hard one for her," Ellen says, her tone neutral. "It'll bring back the whole week. Those days in the hospital. The funeral. How she felt."

"And what I did."

"She'll have forgiven you by now."

"That's not the point. I haven't forgiven her."

"Oh, Jamie, she did the best she could."

"And it wasn't good enough," he snaps back at her.

And then there's silence. Each looks away. Ellen watches a young gay couple walk their Jack Russell terrier across the street, holding hands as they stroll. One man lays his head, briefly, on the other's shoulder, then straightens up and, incongruously, begins to sing. Ellen is riveted by his total lack of self-consciousness.

Jamie replays the scene from a year ago in his mind, the act for which he needs to be forgiven. He wouldn't take back a second of it. Even now he feels entitled to the exaltation he felt, the declaration of his emancipation from the lies of his family as he met his mother's gaze and continued on, tossing his father's clothes to the nearest greedy hands—shirts, sweaters, shoes, and then that maroon dressing gown the old man always wore at night.

And a deeper memory pushes in that he doesn't want to have, a much older one. *Not this memory,* he tells himself, *please,* but it rushes forward anyway, the floodgates open. There is his father, wearing that gown. Jamie remembers the tiny black fleur-de-lis scattered across the silk, and he sees it flapping open against Hugh's startlingly white shins as he chases his fourteen-year-old self throughout the house. Hugh is very drunk, sputtering, yelling. Jamie remembers his father's steaming red face. And he sees the enormous butcher knife Hugh brandishes above his head as he runs Jamie out the kitchen door. His mother, at the sink washing dishes, doesn't turn around. Into the November snow Hugh chases him, bellowing all the while, "It's your turn to die, Jamie!" And Jamie, terrified, had believed him, believed that if his father had caught him, he would have plunged in the knife.

A COLLEGE KID WEARING a large white apron and a patterned bandanna around his forehead brings their coffees. He has that haven't-shaved-in-a-couple-of-days look that for the life of her Ellen can't figure out. *Do they ever shave? Or do they shave a little? How is it possible to always look like you need a shave?*

"Hey," he says to Jamie, "nice to see you again," and Jamie nods at him. Then there's more silence between the siblings.

"Look," Jamie finally says, "I moved three thousand miles away so I can put all the O'Connor shit behind me. There's no fixing it."

"I don't know, Jamie," Ellen begins tentatively. She tries to tread very lightly now. "We can't do anything about the past, but I think we can—"

"We were brought up in a combat zone," he cuts her off, "and we've all been crippled by it. Every one of us, except maybe Marianne. End of story."

"I don't feel like a cripple," Ellen says very carefully.

"No?" Jamie challenges her, the image of his sister barely alive at their father's wake vivid in his mind.

Ellen knows precisely what he means. "At least not now."

"Good for you." And he looks away again.

She studies his profile. His jaw is set, his lips a thin line. This isn't the face she wants to see. She offers him something. "Do you want to know why I looked that way when I came to Buffalo?"

"I'm afraid to say yes," Jamie tells her without taking his eyes off the small shops lined up across the street. Ellen waits. Jamie is deliberate, slow to reveal even a small part of his soul. She knows this about her brother. Finally he turns and meets her eyes, his voice a whisper. "I was so afraid you were dying, El."

"More like being reborn."

"Oh my God, Ellen, you haven't been hijacked by some fundamentalist Christian—"

And she bursts into a cascade of laughter. And he smiles at himself. "Well, you said 'reborn.'"

"We're outside, I can smoke, right?"

"If you have to."

"This is a long story," she says as she lights a cigarette, preparing herself for the saga she's about to tell. "Okay, here goes. . . . I went to Spain to get away from Buffalo. Well, really to get away from myself in Buffalo. And Dad, he seemed to be everywhere, you know?"

Jamie nods. He left for the same reason.

"It was my fault. I couldn't leave it alone. I had to tell him about every new job I got, even though I knew—Jamie, I *knew*— that he'd tell me what was wrong with it and how I was an idiot to work there. And there'd come a time with each new guy I was seeing when I'd say, 'Come home and meet my mom and dad.'"

"A suicide mission," Jamie says with quiet assurance. None of this is new to him. "Dad didn't like any of them, and Mom probably said, 'He seems nice enough.'"

Ellen nods. "The phone would ring later that night and Dad would be sure to tell me what a loser I'd picked. And I'd defend the guy, even though I was having my own doubts by the time I took him home. And we'd start shouting at each other and I'd tell him if he ever wanted to see me again, he'd have to clean up his act and he'd shout at me that there was nothing wrong with his act and it was my act that was a pitiful mess. . . ." Ellen shrugs. "And he was right."

"Dad was never right," Jamie says.

"You know," Ellen tells him, "you have to acknowledge truth wherever it comes from."

"I don't think so."

And instead of getting angry, Ellen laughs again. "Jamie," she says, "you don't see the value of the truth?"

"Mostly, no."

"Uh-oh," Ellen says, "this is going to be harder than I thought."

"What is?"

"Saving your life. I'm here to save your life."

"The impossible dream." But he's grinning. "You want another coffee?"

He gets up, goes inside to get it, and she takes a deep breath. The mission is out on the table. He doesn't seem offended or even reflexively resistant. She can slow down a bit, she thinks. They have time, and suddenly she's exhausted. She lays her head on her crossed arms and feels the warmth of the metal table beneath them. By the time Jamie comes back with their new coffees, she's asleep.

SHE LEANS INTO HIM as they walk home. He has his arm around her and is laughing as she trips over her own feet. Anyone watching would think they were a couple stumbling home after a very drunken all-nighter.

When they get back to the condo, Jamie opens the pullout couch in his second bedroom, the one he has made into his office, and tucks Ellen in. She's mumbling "Thank you," barely awake, and then she's not. He takes his fifth period's essays from his desk and closes the door softly behind him.

The day is glorious, quintessential San Diego weather— assertive blue sky, a comforting breeze from the ocean, temperature just right for sitting in the sun. He'll take the papers and another cup of coffee and read them on his patio—"microscopic" as it may be—while he waits for Ellen to wake up.

He assigned his eighth graders *The Miracle Worker.* This is his honors class, and he's hoping at least some of them will be able to think beyond the "triumph over adversity" reaction most people have when they read the play or see the movie. That treat, screening the movie, Jamie always saves for last. He wants them to come to the play without the overlay of Anne Bancroft and Patty Duke.

For Jamie, Annie Sullivan is the more interesting character, more nuanced, and yes, ultimately the more "heroic." Her own childhood was horrendous—institutionalized in a mental hospital because there was nowhere else to put her. Blind before an operation restored some measure of her sight. Literally falling at the feet of "important men" who came to visit the asylum and pleading for an education. And then, without any real training, coming to the Keller household as a young woman barely out of her teens and refusing to give up on the wild animal she found there— Helen. There's a reason the play is titled *The Miracle Worker* and not *Helen Keller.* He hopes at least some of his students will see that. He doesn't expect any of them, except maybe Colleen McAllister, who is serious beyond her thirteen years, to understand that Annie Sullivan is also heroic because she allows herself to love Helen fiercely. After all that life had thrown at her, she still opens her heart. That's a kind of heroism Jamie doesn't expect middle schoolers to begin to understand. That's the kind of heroism he most admires.

He picks up the first essay. It's Chloe's, outgoing, gregarious Chloe, who always greets him with "How's it going, Mr. O'Connor?" and never seems to have a bad day. "Helen Keller was an amazing person who overcame all the challenges life threw at her" is her topic sentence. They've been working on creating good

topic sentences. This one doesn't bode well for an essay he'd want
to read. Jamie puts the paper aside and tries the next one. "When
Helen Keller met Annie Sullivan, it changed her life." This one
is from Kim-Ly, granddaughter of Vietnamese immigrants, who
wears the shortest skirts in the class. Beside the ambiguous "it"
that Jamie circles with a red pen, the sentence doesn't promise any
new thinking, either. He tries the third essay. "Being deaf, dumb,
and blind didn't stop Helen Keller from having a full life." This
one is from Sam, a too-earnest kid who always seems to Jamie as
if he's half Labrador puppy. Jamie circles the word "dumb" and
writes, "Helen Keller was anything but 'dumb.'"

Jamie puts the essays aside and gets up. It's moments like this,
when he suspects that he hasn't managed to motivate his kids
to any creative thinking, that would depress most teachers he
knows. But that's not the effect they have on Jamie. Instead, he
asks himself what he could have done differently. How could
he have led his students away from conventional thoughts and
into creative ones? What should he say when he hands these
papers back to them? It's like a puzzle where he has to find just
the right pieces in just the right order to make the picture he
wants them to consider appear in their heads.

Jamie loves his chosen profession. He will readily admit that
there may be nothing else in his life that isn't compromised,
thwarted, distorted, or unfulfilled, but the knowledge that he has
found his true calling keeps him going.

He searches through the stack of essays for Colleen's and pulls
it out. Her topic sentence is "*The Miracle Worker* is a play about
finding your special gifts in life." Ah, better! Interesting take.
Colleen, you've saved me, he thinks as he settles back to read her
essay.

By the time the light has mellowed into dusk, Jamie has read
more than half of his students' essays and written them lengthy

notes that he suspects very few of them will even read. He's seen them. They flip to the grade and then quickly stash the paper in their backpack, where it disintegrates in short order and joins the other wads of trash at the bottom of the bag. He gets up and stretches his back. He's stiff from sitting in one position for so long. *Ah, creeping middle age,* he thinks, as he often does these days. *Once you pass forty, there's no denying middle age.*

He checks in on Ellen, cracks open the door to see her sleeping like she's in a coma. He smiles in recognition. All the O'Connor siblings sleep that way—through anything, oblivious to noise, a survival technique they all learned early on in a household that was perpetually loud and had no detectable schedule. You were as likely to see a toddler with a full diaper wandering around at midnight as you were to come across one of the boys snoring on the basement floor at twelve noon.

Jamie figures Ellen is out for the night. He'll see her in the morning before he leaves for school, waking her up if he must to tell her he's going.

He heats up some leftover soup for his dinner and sits at the dining room table to tackle the rest of the *Miracle Worker* essays. It's a Sunday night like countless other Sunday nights he's had since moving to San Diego. If he had stayed in Buffalo, he'd probably be at some neighborhood bar right now with friends from high school or one of his brothers and they'd be spending the evening watching whatever game was on TV, probably basketball this time of year, and there'd be a good deal of drinking and boasting and storytelling and betting on the game. Does he miss all that? Sometimes, mostly the easy companionship that asks little and expects only that he stay the same Jamie they've always known. That last part, that was the part he couldn't fulfill. The Jamie who drank too much in order not to feel, the Jamie who was quick to argue as a defense against being steamrollered, the Jamie who needed to constantly declare himself lest he feel like he was

disappearing—that Jamie was abandoned in Buffalo. The Jamie
who settled himself in San Diego needs far less from the world
and wants only quiet, predictability, and the safety of no
demands.

ELLEN STRUGGLES THROUGH THE SLUDGE of her exhausted sleep
and pushes herself awake. She has no idea how long she's slept.
The bedside clock tells her it's 10:35, but she's not sure if it's
nighttime and she's just napped a bit or whether it's the morning and she's slept right through. She opens the door quietly and
pads in bare feet to the archway that defines the living area of the
condo. Immediately she sees her brother, bent over, elbows on the
dining room table, writing copiously with a red pen. A pendant
lamp hanging straight down in the middle of the table illuminates
its surface but casts shadows on her brother's face. The lighting,
the sparseness of the room décor, the intensity with which he's
writing remind Ellen of one of those cop shows where the accused
is being forced to hurriedly write out his confession in a tiny
room with a single bulb hanging overhead.

"I hope you're staying home because I'm here and that this
isn't your normal Sunday night routine," Ellen says as she walks
in. Her face is creased from sleep and her difficult hair is now flying about her head like exclamation points.

He gestures at the stack of essays. "I teach five classes of
English. This is pretty much where I am most nights."

Ellen sits down, points to the empty soup bowl. "And that was
your dinner?"

"Mexican black bean soup from Whole Foods."

"Pitiful."

"Actually, it's quite good."

"Is there more?"

. . .

ELLEN EATS HER SOUP. Jamie grades his papers. There's the companionable silence of siblings who have spent thousands of hours together. If Jamie weren't such a tight ass now, Ellen thinks, she'd reach for a cigarette. Instead, she begins to talk. No preamble. She simply continues the story she had begun at the café.

"Miguel was supposed to be my savior."

Jamie looks up at her, puts his pen aside, settles back in his chair, arms crossed over his chest, content to allow Ellen to spool out her story as she can.

"Spain is good for me. I love the pace of it all. The sense that time isn't demanding anything of you, simply that you are passing through it. The weather is wonderful—no more Buffalo winters. That's enough to lift my spirits permanently. And Tracy is there, you know. Do you remember Tracy Keppinger?"

"Donnie's older sister?"

"Yes, she was in my class at Immaculate Heart. Do you remember her? Tiny with all those blond ringlets? She sort of looked like Little Orphan Annie."

Jamie nods. He does remember her hanging around the house when they got to be teenagers. He had thought she was kind of cute but never acted on it.

"When she was in college, she went to Malaga for her junior year abroad, met Rafael, and never came home. They've got four kids now. All of them have those curls. Anyway, she's been telling me for years I had to come over, and when I hit thirty-five and looked at my life in Buffalo, I thought, 'Why not?' Things couldn't get any worse."

"What was so bad?" Jamie asks her.

"What wasn't? I had been working at the same kind of dead-end job for over ten years. It didn't really matter what construction company it was—it was essentially the same job. Bob Wardlow called me his bookkeeper. Keith Lutz called me his right-hand man. Tony Stradello called me his office manager. Whatever, all it meant was that I had to sit in a filthy office, or worse, a construction trailer that was an oven in the summer and an icebox in the winter, answering the phones, making sure the bills were paid and that the guys got to the right job site on time. Hardly taxing on my mental abilities."

"No," Jamie agrees.

"No chance for advancement."

Jamie nods.

"And putting me in close proximity to exactly the wrong kind of guys for me."

"Which were?"

"Guys who drank too much. Guys who were married. Guys who thought an endearment was 'Fuck me harder.'"

Jamie laughs out loud and Ellen smiles back at him. Now she can make jokes about it all.

"In other words," Jamie says, "guys we grew up with."

"The very same."

Ellen puts her forearms on the table, laces her fingers together, and looks at her hands. It's quiet for a minute. Jamie feels Ellen shift into another, more somber, gear. "I somehow found a way to pick the very guys who would infuriate me. Who would scream at me so that I could scream back . . . A lot of yelling . . . A couple of smashed car windows . . ."

"Someone deliberately shattered your car window?"

"No, Jamie, I did the smashing. I was always so angry . . . and there wasn't any way to get rid of it. . . . Oh, of course, if only I hadn't picked guys who treated me so badly, who disappointed me before I even learned their last names . . ." She trails off, doesn't finish the sentence.

Jamie nods. He understands the "if only" part of it. "If only" their father hadn't beat the crap out of them. "If only" they didn't wake up every morning with that worm of fear twisting in their intestines. "If only" victimhood hadn't been fed to them with their Lucky Charms and Jell-O Pudding.

"Remember Mickey Fogarty?"

"Big guy with that eagle tattoo running down his forearm?"

"Yep. He was the last straw."

"I never really liked—"

"He was a pig. I was sleeping with a pig." Ellen says it with such fierceness that Jamie has nothing to say. He doesn't disagree.

"And then Tracy called from Spain just to check in and asked me again when I was going to come visit and I said, 'This weekend.' Just like that. It popped out of my mouth and I didn't take it back and so I packed up all my clothes and flew to Malaga. . . . I was thirty-five and I thought it was my last chance. . . . I thought if I stayed in Buffalo I would either have killed some guy or he would have killed me."

"Come on, Ellen," Jamie says, standing up now. He doesn't want to hear this. He doesn't want to believe his sister could have had so much violence in her. "You always exaggerate. Can't you just say you went to Spain for a fresh start?"

She looks at him as he gathers up his papers into a neat pile, clears the dishes off the table, and loads the dishwasher. When he comes back to the table with a sponge in his hand to wipe it down, she puts a hand on his wrist, stopping him and forcing him to look at her.

"I'm not exaggerating. I'm telling you what my life was like then and what I was afraid of. You need to believe me."

But he shakes his head. He doesn't want to. He won't. It's too painful for him to believe that their father's legacy of violence has infected this sister just when he's reminded of how much he loves her.

"I need to get some sleep. Tomorrow's a school day. Do you think you can go back to bed?"

"Not now," Ellen says, clearly disappointed that Jamie is bailing out of this conversation.

He hands her the remote from the living room coffee table. "Knock yourself out, only keep the volume low."

"Yes, sir."

She watches Jamie walk down the hall and hears him enter his bedroom. She needs to slow down, she tells herself, or he won't hear her and she hasn't even gotten to the difficult part yet.

WHEN JAMIE GETS HOME FROM SCHOOL, HE finds that Ellen has decorated his house. There are fresh flowers in vases he doesn't recognize on the dining room table and the bookshelf in the living room. There's a deep blue bowl piled high with symmetrical yellow lemons on the breakfast bar, the contrast of colors somehow perfectly right. And the living room couch, a deep utilitarian forest green, now boasts striped and patterned pillows in corresponding hues of yellow, blue, and cream.

He stands with his back against the front door and takes it all in, briefcase in hand crammed with more student essays.

"They're all removable if you don't like it," Ellen says, coming in from the patio. Jamie gets a wave of cigarette smoke before she closes the sliding glass door behind her. "The flowers will die, the lemons will rot, and the pillows can be stashed in a closet."

"Well, there's a happy thought."

"I just mean, this is all temporary if you need to go back to the monk's cell you favored before."

"It looks nice, Ellen."

And she grins at him, relieved. "Good."

They look at each other—*What's next?* "I usually take a run when I get home . . . ?" He lays it out there as a question.

"Go," she says, "I'm cooking you dinner."

"You don't have—"

"Go—"

IT'S ON JAMIE'S RUNS THAT HE SORTS things out in his life. He takes a route that follows the water, passing a few other runners, maybe a mother or two with a stroller, or a couple of people walking their dogs, but that's fine because most simply nod and he can avoid eye contact and keep running.

What does he think about this impromptu visit by his sister? On the one hand, she seems to be doing so much better, and that cheers him. She's laughing and has that blunt honesty he always admired. On the other hand, she seems to be on a mission. Is that crazy? Does he need to be saved? Maybe from the outside it looks as though his life is sparse, barren even. He's sure many people see it that way, but from the inside of this life he's constructed a continent away from the turmoil of his family, the choices he's made feel lifesaving.

Of course, there's been a price to pay. And there are times when he aches with the losses he readily acknowledges. Those brothers who once felt like his second selves would never embrace this West Coast Jamie. And he knows it's his lack of nerve that has kept his friendships here at the most superficial of levels. *Something happens when you shut down,* Jamie thinks as the path curves and continues around the bay. And the fact that he's single, the fact that the women in his life up and leave him—he takes responsibility for that as well. They want more. So does he, but he knows that what they want is locked too far away to give.

Yes, there's plenty Ellen could latch onto in this campaign she seems to be embarked upon. Will she listen? That's the question he asks himself. Will she believe him when he assures her he sees the perimeters of the bargain he's struck with himself and he's made peace with them?

WHEN HE OPENS THE FRONT DOOR forty-five minutes later, sweaty and winded, it looks like Armageddon in his kitchen. Dirty pots are piled in the sink and across the countertops. Does he own all those or did Ellen buy some? Used plates and bowls are piled on every available surface and the floor. The bright red skins and pulp of tomatoes are smeared across a wooden chopping board like bloody entrails. Part of a chicken carcass rests, inexplicably, on his breakfast bar next to bowls of mussels and shrimp. On the stove some kind of sausage—chorizo, Ellen tells him later—is sizzling away at too high a heat and suddenly his smoke alarm goes off with a deafening shriek. And in the middle of all this, Ellen turns around, grinning with manic goodwill, and greets him, "Welcome to paella Espagnia!"

"Turn the burner off!" Jamie shouts.

"What?!"

And he does it himself, switching off the gas, moving the frying pan away, and then ripping the batteries out of the smoke alarm. The sudden quiet is like a slap in the face.

Ellen sneaks a quick peek at her brother's face and knows she has to quickly salvage this. "I had it all under control until that damn thing went off."

"That 'damn thing' goes off when you're in danger of burning the whole place down."

Ellen takes a deep breath. She doesn't want this evening to start off with an argument. She gathers her calmness around her with a second deep breath. Firmly, without rancor, she tells him, "Go take a shower and I'll finish up here. You'll be amazed when you get back."

He grunts and goes.

When he comes out of his bedroom twenty minutes later, his black hair wet, sleeked back and curling around his neck, bare-foot, wearing a pair of comfortable jeans and an old T-shirt, he sees a large platter of just-finished paella resting on the dining room table. It smells amazing. New straw placemats hold his old white dishes. Patterned napkins Ellen must have also bought— Jamie would never buy anything with a pattern—finish the place settings. A bottle of red wine and a round loaf of crusty bread he recognizes from Sweet & Savory take up the middle of the table. It all looks so sumptuous, so lovingly prepared, that his heart melts. He scrupulously avoids looking into the kitchen.

"Wow," he says softly.

"Sit down," Ellen says, "I'm going to feed you."

And she does. She spoons out the paella, cuts the bread, pours him some wine. He feels taken care of in a way he hasn't since Nicole left three years before.

When they were first dating, Nicole would cook for him, but by the time the relationship was in trouble, six months later, the cooking had stopped. *There is no upside,* she had told him, *to giving to someone who isn't giving back.*

The thing is, he was giving, only not nearly enough for most reasonable people. Why didn't he confide in her, she asked, or "share his feelings" about anything important? He couldn't explain beyond the imperfect and inadequate "That's how I am."

He wouldn't agree to have her move in, and he needed to be alone too many nights a week for her to feel truly wanted. At first she had thought she'd win him over; hence the cooking and the acquiescence to his need for nights alone. But when nothing progressed, when she felt as though they were still in week three of their dating, she began to complain and then push him to argue, but he wouldn't. He knew what was coming and he wouldn't try to talk her out of it. He simply shook his head when she told him she was leaving.

"Say something!" she threw at him. "Argue with me. Tell me

you need more time. Convince me there's really a loving, giving Jamie trapped in old habits! Speak to me! I'm walking out the door here, Jamie."

"I understand" is what he said so quietly she almost missed it.

She stared at him in disbelief and then, when he didn't say another word, the sorrow that flooded her pretty face made him turn away. "Pathetic" was the last word he heard before the slam of the front door.

After the paella, Ellen serves him coffee and a caramelized pear tart she bought along with the bread. It's then that she picks up her story from the night before.

She says, with a grin to acknowledge that she's quoting him, "So I went to Spain for a fresh start."

"That I understand." Jamie is playing along.

"And at first it felt like that. I stayed with Tracy for a few weeks while I found a job and a tiny room. I took Spanish lessons. I walked around the city a lot on my own. It all felt sort of pure, you know? Like, the simpler the better. No entanglements. Just me getting through each day, learning the city a little more, learning Spanish a little more. Seeing Tracy and Rafael but really no one else. It all felt manageable and I felt like I was calming down. I didn't call Mom or Dad. I e-mailed them occasionally, but part of my recovery, I realized, was scaling those old relationships way back."

"Why do you think I'm three thousand miles away?"

"I get it, Jamie. I never questioned your move away, did I?"

He shakes his head.

"When my Spanish got better I was able to get a job at a construction company. All that experience in Buffalo helped. It turns out construction is pretty much construction anywhere in the world."

"Was that smart?" he asks her, his eyebrows raised.

"You're getting ahead of me here, and no, it turns out it wasn't smart at all. That's where I met Miguel."

"Your 'savior'? You see, I was listening last night."

"At first, I couldn't believe my luck. For starters, he was single and I hadn't made it a practice to date single men. And he was gorgeous. Not that I'm all that superficial, but when you've just left Mickey Fogarty with his two dozen tattoos and questionable personal hygiene, gorgeous and clean go a long way." Ellen pauses, mashes the crumbs of her pear tart into her plate with the back of her fork. Her eyes down, she finally says softly, "And he wanted me, really wanted me and told me why. Told me what I had and what I was that was worthwhile. He was the first person who ever . . ." And she trails off. She won't get teary in front of Jamie.

But when he says, "Oh, Ellen," understanding exactly how unique that kind of validation would be to one of them, the O'Connor children, who never heard about their specialness from either parent, Ellen's eyes fill anyway.

She needs to back up to more neutral ground. She lays out some of the facts. "Miguel's a lawyer, and he was counsel for the company building the shopping center we were working on. They'd had neighbor complaints about the height of the parking structure or something. Anyway, Miguel came into the office one day to go over the building specs with my boss, and when he walked in and we looked at each other, that was that." Ellen shrugs as if all that followed was inevitable.

"I'd never felt that before," she tells him, "that instant connection. Miguel said he hadn't, either. Do you know how powerful that feeling is, Jamie?"

"Sounds exhausting to me."

"Oh, it was. Exhausting and exhilarating in equal measure, but mostly it was mesmerizing. For both of us. You've got to understand I wasn't some infatuated teenager mooning after some guy who didn't give a damn. Miguel was in this with me. It's important that you understand that. He needed to see me every night. He'd call me sometimes every hour, all day. The rest of my life—my friends, the class I was taking, the attention I put into my work—they all fell away, and I was alive only for those hours I spent with Miguel."

There's something about this Jamie doesn't like, but he doesn't say anything, simply nods as she continues to tell the story.

As if Ellen were reading his thoughts, something they would often do as children, she quickly says, "And he was kind to me. He filled my little apartment with flowers, day after day, week after week, and then he began to buy me things. He had a set of dining room chairs delivered to my apartment."

"Did you need dining room chairs?"

"No, but he said the ones I had weren't comfortable and if he was going to have dinner with me every night, he wanted to be comfortable. And then he began to buy me clothes and jewelry. He'd take me to really expensive restaurants so I could wear the dress or the shawl or the jade earrings that he'd just bought me and he would tell me how beautiful I looked.

"When he asked me to move in with him, there seemed to be no other answer but 'Yes, of course, I love you, of course I will.'"

"How long had you known him?" Jamie asks.

"Two months."

"Did you bring the dining room chairs?"

"Very funny, Jamie, and the answer is no. I left them with the apartment along with everything else I had acquired since I had moved to Malaga. It didn't matter. They were just things. You've got to understand, I couldn't believe my luck. I had gone to Spain to change my life, and here was proof that I'd been right. I had a man who loved me, who treated me like I was a prize. I had done it. I had escaped the O'Connor curse."

"How long did that feeling last?"

"Okay, I know you want me to cut to the chase, but you need to believe that we had something that people long for all their lives."

"I get it, Ellen, but you're not telling me this story because it all stayed that way, are you?"

"No."

"When did it turn bad?"

"I don't know."

He snorts. "Weren't you there? How can you not know?"

"Stop being such a prick and I'll tell you."

"Okay," Jamie says, a bit chagrined. "Sorry."

"It started so quietly I wasn't even aware of what was going on. His daily phone calls became sort of 'Where are you? What are you doing?' instead of 'I miss you. I can't stop thinking about you.' Do you see the difference?"

"He was checking up on you."

"Yes! But would you have recognized that right away?" Jamie shrugs and Ellen shakes her head at her own gullibility. "Well, I didn't. Then he began to say things like 'I don't like you in that dress, wear the green one I bought you.' And I'd think, 'What difference does it make?' And I'd go and change into the dress he liked. . . . Then he began to tell me my friends were boring and we'd only go out together if we were seeing his friends. He said I could see my friends during the day. But I didn't. Somehow, because Miguel didn't like them, I wasn't interested in seeing them."

"Tracy, too?" Jamie asks.

"Not at the beginning, but when it got bad, then, yes, I cut Tracy out of my life, too."

"When did it get bad, Ellen?" Jamie asks quietly.

"When I quit my job."

"Because he wanted you to?"

"Because he told me to. He made a lot of money and he had

family money, and after we'd been together for about a year, he told me that my job was getting in the way of our life together. He wanted me to travel with him. He wanted me at home when he got home. What did I do all day at my job that was so important? Nothing, I realized, it wasn't important. Miguel was what was important.... So I quit my job."

Ellen won't meet Jamie's eyes as she tells him, "And then I became his prisoner. He set new rules—I had to call him before I left the apartment and when I got home, the minute I got home. If he didn't like where I said I was going, he told me to stay home. I began to lie to him so I could go out, and when he found out I was lying, he got very angry."

"Did he hit you?" Ellen won't answer. "Ellen, did he hit you?" Jamie asks again, more insistent.

"That wasn't the worst of it," Ellen finally whispers. "It became this sort of ritual for him. He'd tie me up...."

"Oh God ..." escapes from Jamie.

"He had this elaborate way of doing it depending on which part of my body was going to get the punishment."

"Don't!" Jamie says. He can't hear this, but Ellen continues on anyway.

"And then he'd find the spot he wanted. It was always a soft spot, somewhere that could be covered up with clothes, and he'd cut me...."

"No ..." Jamie is moaning now. "Please ..."

"And he'd tell me this would all stop if I'd only be good, what he was asking for was only reasonable. Wasn't it reasonable that he know where the woman he loved was? Wasn't it reasonable that he be able to believe what she told him? Wasn't that reasonable, he'd ask me, and I had to agree or he'd find another soft spot."

Jamie gets up abruptly. He can't hear any more of this, but Ellen grabs his forearm. "Sit down. I'm not finished." And as much as he's desperate to walk away, to wipe from his consciousness what she's just told him, he looks into his sister's urgent face and sits down again.

"But I didn't just give in. I began to fight back. And that's when it got really scary. We began to inflict major damage on each other. Not just black eyes and bruises, but I broke his wrist once and he pushed me across the kitchen one night and I fell against the stove and blacked out. And he couldn't revive me and so I ended up in the emergency room with a serious concussion."

"And that did it?" Jamie asks, begging her to tell him that this horrendous story is over.

"You would think, wouldn't you, that that would have been enough." Ellen sits back and says this without emotion, as if she's telling the story of someone else, someone completely crazy. Someone who has no relationship to her.

"You didn't leave him then?!"

"Not the first time I showed up in the hospital, but the second time, yes. But only because he was arrested and when I was well enough to go home, he wasn't there. . . . Before he made bail, I did the one smart thing in the middle of all this mess: I called Tracy and she came and got me."

"Is that the end of this story?" Jamie asks her. "Because I don't think I can hear any more."

"The rest of the story is good," she says. "The rest of the story is how I became this paragon of health and happiness that you see before you. The rest of the story is what I came to California to tell you."

"You know what, El, I don't think I'm ready to hear it now."

"Okay," she says reasonably, "I've given you a lot to take in."

"Would you call that an understatement?"

And she grins at him. "Yep."

. . .

WHEN HE LEAVES FOR SCHOOL the next morning, she comes
with him. She wants to see where he works and then she wants
to explore San Diego. She'll drive around a bit and then pick him
back up at three thirty. They arrange it over breakfast, sitting
at his breakfast bar, drinking their coffees, and idly reading the
morning paper.

She seems so calm to Jamie, so present, so unaffected by the
story she told him last night that part of him doesn't believe her.
How could she have gone through what she described (and he has
a feeling she left a great deal out) and still be the Ellen he knows?
The two things can't quite coexist in his mind.

When she looks up from the paper and sees him scrutinizing
her, she again knows what he's thinking. "I survived, Jamie, and
something miraculous happened because of all the pain. Don't
judge until you hear the rest of the story."

"Give me a breather here, El."

She laughs. "I can wait."

Jamie's school is close to the water. It seems to Ellen that practically everything in San Diego is within sight of the Pacific Ocean.
The middle-school building is part of a vast old military base.
Some of the other buildings have been renovated, too, and Jamie
points out the elementary school and the high school as he parks
in the teachers' lot.

"We're all part of a charter school run by a private corporation.
They leased the land from the Defense Department, refurbished
the buildings, and set all this up."

"So it's a private school?" Ellen asks as they open the large
glass double doors and walk into the main hallway. Inside, the
building has been opened up with skylights and bright paint colors horizontally striped along the walls.

"No," Jamie explains, "we're part of the San Diego Unified
School District. The kids have to meet their standards, but because
we're a charter, they pretty much leave us alone."

"Well, that should suit you just fine," Ellen says, and she looks at him sideways as they enter the main office so he can check his mailbox.

"Very funny." But he doesn't seem at all offended as he grabs a fistful of mail from a cubbyhole, one in a row of several dozen along the left-hand wall of the office."You want some more coffee before class starts?"

"Do you even have to ask?"

He points her across the hall to the teachers' lounge. It's a long, narrow room with windows overlooking the front of the school. Someone's taken the trouble to put together a cozy room—easy chairs in the same primary colors as the hallways. *Everything in this school seems to pop out at you,* Ellen thinks. *Do they need to wake people up?* Some of the chairs have ottomans next to them, useful for putting up aching feet or as a place for the paper overload that always seems to accompany any teacher. There are two small, round tables for catching up on work in one corner of the room and an efficient coffee area with a tiny sink and under-counter refrigerator and the ever-going coffeemaker opposite it.

Jamie pours them each a mug of coffee and introduces Ellen to the handful of teachers who are getting ready for their day. "My sister Ellen, everyone. She's visiting from Spain."

The teachers are friendly. They greet her. She sips her coffee and looks around the room. More teachers have come in to grab a cup of coffee or simply as a respite before the day officially begins. They stand in twos and threes, chatting. But, she sees, not Jamie. He's over by the windows, by himself, reading what looks like a memo. No one approaches him and he doesn't look up. It bothers her that he is the singular person in a room of groups and conversation, and she's watching him, waiting for him to turn and talk to someone or have someone talk to him, and so she doesn't see a very pretty woman in her thirties come over to her.

"I didn't know Jamie had a sister," she says.

"Jamie has four sisters."

"Really?" The woman seems puzzled.

She's fine boned, wrenlike, with honey-colored hair that today she's pulled back into a sleek ponytail, not a tendril escaping. Immediately Ellen can tell that this woman has been pretty all her life and takes it for granted. No makeup. Clothes that seem too casual for teaching—cargo pants, a T-shirt advertising San Diego State, and running shoes. Next to her Ellen feels like an unruly Amazon, her wiry reddish hair unattended, her five-foot-seven height oversized.

"I'm Nicole. I've known your brother forever."

"And you didn't know he has four sisters and three brothers?"

"I wouldn't call your brother much of a talker." And this last is said with just enough of an undertone of bitterness that Ellen pays more attention.

"Well, you know," Ellen says, defending Jamie without even thinking about it, "when you grow up in a family of eight, there's not much of a chance to talk. We shout. We're really good at shouting."

"There were times I would have been thrilled to hear him shout, but I never did," Nicole says as she moves off, glancing at Jamie as she does. "Enjoy your visit."

Okay, Ellen thinks as she watches Nicole move across the room, *did she just mean what I think she meant?* She glances at Nicole's left hand as she grabs the doorknob, surprised to see a wedding ring set with diamonds on her fourth finger. *Ancient history? Recent history? Recent enough for her to still be pissed.*

IN JAMIE'S FIRST-PERIOD CLASS, his sixth graders, they're discussing "The Road Not Taken," the Robert Frost poem. Ellen sits at the back of the class and takes it all in. She can see immediately that her brother is in his element, and she relaxes.

Jamie has led the kids to see that the two roads that "diverged in a yellow wood" are more than just paths through the forest. He tells them nothing. He asks questions and entertains many answers without calling any of them wrong, and so the atmosphere in the class encourages conversation. Ellen can see that the kids raise their hands eagerly, that they are confident Jamie will listen to them. And he's animated, moving around the class, touching a student on a shoulder here and there, even clapping his hands at one answer from a quiet, dark-skinned boy in the back. "Yes, Ritesh!" he says. " 'The traveler' could be any of us—'and sorry I could not travel both / And be one traveler.' That's right!" The boy shimmers with good feeling that Jamie has rewarded his opinion.

And when they get to the last stanza, Jamie reads it out loud. " 'I shall be telling this with a sigh / Somewhere ages and ages hence: / Two roads diverged in a wood, and I, / I took the one less traveled by / And that has made all the difference.' "

There's a moment of silence after he finishes reading, and then a large boy with a puzzled look on his face blurts out, "What difference?" And there's laughter from the other kids.

"A good question, Kyle," Jamie says, and then to the class, "What is 'the difference' Frost is talking about?" More silence. No one seems to know exactly.

Jamie catches Ellen's eye and they smile at each other. "The difference" has been the subtext of all their conversations the last few days.

Before Jamie can lead his sixth graders to an understanding of Frost's words, the bell rings and the kids get up, gather their things, books into their backpacks, jackets across shoulders. Jamie has a group of kids around him as one class files out and another files in, so Ellen keeps her seat at the back of the room. She doesn't want to intrude, simply to observe.

As much as Ellen is thrilled to see Jamie in his element, when his second-period class starts with a discussion of the same poem, she's not sitting still for a repeat. She gestures to Jamie that she'll see him later and slips out the door.

As she's walking down the quiet hallways, murmurs of teachers' voices coming from open doorways, she recognizes the yellow doorway into the teachers' lounge and slips in to return her coffee cup.

At first glance, she thinks the room is empty, but as she rinses the mug in the sink, she notices the woman she spoke with that morning, Nicole, sitting at one of the round tables, grading papers. Her head is down. Her body is still, no wasted motions, only her hand with a red pen in it moves. She takes up such a small space in the room that it isn't hard to miss her.

"You teach math?" Ellen asks when Nicole looks up and smiles at her.

"Algebra, I and II." Then, "Did you watch Jamie teach?"

"Yes."

"He loves it, doesn't he?"

"A lot," Ellen says as she comes and sits at the table with Nicole. Then, "How well do you know each other?"

"Oh, I could say intimately and not at all."

Ellen nods. She knows exactly what this woman is talking about.

"But he disappointed you?"

"Just till I got it through my thick head that he'd rather be alone than with me."

"Or anybody?" Is that what Nicole is saying—that her brother doesn't want anyone close to him?

Nicole shrugs. "Maybe there's someone out there, but 'it ain't me, babe.'" She gathers her papers together into a neat pile, edges aligned, and affixes a metal clip to the corner before she slides them into a backpack. "Doesn't matter . . . I'm married now, so . . . ancient history."

"It matters to me," Ellen says quietly and the other woman nods. There isn't anything else to say. Nicole gets up, carefully pushes her chair back under the table. "He's a good man, but . . ." There's a shake of her head, as if she still hasn't figured Jamie out. And then she's gone.

Ellen sits in the empty room for a moment, more unsettled than she'd like to be by this confirmation of her brother's life as solitary and self-denying.

She needs to go back to Sweet & Savory, she suddenly realizes.

WHEN ELLEN'S SEATED UNDER THE AWNING, at one of the bright metal tables, the same waiter brings her cappuccino and a wedge of spinach quiche she ordered inside. Today he's wearing a yellow patterned bandanna across his forehead instead of the red he favored the morning she arrived.

"Hey," he says as he sets her food down, as if he remembers her.

"Hi. I was here on Sunday morning with my brother. Do you remember? You brought us our coffees."

"Sure. You were my first customers, like at seven, right after we opened."

"Yes." Ellen is more pleased than she has a right to be that he remembers them. "You seemed to know my brother."

"Just from here. I musta seen him ten, twenty times."

"Can I ask you something, then? About Jamie?"

And immediately the kid looks wary. "I don't really know him at all, like personally, you know?"

"Was he usually alone?"

The kid stops to think, as though a lot of money rode on the answer. "Yeah, I can't remember him coming in with anyone, except, of course, for you."

"Okay, thanks, that's it."

And the kid smiles again, hugely relieved, that was easy. He passed whatever test Ellen had put out there in front of him. "Anything else I can get you?"

Ellen just shakes her head and he leaves her. She sips her coffee—*God, that's good*—and takes in the morning information, from Nicole, from this kid. None of it surprises her. It just confirms for her that she made the right choice in coming.

And then she starts to get angry. *Calm down,* she tells herself, but instead her mind runs endless loops of images of Jamie's life—the spartan apartment that looks like nobody lives there, his separateness in the teachers' lounge, that pretty teacher he wouldn't have, his solitary meals sitting right at this table. She's growing angrier and angrier.

Get a grip, she tries to tell herself again, but it's not working. She can feel the heat of anger rising. She knows the pale skin on her chest, now her cheeks, is flushing red. And she knows it isn't good. She reaches for her cell phone, punches in a number she knows by heart.

The woman who answers speaks in Spanish. Ellen answers in kind as she asks for Dr. Smithfield. And then Ellen's face breaks wide with relief before she switches to English, "Amanda, thank God you're there."

A decidedly English voice, with a lilt of humor, answers, "Ellen, I'm always here."

"I'm angry. I'm too angry at what I've found here. Jamie is denying himself everything but his teaching. There's nothing else."

"That's Jamie's life. His responsibility. You know that, so why are you so—?"

"Because the son of a bitch is winning! Because he's still

destroying Jamie's life, only now it's from the grave!" She's yelling, her voice strident, suddenly much too aggressive and very loud. People at the other sidewalk tables are looking at her, then turning their eyes away, embarrassed.

"That's Jamie's life. You need to take care of your own."

Ellen doesn't answer. Instead she closes her eyes and tries to take a few good, deep breaths.

"Ellen?"

Finally Ellen lowers her shoulders, sits up straighter. "I know. I'm here. It's all right. You're right. I can only do what I can do."

"You can love him, Ellen. I know you can do that."

And Ellen smiles. "I can. Thank you. Again and again and again."

"I'll see you when you get back," Amanda Smithfield says, and she hangs up.

I can love him, Ellen tells herself again. And it calms her. Yes, that is something she can do.

"THERE'S A PLACE IN THE COUNTRYSIDE outside Malaga where people get a second chance to be alive."

"This is the good part, right?"

Ellen nods, smiles at Jamie. "This is the good part. . . . I went from the hospital to Tracy's and then to 'A Safe Place'—that's the name of it, 'Un Lugar Seguro.' And they're not kidding. No one who isn't wanted can get in, and no one who's in can get out."

"Sounds like a prison."

"No, no, more like a womb."

They're driving from Jamie's school, where Ellen has picked him up, into the heart of the San Diego downtown, to the annual ArtWalk. Hundreds of local artists display their work. There are usually several bands, including a mariachi, and food stalls. It's a street festival, and Jamie goes every year. He wants to show it to Ellen.

It's late on a Friday afternoon, and Ellen, who spent the week exploring, is at the wheel. She feels like she knows her way around now.

The week has gone well for both of them. Breakfasts and dinners together. Each day inching closer to that sense of seamlessness they shared as children. Jamie went to work. Ellen explored. One day she went to the Wild Animal Park and rode the little tram around its acres and acres, visiting the Elephant Valley and the African Outpost, where she saw cheetahs and warthogs, and the Gorilla Forest, and the giraffes, of course the giraffes, her favorite. Another day she drove to La Jolla and walked the wide, clear beaches for miles. When Jamie got home he found her sun- and wind-burned and lazy with relaxation. They watched a DVD that night of *Doubt* because neither had ever seen it and both had plenty of memories of nuns and priests to add to the mix. They stretched out on Jamie's forest green couch, now with colorful throw pillows under their heads, and ate popcorn for dinner and talked to each other and the TV screen all the way through the movie. A perfect evening.

"If you want to be crass about it, it's a rehab hospital," Ellen continues as she drives, "only it looks like a spa—all the buildings have thick white walls and tile roofs, there's bougainvillea draped over everything, I mean everything, in that shocking magenta. There are two pools, a massage room, a kitchen that turns out only organic food that is amazingly good, and acres of olive trees with paths and patios everywhere. You get the picture. Very tranquil. *Muy tranquilo.* Very expensive. *Muy caro.* Miguel paid for it. He sort of had to—he'd put me in the hospital twice. He didn't want me to press charges."

Jamie watches her as she talks and steers the car down the

Pacific Coast Highway, through the crowded Friday afternoon traffic, the endlessly blue ocean on their right. She does it effortlessly, as if she were the world's most competent person.

"What were you rehabbing from?"

"Are you kidding me? From our childhood."

"Then all eight of us should be in a place like that."

"Wouldn't be a bad idea."

"Really, Ellen, can you be a bit more specific?"

She doesn't answer him directly. She thinks about how to go about this conversation for a minute and then says, "You would think, wouldn't you, that if you were subjected to the kind of violence we were as kids, then as an adult, you'd avoid any situation that might conceivably lead there."

"I have," Jamie says.

"We'll get to you in a minute. There's a flip side to all this."

"Oh, good." Jamie turns from her and looks out his window at the ocean. The sky at the horizon line is turning purple. It will be dusk soon. "I can't wait to hear the flip side," Jamie says, his voice brittle and chopped.

"Jamie, I almost died because I wouldn't look at what was driving my life. Don't check out on me here."

With effort he turns back to her, but he knows now that this "good part" is going to include things he doesn't want to hear.

"I had to let go of everything I believed about who I was and how I worked and what had made me. They have doctors there who help you do that—to see clearly, to be naked, psychologically speaking. When I came to Dad's funeral, I had only done that work. I had stripped myself to the bone, and I was terrified. I hadn't put myself together in a new way yet. That's what you saw when I came to Buffalo."

"Who was that grim woman with the mustache?"

Ellen laughs. It's open and free. "Estella. She works there as a sort of psychiatric aide. The only way they'd let me leave was to have someone with me, to take care of me, sort of. And they were right. I was barely functioning. It took another six months before I could see another way to be. Before I could leave all that need for violence behind."

She looks over to see how Jamie is taking all this. His face gives nothing away, even to her.

"Here's the thing—you can't just bury all the shit we lived through and expect to have any sort of life."

"I have a life," he says through tight lips.

"Barely, Jamie, barely. Don't you see how much you deny yourself?"

He shakes his head. *Here it comes,* he thinks, *here comes the attack.*

"Ellen," he says as calmly as he can, "I hope you didn't fly all this way to tell me how to live."

"I did!" she crows, as if he's won the jackpot. "That's exactly why I'm here! Because I learned something vital. Because I know now that what you're doing is just burying everything. I chose to act it out. You choose to stuff it down. It's the same shit, and it's ruining your life as much as it ruined mine."

"Ellen . . ." and now his tone is a warning.

"I want you to see what I now see—"

"We're different people, Ellen, you're—"

"I want you to have more, Jamie—"

"I can't!" And this last is a cry and it shuts Ellen's mouth. She stares straight ahead as she takes Grape Street east, away from the ocean. At the first red light, she looks over at him. He looks so miserable.

"I love you, Jamie."

"I know that, but we all have to find our own way through all this. I have something I love in my life, my teaching, and I consider myself lucky. Leave it be."

As the light turns green, she pulls ahead slowly. It's crowded here already. People walking in groups toward Little Italy, some on the sidewalks, the overflow at the edges of the street.

"Which street do I make a right on?"

"India, and then park anywhere after Fir that you can."

"Okay."

There's silence, but it is an unresolved silence. Ellen hasn't given up. Jamie can sense her pent-up frustration. Her hands on the steering wheel are tight. She pushes herself against the back of the driver's seat as if she will stand up at any moment. Her foot on the accelerator is heavy, and he can see she's trying to figure out how to frame the next volley. He braces himself for the onslaught as she starts to talk again, tightly restrained.

"I had to understand the violence in my life so I could eliminate it forever. Jamie, do you even realize how free I feel?"

He shakes his head no.

"That was my task, and yours is to open up the lockbox where you've stuffed everything since you were a teenager. The beatings. The night Dad almost killed you . . ."

"Stop it, Ellen!"

"I won't stop it! I won't give up on you!"

She makes a right on India Street, too fast. Jamie can feel the car tremble. She doesn't realize. She's focused on Jamie, on having him understand, on saving his life. The ArtWalk is right in front of them, down about a block. The street and sidewalk are packed with people, walking toward it. Families with children in strollers. People who've come with their dogs. There's a live band at the corner of Fir and India, and their amplified sound blasts out into the twilight air.

"Ellen!" he yells above the music. He wants her to slow down, but he's not sure she can hear him.

"You have to listen to me, Jamie!" Her voice is urgent. She's searching his face to see how far she can push.

"Look!" He's pointing at the people in front of them clogging the street, but she's too intent upon her mission. She will save her brother. She won't be derailed.

"Your life is at stake!" She's screaming now over the music, her body taut, rising up from the seat, her foot pressing down on the accelerator, but she doesn't realize. The car is speeding. The streets are clogged with pedestrians.

"Stop!" he screams at her. "Stop, Ellen, stop!"

He grabs the wheel, but it's too late. The first body hits the car with a sickening thud. The next with a scream that pierces his heart and shatters it.

Ellen slams on the brakes and the car comes to a shuddering stop. She stares with horror at the carnage in front of her, unable to move. Jamie pushes open the passenger door and gets out. To see what happened, to help if he can. But it's too late, he sees. *Oh God, it's too late.* The damage has already been done.

 *Aftermath*

HAVING SPENT MOST OF HIS FORTY-THREE
years intimately acquainted with the notion that the sins of the
father are visited upon the son, Jamie O'Connor now contemplates
the sins of the sister. Deep in the middle of the night, as he drives
from his home to University Hospital, he tries to determine what
his responsibility is to carry those.

Twenty-four days ago his sister Ellen plowed into a crowd of
people walking to a street fair. She was driving his car. He was
there, sitting in the passenger's seat. Should he hold himself culpable for her act? For not insisting when she picked him up from
school that Friday afternoon that she slide over and let him drive?
Should he have seen she was in no shape to be behind the wheel?

But she seemed fine, Jamie argues with himself. By now, he's
had this internal debate too many times to count. It's boring and
compelling and urgent all at the same time. *She drove with confidence. Like a pro. She could have given a master class on how to
navigate the I-5 Freeway,* he reminds himself yet again.

All right, then, maybe he can't fault himself for not taking the wheel at the beginning of the ride, but what about once she became agitated? Once he saw her knuckles whiten, her hands clutch the steering wheel too tightly? What about when he saw her back press up against the driver's seat as if she wanted nothing more than to burst through her skin?

But how do you do that? How do you force a person to stop a car safely? When I yelled at her to stop, did that just make things worse?

A groan escapes from deep within him and Jamie shakes his head slightly, alone in his car. What part of this disaster was his fault? What should he have seen that he missed? How much of the carnage could he have realistically prevented? There are no answers to his questions. He knows that now. It is the weight of this burden that propels him through the streets of San Diego.

It seemed to Jamie for weeks after the accident that there was nothing else on the local television news or in the papers—"Sister of San Diego Teacher Crashes Car into ArtWalk Crowd." Several people had whipped out their cell phones at the first horrified scream, and their grainy videos were played on the networks obsessively. Various police officers were interviewed on camera. The accident-reconstruction people brought out their renderings of tire tracks and skid marks. And one channel ran animated drawings of the bodies' trajectories as they flew, endlessly, through the air.

Jamie's colleagues at Pacific Village Middle School turned up on news cameras regularly, all expressing shock. *Jamie was so quiet, such a gifted teacher,* they uniformly said. Some had met Ellen when she visited school to watch Jamie teach. *She seemed so nice,* they said. Everyone seemed genuinely puzzled how something so awful could happen to such decent people.

That question had led to the second round of media speculation. Mental health experts, from the safety of their armchairs,

offered opinions about the driver's possible mental state—
repressed hostility, depressive disorder, a subconscious suicide
wish. Then legal experts weighed in on probable trial strategies
for both sides. None were shy to predict outcomes and sentences.

But no one had talked to Ellen. She was in jail. Her bail had
been set at five hundred thousand dollars, and neither Jamie nor
anyone he knew had the kind of money it would have taken to get
her out.

Seven people had been injured, two seriously. A forty-seven-
year-old manager at a Sears store in Chula Vista had suffered
broken bones, a lacerated spleen, and internal bleeding. He was
recovering. The other, a graduate student at the University of California, San Diego, was still in the intensive-care unit, where her
survival chances had been broadcast almost hourly by every local
news outlet.

It is Celeste that Jamie comes to see in the middle of the night.
The first time, five days after the accident, he felt compelled to go.
He knew it made no sense. What could he offer? Why would anyone want him there? Logical questions, but completely irrelevant
to the imperative he felt. He needed to be there.

He waited until very late at night, after the news cameras
were gone and the hospital staff was a skeleton crew. Then it was
simple to slip through the emergency entrance. No one paid him
much attention at two o'clock in the morning. He took the elevator up to the seventh floor. He knew where the intensive-care unit
was from the time one of his students had swallowed too many of
her mother's pills. Jamie had kept the vigil with her family until
the girl was out of danger and moved to the psychiatric floor.

When he walked into the waiting room of the ICU, he knew
immediately that the man sitting alone in there was her father.
The papers had said she was from Montana, doing graduate work
in marine biodiversity and conservation. They all mentioned she

had grown up on a horse farm not far from Helena, as if there was something faintly exotic about it all—life on a ranch, raised by a single father.

The man sitting there looked like everyone's image of a cowboy—a body made lean from physical labor, a face weathered from being outside through all seasons, dark hair needing a cut and laced with gray, spilling over the collar of a blue work shirt. Late fifties, Jamie guessed. The man sat very still, the weight of his body on the balls of his feet, his back not touching the vinyl of a yellow molded chair. To Jamie he looked as if he was holding himself back from springing up and rushing out of this godforsaken place. Jamie's eyes went to the man's hands. They were open and splayed flat on his thighs, the only part of him that didn't seem poised for flight.

Jamie sat down next to him, knowing he needed to say something but without a clue what that might be. "Mr. Jewell?"

Chet Jewell turned his eyes to Jamie. They were a pale blue, almost gray, and they contained so much bewilderment that Jamie almost got up and left. He didn't know how to answer the question he saw there. *Why? Why?*

"Are you a doctor?" is what Chet Jewell said instead.

"No."

"What is it, then?"

"I thought I might sit with you."

Chet's eyes swept the clock mounted on the far wall. "Don't you have anyplace better to be at two ten in the morning?"

"No."

"No wife or kids?"

"No."

And then he swiveled in his chair and really looked at Jamie. "What is all this to you?"

"My sister was driving the car."

There was a long moment of silence. Jamie had no idea what Chet Jewell might do. Punch him? Toss him across the room? He looked capable of either. Instead, Celeste's father nodded—he certainly understood grief when he saw it—and then turned his eyes away from Jamie, out the darkened windows that gave back nothing but his own haunted face.

That first night they sat side by side for many hours, until the sun came up and Jamie had to go teach. Neither man spoke, but now there were two sets of eyes to scan the faces of the ICU nurses as they swept past the waiting room, busy, preoccupied. *Something About Celeste?* each man asked silently, afraid to speak. Not that night.

And throughout the always dangerous predawn hours, when the world seems at its bleakest, Jamie offered what he could—a second body immobile in a chair, a second set of shoulders not quite touching, a second heartbeat to match the first.

AFTER THAT, MORE NIGHTS THAN NOT, Jamie found himself making the twenty-minute drive from his condo to the hospital. Always late at night. Always without much premeditation. Oftentimes when sleep eluded him, he'd get up out of his solitary bed, gather the things he'd need for school the next day—the set of seventh-grade essays he'd graded earlier that evening or the questions for the poetry test he'd be giving his honors class—and make the drive with what he came to acknowledge as a quiet sense of anticipation. The desire has been born in him to sit beside Chet Jewell.

For many nights the men don't speak. That Chet nods when Jamie shows up and allows him to take the seat beside him is enough. Sometimes Jamie brings in coffee for the two of them, and that is appreciated.

Both men come to know the night nurses who attach the tubes and watch the monitors and change the dressings and respond to the alarms when they go off: Patty Joe, blond and heavy, who is curt with everyone and seems too angry to work in such a tenuous place; Felicia, Filipina, demure and worried, who never makes eye contact with any of the relatives; Sandra, who is built to play basketball and never seems to speak. But it is Tamara they pay the most attention to. Both men sense she is the one who would give them what little information there is about Celeste.

Tamara is small and tidy and efficient, that's clear. A light brown woman in her forties, she seems confident without being showy. They can pick all that up by watching her work, and their eyes never leave her on the nights she's on duty, following her as she weaves in and out of patients' rooms.

When she comes to the door of the waiting room to speak with Chet, she includes Jamie, assuming he is a family member, and no one corrects her. Her updates are usually short, delivered on the fly, but gratefully accepted. "Her temperature is down," she tells them one night. "Her pupils are responding to light, that's a good sign," she tells them a few nights later. The men receive her words with nods and always a "thank you" from Chet but never a question of his own. It is almost as if he feels his only role is to wait and accept. As if what is happening in that ICU is beyond his ability to fully take in. Forming a question would be an impossibility.

Several nights after Jamie begins to sit with Chet, Tamara comes to them one early morning. The sky is lightening out the window, a dove gray, then a slight blush of pink. She sits down, turns her chair to face them both, and Jamie's heart sinks. Something serious must have happened to Celeste. Tamara never sits down to speak with them. But no, that isn't it. It's the seriousness of her instructions that makes her sit down. She tells them that Celeste's coma is the body's way of quieting the brain so it can begin its repair. She says they mustn't lose hope; she's seen amazing things in her twelve years working the ICU. Both men believe her when she speaks. She has that kind of gravitas.

"Talk to her," Tamara tells them, "hold her hand and tell her that you're here. Tell her that you're not going anywhere and that you'll be here when she wakes up."

Chet nods but he doesn't move. "Now," she says, "now you need to do that. Come on." And she prompts him to stand up. "You, too," she says to Jamie.

"No . . . I'm not really . . ." he begins.

"She's got two hands and there's two of you."

Jamie finds himself following the straight back of Chet Jewell into the sedated light of Celeste's cubicle.

She lies absolutely still. *This is what death looks like* is Jamie's first thought, although he knows she isn't dead. Her chest rises slightly as the machines breathe for her. The electronic screens all record some kind of activity, evidence that the body is alive, if not the mind.

She doesn't look like her pictures in the papers, of course. Those showed a girl who thought life was an adventure. There was a kind of friendly challenge to the cock of her head, to her open, grinning face. This young woman who lies so undefended in a startlingly white bed seems younger and somehow purified.

Jamie hangs back in the doorway—he doesn't belong here, he feels—and watches Chet pull a straight-backed chair close to the right side of the bed. The father takes his daughter's lifeless hand in his two large, callused ones. They are trembling.

"There's another chair," Chet says without looking at Jamie, but it is an invitation. Jamie comes into the room and positions a chair close to the other side of Celeste's bed. That first night he can't bring himself to reach for Celeste's hand. He doesn't have the right. Or the courage.

Chet doesn't seem to notice. His head is bowed. His eyes are closed. His hands cling to his daughter's. Softly, he begins to talk, whispering really, a prayer: "Please . . . please . . . please . . . please . . ."

That night and during the ones to come, over Celeste's motionless body, the men begin to talk. In hushed voices, haltingly the first few nights, then more expansively. The whisperings of the machines against the quiet, the delicacy of Celeste's condition, the cocoon of the ICU where the outside world doesn't exist—all these make confessions possible.

"Her mother left when she wasn't even two," Chet begins. "How does a mother leave her own child?"

Jamie shakes his head. He doesn't know the answer to that.

"She said she didn't know what she had signed on for. I took that to mean me. And probably life in Montana, on a ranch . . ." He shrugs. "Maybe that meant being a mother, too. I don't know. She just left and never came back."

Chet looks up at Jamie. "Do you know what it is to raise a child? Yours or someone else's?"

"No."

"It lifts the spirit. If you've got someone like Celeste, it does that."

Jamie can't imagine his own father, dead just over a year now, embracing anything resembling Chet's sentiments. To Hugh O'Connor, his eight children were lumped together as "the little shits," and he made it clear that they were a drain and a trouble and a cause of endless fury for their multiple shortcomings. The beatings the four boys endured for most of their growing up were their own damn faults, Hugh maintained, instead of the heedless cruelty Jamie has come to understand them to be. So this notion that raising a child "lifts the spirit" is as alien to Jamie as the environment the two men are occupying as they speak.

Jamie tries for a minute to imagine his father in this room watching over one of his children, and he knows immediately that his father would never be here or anywhere near a hospital. When Marianne, the youngest of them and the favored, was tiny, she got in the way of one of her older brothers as he was carrying a large pot of spaghetti from stove to sink. She was burned very badly. Second- and third-degree burns over her chest and legs and in the hospital for weeks and weeks, Jamie remembers. His mother went every day and sat by Marianne's crib and read to her from the worn children's books that were always piled in an old basket in the basement of their brick house. But his father never came. There were excuses—"I'm working overtime to keep you kids in Catholic school," or "Your mother does the visiting for both of us"—but even then, when he was just twelve years old, Jamie thought his father was a coward. He couldn't face the hospital and the sight of Marianne bandaged and whimpering in pain.

Jamie remembers his parents standing in their old kitchen, which was narrow and cramped like the whole house. And, like the whole house, it was filled up with useless stuff—ceramic figurines and broken sports equipment piled in a corner, discarded clothes thrown across chair backs, and Christmas decorations that have never been put away. It's early morning and his mother is packing lunches for himself and Ellen.

His father is wearing his white overalls with the name "O'Connor Plumbing" on the back in brown script, and he's pouring hot coffee into a large thermos.

She wants to see you, Hugh, his mother is saying in his memory.

Aw, she'll see enough of me when she comes on home.

Just a few minutes would do her a world of good.

You tell her that I love her. His father is grabbing his heavy plaid jacket, preparing to leave.

Hugh, his mother says, and this is as close to a rebuke as she ever gets, *the child's two years old.*

Don't tell me I don't know how old my children are. Hugh is angry. He slams the back door as he leaves.

No, Jamie knows with certainty, his father would never show up in the intensive-care unit and hold the hand of his daughter and plead with her to live. To wake up and live.

SOMETIMES JAMIE AND CELESTE'S FATHER talk about mundane things. It is an escape route from the surrealism of where they are. And the stories pull them both back to a time before Jamie's sister turned his car into a lethal weapon and before Celeste lay supremely helpless in a hospital bed. Chet talks about how the family he works for, the Swensons, has transformed what had been for generations a working horse and cattle ranch into what is euphemistically called a "guest ranch." Chet spits out the two words. Jamie doesn't have to ask him how he feels about the transition.

"Now we have to take these people along when we move the cattle from one pasture to the next or let 'em watch the colt training or drop what we're supposed to be doing and take them out on a 'ride,' as if that's an activity, 'a ride.' That's how we get from place to place—on a horse. It's not an activity."

Jamie smiles slightly. He can't help it. Chet is so indignant.

"You ever been on a horse?"

"No. I'm a city boy. From Buffalo."

"Well, let me tell you—you have a relationship with a horse, a real one, then you don't need many people in your life."

"I've gotten to that point without the horse," Jamie says, grinning.

"I thought so."

ONE NIGHT, WELL AFTER MIDNIGHT, Chet starts to talk about what Celeste was like as a child. How she took to all the ranch life like a natural. How she could ride well by the time she was four. How, when she got older, she loved to help him in the spring, during foaling season. That they'd stay up all night together if a mare was having a hard time and Celeste would never complain. And about how excited she'd get when the foal was finally born. She always said it was worth it, the long hours, the cold in the middle of the night, because *Look,* she'd say, *Dad, look what we got!*

That's why, Chet admits to Jamie, he couldn't understand her need to go so far away for college. She insisted she had to be somewhere she could see the ocean. That was the criterion—not how good the school was, or how much it cost, or how big or small it was, just that the ocean be nearby. Like there was some magical pull to be near the sea.

"That's what we do," Jamie tells Chet, "we find the opposite and we move toward it. It's part of finding yourself."

"Celeste was herself. More than anyone I ever knew."

"That was one self," Jamie says quietly, "the one who was your daughter and who lived on a horse ranch in Montana and had never been to the West Coast. She needed to find other selves. That you didn't know, precisely because you didn't know them . . . It's what they're supposed to do in order to grow up."

Chet is silent a long time. He watches his daughter's face as if the answer is there, but not so much as an eyelash flutters. Then Chet asks in a harsh whisper, "Then it wasn't me?"

"No," says Jamie without equivocation, even though he's just met this man and has never spoken a word to his daughter. He knows that the right answer is "no" and he says it again, firmly. And he sees Chet sigh with what Jamie interprets as relief.

"HOW DO YOU KNOW SO MUCH about what teenage girls have to do?" Chet asks him later that night, after he's had time to mull over what Jamie has told him.

"I don't really, but I've been teaching middle school for thirteen years now, and you pick up some things just from being around them so much."

"What do you teach?" Another personal question from Chet.

"English."

"And you like it?"

"It saves my life."

Chet nods. He understands how something can do that. He knows that without the horses he wouldn't be much alive.

"And the rest?"

"There is no 'rest.'" Jamie shrugs, a bit embarrassed but he says it anyway. "Just an old-fashioned Irish bachelor."

"That mean you're gay?"

At that Jamie laughs softly, not offended as Chet feared. "No, that means I've never married and don't really see any chance of it."

Maybe it's the late hour. Maybe it's the exhaustion of too many nights spent here in the ICU. Probably it's the sanctuary of Celeste's room, but Jamie finds himself doing something he never does. He begins to talk about himself, about his past. About his father's drinking and his brutality. About his mother's complicity even though she never lifted a hand to any of them. About how she refused to intervene between his father's titanic rages and any one of her children.

It's time for Jamie to go. To return to his condo, grab a quick shower, and get to school. He stands and stretches. The two men have been sitting there for five hours.

"That's all three thousand miles and twenty-five years ago.

Now," he says, "I'm doing the best I can." Jamie isn't sure, even as he says it, whether it's the truth.

ON A THURSDAY NIGHT SOMEWHERE BETWEEN eleven and midnight, when Jamie arrives in the ICU, he finds Chet pacing outside Celeste's room. All the curtains are drawn and it's impossible to know what's going on, but he can immediately see that Chet is upset.

"What's happening?"

"She's thrashing around in there."

"She is?" Jamie is stunned. He hasn't seen her so much as move a finger. "What are they doing with her?"

"Giving her some kind of test to figure out what's going on."

The men wait together, Chet pacing when he can no longer stand still. They can hear groans and angry sounds coming from the room, and then the door opens and Dr. Banerjee comes out. He's a neurologist, originally from India, and he's inordinately polite.

"Please," he says to both men, "would you join me in the waiting room?"

Chet says yes, but looks past the doctor to see if Celeste is all right and meets Tamara's eyes. She stands in the doorway of the room and indicates with a tilt of her head that they should hear the doctor out.

The men find the well-worn plastic chairs in the waiting room and the compact, brown-skinned doctor leans forward so they can talk quietly.

"She's struggling to wake up," he tells them in a soft voice, marked with that distinctive Indian lilt, "and many times that struggle is fueled by anger. That's what you're hearing. The more aware the patient is of what she's feeling, sometimes the angrier she becomes."

Chet stares at the doctor as if he hasn't understood one word he said. There's a long, drawn-out silence. Jamie looks at Chet, waits for him to respond to the doctor's words, but Chet appears frozen in space. So Jamie, totally unaccustomed to asserting himself, finds his voice for the two of them. "Are you saying she's coming out of the coma?"

"We think so."

Jamie glances again at Chet before he continues. "And what will she be like, if she does?"

"Ah, you're asking for my crystal-ball properties. I'm afraid I haven't any. We must just wait and see. Wait and see." And the doctor stands up to indicate the moment is over. "We'll talk tomorrow, then." And he's gone.

JAMIE TAKES THE NEWS TO HIS SISTER Ellen at the San Diego County Jail, where she's been since the accident. Her public defender, a young woman named Carmen Arteaga, uses Celeste's recovery to bolster her case for deportation instead of incarceration. Ellen has been living in Spain for the past seven years, Carmen reminds the prosecutor as they discuss her case, one among too many they both have to handle.

They're in his office. It's late in the day and there are shadows in the room, but he doesn't seem to notice, doesn't reach to turn on a light. Carmen watches as Roger Koenig moves files from one surface to another, looking for Ellen's. What hair he has left is steel gray. His body speaks of decades without exercise, and if they allowed smoking in city buildings, Carmen is sure he would have a cigarette burning between his fingers.

Roger knows he's been doing this too long. It gets harder instead of easier to wade through the misery of most people's lives. He asks himself at least once every day why he doesn't just quit, and then he moves on without an answer.

He must be at least sixty, Carmen thinks as she watches him search and curse quietly under his breath. *More than twice my age. If I'm doing this kind of work in thirty years, shoot me,* she makes a note to herself.

Carmen is always in forward motion, never resting anywhere for too long. It's the only way she got to college and through law school. One brother was murdered by a gang member when he was fifteen and the other works in an auto body shop. Her father moved the family to San Diego for the agricultural work and never really learned English well enough to get any other kind of job. It was her mother who cleaned houses to keep them going. And it was her indomitable mother who pushed Carmen to get out, to reach higher. She feels the obligation of her success every day of her life.

"The girl was moved from the ICU to a regular room." Carmen speaks to Roger's back now. "She's going to live. So now we know we have reckless driving bodily injury, not vehicular manslaughter. There was no intent."

"The woman mowed down seven people, and the fact that the girl's going to live doesn't tell us anything about *how* she's going to live. What shape she's going to be in."

"It was an accident, Roger. I have to keep telling you and Ellen the same thing. The woman's devastated. She feels so guilty she wants to die. You want remorse—she's a poster child for remorse."

Finally, Roger finds Ellen's file and sits down behind his desk to scan the papers in it. Carmen leans over, snaps on his desk lamp—she can't bear that he's squinting to see—and continues to talk while he reads. She has a solution to all this and she wants him to sign off on it.

"Her doctor from Spain, her shrink, will be here tomorrow. Ellen spent a year in her center, institute, rehab place, whatever you want to call it. And Dr. Smithfield will take her back and be responsible for her. There—perfect solution. Ellen will be out of the country. She won't be driving anywhere near San Diego ever again, and she'll be getting the treatment she obviously needs. Anger management, et cetera, et cetera." Carmen waves her hand in the air to indicate the et cetera, et cetera. It's not that she doesn't care what happens to Ellen. She's come to like her and to understand that this accident has undone all the careful rebuilding Ellen's attempted in her life. What she's trying to do is move this case along without any push-back from Roger.

"Don't you have enough seriously bad people to put away?" she asks him, a genuine question. "Ellen isn't one of them."

He leans back in his chair. "What a mess."

"Roger, look at the psychiatric eval." Carmen leans across the overloaded desk and searches in Ellen's open file, pulling out the shrink's report. "Did you read it?"

"I must have," he says.

She puts it in his hands and says very quietly, "The woman barely speaks. She's stopped eating. You want to deal with a defendant who's refusing food? We're there."

"Shit."

They look at each other. Carmen waits. She's giving him room to agree, and finally he does. He nods at her and she stands up, more relieved than she realized she'd be.

"We're doing the best we can here," she tells him as she opens the office door.

"You tell yourself that," he says, but he's already turned his back and is searching through a stack of case folders piled on a bookshelf.

WHEN THEY ALL MEET IN Judge Fornay's courtroom, they present a united front. Roger proposes the settlement Carmen presented in his office and she concurs when asked. Dr. Smithfield, who is British and impressive and brisk, agrees to be responsible for Ellen's treatment and Ellen says yes, very softly, she will return to Spain and stay there.

Jamie watches all this from the second row of the visitors' seating. It looks like a form of theater to him, with all participants knowing their lines and delivering them on cue. He understands that everyone in the room wants to make this go away and that Carmen has crafted a path for that to happen. He's grateful.

Afterward, he has only a few minutes alone with Ellen before she leaves with the doctor. In the two months she's been in jail, Ellen has lost enough weight to look once more like a famine survivor. She's punishing herself before anyone else can do it, and in the corridor of the courthouse he tries to tell her again, yet again, that it was an accident and not her fault.

"The sin of pride, Jamie," she says in a voice so low that he instinctively leans forward toward her. "I was so sure I had the word and had to deliver it to you."

"To help, Ellen—" he starts to say, but she isn't finished.

"And look what I did! Destroyed. Everything I try, everything I touch . . ."

He can't bear to hear the words of their father coming from her mouth—*you are nothing, you deserve nothing.* He gathers her into his arms, where she shuts her eyes, arms around his back, holding on tight, holding the memory of embracing her brother. They both know that it might be a very long time before they see each other again.

It is Ellen who pulls away first. As much as she loves Jamie, it is Dr. Smithfield she needs now. The doctor stands waiting, discreetly, several feet away. But she's ready when Ellen comes to her. Jamie watches the two women walk away from him, and he sees his sister reach for the hand of the older woman and hold it tightly. If he believed in the language of touch, he would be reassured.

BECAUSE HE'S TAKEN A SICK DAY from school to be in court with Ellen, he is at loose ends once the proceedings are over—nowhere he has to be, no one who's waiting for him. And so he goes home to his condo, where he's lived for the past decade.

When he walks in at noon, the first things he sees are the brightly patterned throw pillows Ellen bought to liven up the space. All those years she was away in Spain, all those years he let go by without any real contact. There's e-mail and smartphones and now there's Skype. Why is it that neither of them is very good about being in touch? Ellen never even let him know she was coming.

As he looks around his living room now, he knows she was right. He is content to live with so little. He never replaced the fresh flowers Ellen arranged in vases on the top of the bookshelf, in the center of the dining room table, or refilled the blue bowl she bought and piled with lemons. "I love the contrast of the blue and yellow," she explained to Jamie and he had nodded. He liked the contrast, too, but once the lemons were gone, the bowl sat empty.

Today, without work to structure his time, he has no idea what to do with himself. He could grade papers, he thinks. As an English teacher with five classes to teach, he always has papers to grade, but he's restless. It's a feeling he distinctly doesn't like and has managed to almost eliminate from his life by carefully scheduling his time: the hour he gets up, his forty-five-minute run after school, his singular nights at the dining room table grading papers and eating something he's warmed up in the microwave.

All that routine has served to hold the restlessness and anxiety at bay, but now he can't settle down enough to really concentrate and he finds himself grabbing his car keys and closing the front door behind him.

When he enters University Hospital, he's struck by how busy it is. For two months he has been visiting in the slightly surreal hours surrounding midnight. But he knows the way to Celeste's room on the fourth floor, three floors below and a world apart from the ICU, and makes his way through the crowded corridors to get there.

Now she's out of danger. Now she's recovering. Her broken bones are mending—her left leg has a steel plate and wire and screws holding it back together. Her shattered pelvis is healing. But it's the trauma of the head injury that will take months, if not years, to resolve. Everyone—the various doctors who sweep in and out and whom they barely know, the therapists, and Dr. Banerjee, who has been with Celeste from the beginning—has told them not to expect the same carefree graduate student who made friends easily, spoke up in class frequently, and had strong opinions about almost everything.

Today she speaks with effort. Often there are pauses as she searches within her injured brain to find the word she wants. There are gaps in her memory, and these pain Chet the most, Jamie thinks, because it means he's lost part of the little girl he raised. Will they come back? None of the doctors will make definitive statements about anything except the fact that she's out of danger.

When Jamie walks into her room now, he finds Celeste sitting up in bed, attempting to read a simple Dr. Seuss book, *Horton Hatches the Egg,* and she's frowning. It's not going well. Her luxurious dark hair was cropped off sometime in the first week of her stay in the ICU. They needed to lift off part of her skull to relieve the cranial pressure, and when she slowly came through that crisis, the doctors returned the piece of bone. Now the hair that has grown in covers her scalp in soft curls not even an inch long. Her complexion is the milk white of skin that hasn't seen the sun in too long.

In the pictures in the papers and on TV from before the accident she looked so animated, so healthy and eager. Here was a girl who rode a horse with confidence before she started kindergarten, who held her own at a dining table full of opinionated, wisecracking cowboys. A girl who demanded she be able to see the ocean every day or she wasn't going to college. Anyone who knew her then might have trouble recognizing her now. For Jamie, this is the Celeste he knows, and to him her fragility is part of the package.

She looks up, surprised to see him. "You come . . ." she says and there's a pause before she finishes her thought. ". . . at night."

"Yes. You remember that?"

She nods. "My dad."

"Yes, usually when Chet is here." In fact Jamie has never been in her room without Chet as a buffer. He realizes he's uncertain exactly how to behave.

"His . . . friend." It's a statement.

"I hope so," Jamie answers and she immediately understands what he's saying, the implication of it, a higher brain function.

And she smiles. "Yes," and Jamie smiles back at her.

"Where is your dad?"

And the smile fades. She can't remember where he went. She shakes her head. She knows he was here but doesn't remember where he said he was going. And Jamie sees the anxiety—that her father has gone, that she can't remember.

"I'll just go find him for you."

"Oh . . . thank you." And it's said with such relief. Such a simple thing that he can do for her.

JAMIE FINDS CHET IN THE ATRIUM at the end of the hall. A plaque at the door lets everyone know that the money to build it was donated by a grateful family whose loved one was saved by the medical staff at University Hospital. It's a place for patients who are allowed out of bed to sit with their families and remember what the outside world looks like. The room is filled with plants—palms and ficus trees—and wicker patio furniture and glass-topped tables.

Chet is standing at the far end, looking out through the glass wall, lost in thought.

"Chet," Jamie says quietly as he walks toward him, watching Celeste's father turn to him.

"What are you doing here during the day?"

"No school" is all Jamie says. He won't talk to Chet of Ellen and the court and her flight back to Spain.

"They want to move her to this rehab hospital."

"That's good, then, isn't it? It's the next step."

Chet shakes his head. He doesn't know if it's good.

"For how long?" Jamie asks.

"No one knows." Then, "I have to get back. They've been great, the Swensons. Understanding about it all, patient, telling me to take all the time I need, but there's a limit. You can understand that. They've got a business to run, and without me there things are beginning to fall apart."

Chet stops, turns away, and stares out over Balboa Park, a carpet of green from this height made up of the tops of all the trees. Jamie knows this man well enough now after weeks and weeks of nighttime hours spent in conversation and silence to know there's more. He waits.

"I'm going to ask this of you, but you can say no. You hear me. You need to feel free to say no."

Jamie says simply, "Don't worry about that. Whatever the question."

Chet turns his pale eyes on Jamie's face, searches there for the grit behind the quick words. "Be here for Celeste because I can't be."

"I will."

HONORING THAT PROMISE, Jamie now makes twice-weekly trips north to Encinitas and the Scribner Rehabilitation Hospital, every Wednesday and Sunday afternoons. Chet travels eighteen hours from Helena, Montana, to Encinitas twice a month, leaving the middle of the day on a Friday, driving through the night, sometimes pulling over for a few hours of sleep before continuing on, usually arriving late Saturday afternoon and having to leave again by noon on Sunday to get back to Helena by Monday morning.

Jamie makes sure to give them, father and daughter, their time alone. On the weekends Chet visits, Jamie is careful to arrive after two on Sunday. Celeste is often quiet when he first gets there. He knows he's a poor substitute for her father, but he does what he can.

At first, he didn't know how to fill the time. Especially when Celeste was newly arrived, conversation was stilted and painful. For Jamie, it was very difficult to watch her struggle to find the words she wanted to say. He found himself talking way too much to fill up the dead air, and he felt that what he brought to her was of no interest, not that she gave any indication that was so. She listened carefully and sometimes struggled to ask a question when he fell silent and always remembered from visit to visit what he had told her.

He talked about what mattered most to him, his students, weaving stories so that Celeste got to know particular ones. He spoke about Colleen McAllister from his honors class, serious beyond her thirteen years, and he confessed that he searched for her essay when grading their papers. It lifted his spirits to read her carefully crafted paragraphs, always holding something thoughtful in them. Embarrassed to be so self-revealing, Jamie nevertheless admitted that her essays validate the effort he puts into his teaching. He reddened a bit when he admitted that to Celeste and shrugged to take the edge off his words, but she understood. Slowly, she said, "She gets it."

"Yes!" Jamie said. "She hears me and then does some thinking on her own. Original thinking. A teacher can't ask for more."

He's pacing in her room as they talk, and she's watching him from a wheelchair. Recently, they've allowed her to get out of bed, with help from Nadia, her physical therapist, and sit in a wheelchair for a few hours a day. It's a task that's exhausting and disheartening that it's so exhausting. For a girl who would ride a horse all day without tiring, Celeste feels defeated by the simple act of sitting upright in her chair for two hours. Everyone tells her this will improve, but her body tells her it will be a long time. And so she tries to concentrate on Jamie and not on the weakness in her muscles or the fatigue that sweeps over her in waves.

She watches Jamie's excitement as he paces, and it makes her smile to see him so enthusiastic. *He's such a nice man,* she thinks but cannot say. *But he doesn't think so.*

And then there are the days he talks about the students who concern him the most. He doesn't want to worry her, he says before he begins, but she shakes her head—no, it won't. Peter Brosner from his sixth-grade English class is the student he lies awake at night thinking about.

"He never meets your eyes," Jamie explains to Celeste, "even when I speak with him alone, after the rest of the class has gone. He only looks at his shoes, nods, mumbles, then hightails it out of the room as fast as he can. When I walk around the class to lecture, I can see that instead of taking notes, he's constantly drawing these grotesque images of weapons attacking flesh. Comic-book images, but still . . ."

"Angry," Celeste says.

"Yes." Jamie sighs. "Very. I know something about that."

"No." Celeste shakes her head. She doesn't experience Jamie as angry at all. "Not now."

"A sleeping dragon inside me." He makes a scary face. "Don't wake it up."

Celeste grins at him. "Okay."

"I've tried talking to his parents, but they really don't want to know. They tell me it's all the video games and they shrug, what can you do, they say, all the kids play them." Jamie shakes his head. He doesn't believe for a moment that it's the video games. Celeste reaches out and places a hand on his forearm in comfort. It's the first time she's touched him, and it stops their conversation. He finds he wants to take that hand in his and bring it to his lips—a revelation—but, of course, he doesn't. He moves away, goes to stand next to the large window. What is he supposed to do now? He needs a moment to regroup, damp down the emotion, smooth the surface. It's a skill he's perfected.

He looks out at the cloud-dotted sky, endlessly blue, and knows that the weather will be like this for months. Beautiful San Diego in the summer. *Will she have to see it all from this window?* he wonders. Celeste watches him and waits.

"I've been talking too much" is what he finally says, not looking at her, very afraid of what he might say next.

"No."

"We should do something more fun."

"This is . . . fun."

Finally, he turns from the window, an action plan in mind. He grins at her, shaking his head to disagree with her. "Girl, you have been cooped up too long. I need to remind you what fun is!"

SO NOW, ON SUNDAYS, HE BRINGS a DVD for them to see. They make a pact that they will go through the American Film Institute's one hundred best comedies. They like the silly movies best, the sillier the better, films he would never have seen on his own: *Duck Soup, Blazing Saddles, There's Something About Mary, It's a Mad, Mad, Mad, Mad World*—the title of which resonates particularly with both of them.

They're outrageous and crude and very funny. Celeste gets all the jokes, another positive sign, Dr. Banerjee says. Jamie has dubbed Sunday afternoons "Movie Matinee Day," and it gives them something to look forward to. It's when they can laugh together, Jamie always leading the way, getting the jokes a split second before she does. He assumes it's her injured brain still having trouble processing quickly, but mostly it's because Celeste's attention is often focused on Jamie. Because she watches his face light up with laughter, hers comes second.

And then, there is Celeste's secret. Despite the relaxed happiness of Sunday afternoons, it's Wednesdays that she looks forward to the most. Jamie arrives after teaching summer school, and there isn't enough time for a movie then. They have to talk or sit quietly, and it's those hours that get her through the long week of physical therapy and occupational therapy and cognitive therapy and speech therapy, the hardest one of all.

She needs her speech therapy. She needs to be able to say all the words that are swimming around her brain, just out of reach of her tongue. She needs to tell Jamie that he has saved her life. That if she didn't have his visits to look forward to she thinks she'd give up. She needs to make him see how good he is. She's listened enough to understand that he feels he's worth something only when he's teaching, and she wants to tell him that this isn't so. That the Jamie she knows from the hospital rooms she's inhabited these many months, to her that Jamie is beautiful.

But she can't say anything any of those things yet, not with the complexity that might make him believe her.

IN THE TIME BETWEEN THE END of summer school and the beginning of the fall semester, Jamie has several unscheduled weeks. In prior years he used those days to prepare for the coming school year. He meticulously made his lesson plans for all five classes. He reread the books or plays or essays that he would assign so that they were fresh in his mind, even though he had taught most of them for years. He would go to school and rearrange his classroom. But not this year. This summer none of that happens, because he finds himself making the drive north many times a week. He tries to convince himself that he is fulfilling the promise he made to Chet, that the trips north are altruistic, but he knows that's not even half the story.

One Tuesday afternoon when he arrives exactly at one thirty, as he said he would, he finds Celeste waiting at the elevator for him, standing up, holding on to a walker. When he steps out onto the floor, she turns without a word and takes four steps, unaided, before she collapses back into the waiting wheelchair Nadia holds for her.

Jamie is astonished. "You're walking. . . ."

"I wanted . . . a surprise . . ." she manages to say, breathing hard from the exertion.

"You pulled it off, didn't you? Wow, you're walking!"

"A little . . ."

"But a little leads to a lot, right, Nadia?"

"We think so."

"I want . . ."—Celeste struggles for the word and then when she finds it, she grins at him—"a . . . reward."

"And what would that be?"

"The ocean . . . I want . . . to see . . . the ocean."

Jamie looks at Nadia for permission. "Could I take her?"

And before Nadia can answer, Celeste says, "I say yes!"

THE REHAB FACILITY HAS BEAUTIFUL GROUNDS, carefully planted and landscaped with level walkways, fountains with benches around them, but Celeste isn't interested. Only the ocean will do, and so Jamie has to push her chair past the manicured lawns and the curved flower beds bursting on this late summer's day with cosmos and zinnias and salvia in shades of purple. They cross the main driveway and come out onto the winding road that brings visitors to the hospital and then continues on.

Jamie pushes Celeste along the shoulder of the road, being careful to look for cars, conscious that her safety is in his hands, but she seems supremely unconcerned. She puts her head back and takes in the feel of the sun on her skin. Her eyes are closed and she is smiling.

"I smell it," she says to him. And so does he. The ocean.

Carefully, afraid that he might be jostling her newly knit bones too much, he turns off the road and cuts across the yellowing late summer grass of an empty field. He knows that if he can get her to the edge of it, she will be able to overlook the ocean. She will be able to see for miles.

She doesn't open her eyes. She waits. He doesn't talk, because he's concentrating on the uneven surface of the dirt, attempting to pick out the least bumpy path. And then he stops the chair, sets the two hand brakes, and kneels down beside her so that he can see what she will be seeing. And yes, the view is perfect—Swami's Beach is in front of them. The sun is on the water. The waves are shallow and rhythmic, running up the sand in frilly white ruffles. The horizon line goes on forever, blending with the bluest sky of the summer.

"Here," he says to her. And she opens her eyes. It's all there. All in front of her. All that she has longed for these many arduous months.

"Oh, Jamie," she says, "thank you."

And she takes his hand and brings it to her and holds it with both of her hands. He lets her. He wants her to.

"Now," she says, "I can get well."

 *Tell Me One Thing*

ON A BRIGHT BLUE JULY MORNING, LUCIA opened her eyes with the thought already formed in her brain—*Is this the day Maggie starts talking?* She had awoken with this question every day for the past thirty-nine days. And every day the answer had been no, not today.

What she hoped for, what the doctor told her not to expect, was that one day, suddenly, her daughter would start chattering again, word would tumble after word, a cascade of sounds and sentences and laughter where now there was only silence and mystery.

Dr. Greenstein took Lucia aside one day and prepared her for whispers, maybe a word at a time, maybe then followed by more silence. "Be alert," the doctor said, "for the occasional word spoken so softly you might miss it." But Lucia didn't want that, one word spoken occasionally. She wanted her child back, her spontaneous, silly, talkative dream of a child.

It had started slowly. On the early Thursday morning, beginning of June, that Lucia began to pack whatever clothes she could

fit into two duffel bags, she looked up to see Maggie in her pajamas, thumb in her mouth, black hair chaotic from the sleep that
still clung to her like a mist, hugging the doorway of the bedroom.

"Oh, sweetheart . . ." Lucia said and then stopped, fumbling for
what to say next. She knew it had to be the absolute right thing,
but she hadn't expected Maggie to awaken so early and she wasn't
prepared.

Maggie's eyes scanned the chaos on the bed—heaps of clothing jumbled on top of each other, the open duffel bags.

"Mommy, where are we going?"

Lucia was desperate to believe that they were going on to
something better, but she couldn't have described exactly what
that was, so, as she sat down on the bed and reached out for her
daughter, Lucia was as literal as she could be. She hoped it would
ground them both.

"We're going to go live by the beach," Lucia said as her daughter climbed into her lap, "in a place called Ocean Park. We went
there once in the summer, to the pier where they have rides and
cotton candy. Do you remember?"

Maggie took a minute to consider. She took all questions seriously. Did she remember? "How old was I?"

"Let me see, you were very little. Maybe not quite two."

"Oh, Mommy," Maggie said, immediately relieved, "that's too
little to remember. No one could."

Lucia smiled. "Probably not." She understood Maggie didn't
like to fail at anything, including remembering things.

"You're being silly," Maggie said as she snuggled deeper into
Lucia's arms.

"It wouldn't be the first time."

"Did we have fun? Tell me about it. I *want* to remember."

And so Lucia described the merry-go-round and the white
horse with jewels in his tangled mane that Maggie insisted on

riding over and over, Richard at her side, holding her on, but Lucia left that part of the story out.

While her mother talked, Maggie took an inventory of the clothing spread across the bed. She saw her shorts and T-shirts, her sandals and tennis shoes, her mother's jeans and sweatshirt hoodies and her face clouded over. It was clear who was going and who wasn't and she stopped her mother mid-sentence. "Why isn't Daddy coming?"

Lucia took a deep breath. "Because his work is here. He has to go to work."

"But when he comes home after work, nobody will be home."

"That's right."

"But what about Sunday? Will he come pick me up?"

Lucia wanted to say, *Yes, eventually, I hope so, if he comes to some peace with this,* but she knew she couldn't say that to a five-year-old. "When things have settled down, Daddy will come on Sundays, but probably not right away."

"He'll be sad."

"Yes," Lucia admitted, "he'll be sad."

"Does he want us to go?"

"No." And here Lucia sighed. "He doesn't."

What Lucia hadn't figured out how to explain was that she was escaping. That's how it felt. Richard wouldn't know until he got home that afternoon that they were gone. If you're escaping, you don't tell anyone in advance. If you're escaping because you haven't the words to explain your departure, it feels like flight.

Richard would have demanded a logical explanation. He is a scientist, after all. And Lucia could have offered him nothing but deeply embedded feelings. There is the certainty now within her that this marriage is wrong and the belief that she would harden into someone she despised—cowardly, angry, and eventually bitter—if she stayed.

This dread finally has propelled Lucia to her early morning escape. It's not that she hasn't tried over the eight years they have been together to speak up, to shift things between them even a little. Oh, maybe not at first. At first she was simply grateful. But gradually, over the years, and especially after she became pregnant with Maggie, Lucia began to question Richard's version of things. She struggled to have him see the way the world looked to her. He would have none of it. It wasn't even an argument. It was an outright dismissal. "No, Lucia, that's not right." "No, Lucia, we're not doing that." "No, Lucia, you haven't thought that through clearly." "Pay attention, Lucia, you're all emotion, use some logic."

Here was a man whose life had proceeded easily from precocious child to adored son to honored student to responsible husband. Only now, as Richard struggles to finish his dissertation, as he competes with scientists more than his equal, as he finds that teaching undergraduates at the University of California at Riverside isn't to his liking, as his life stalls around him, only now has Richard ever had to examine his circumstances. And he's not doing a good job of it, introspection being a skill he never acquired.

At the beginning, Lucia thought Richard would light the way. It was his rock-solid belief in his own competence that drew her to him. In those early days, she believed he knew how to get the better of life.

"Most people don't know how to set the right goals," he told her in the midst of a noisy Oberlin party the night they met. "That's their first problem."

Lucia's immediate thought wasn't that she didn't have the *right* goals, but that she had *none*. She would graduate in June, and then what? The thought terrified her. Would she end up back at her parents' house in Columbus, Ohio, sleeping in her childhood bedroom, eating Sunday dinner in her grandparents' overstuffed din-

ing room, walking the same neighborhood streets, seeing the same
tired faces as she had every day of her life until she left for Oberlin? She saw no other alternative. She was studying music. How
would that translate into a life that could sustain her? She had no
idea, but she knew that if she didn't come up with a plan soon, it
would be as if her four years at college had never happened.

Richard and Lucia stood in the tiny kitchen of a classmate's
apartment, the crowded party going on around them, empty beer
bottles spilling out of black garbage bags and continuing on across
every available surface—countertop, stovetop, kitchen sink. The
floor was crunchy with broken pretzels and ground-up potato
chips, the air thick with the aroma of pot, and the room swelter-
ing from a late September heat wave. Not a lick of a breeze came
through the open back door.

Richard seemed to take no notice of any of it. A deep green
bottle of Rolling Rock in hand, he leaned his lanky body against
the old lumbering and wheezing fridge, his blue eyes intense with
concentration as he spoke to Lucia. He made her feel as if they
were alone and she was flattered, rapt. Richard Weiss was mesmerizing in his certainty.

"And most people refuse to work hard, really hard. They
don't understand that's what you have to do if you want something badly enough. You do all that . . ." And here he paused and
shrugged, as if to say the rest was self-evident. His thin face, so
somber till then, broke into an irresistible grin, and suddenly he
was boyish and appealing. When he said, "My life is the perfect
example," it didn't occur to Lucia to see it as bragging.

Her own life had been a series of accidents and unexpected
turns, so that Lucia never trusted the outcome of any enterprise
and certainly didn't trust her ability to make things happen.

Named after her paternal grandmother, Lucia grew up the only
child of grateful parents. Her father, Lino, had emigrated from

Calabria, Italy, as a young man, lured by the stories of his relatives who had come before him, and settled in Columbus. Two uncles had opened a shoemaker's shop. At first they did only the most commonplace repair—resoling shoes, replacing broken heels, stretching insteps for ladies who had bought a shoe several sizes too small. But gradually they began to design and make shoes. The uncles were friendly. Their customers spoke to them about their difficulty in finding a comfortable shoe. People with tricky feet were grateful to pay a little more for the luxury of walking pain free. Their business prospered.

Because neither uncle had married, they gratefully taught their nephew the trade. Thirty-seven years later, as Lucia packed her duffel bags in Riverside, California, Lino continued to greet customers at the counter of Pascoli Brothers Shoes in Columbus, the uncles long dead, the shop now his.

Never once can Lucia remember her father complaining. Did he like what he did for a living? The question, itself, was outside his range of inquiry. He was grateful to have had uncles to help him, grateful to have made enough money to provide for his wife and daughter, grateful he has work still.

Lucia named her daughter after her own mother, Margaret, who married Lino Pascoli, this courtly Italian man, and never stopped loving him. Margaret's Irish-Catholic parents weren't pleased. But Lino was Catholic. They could all go to the same church. They believed in the same God. That's all that mattered, Margaret told them, and, as the years went on, they agreed.

Her hopeful, sweet mother, who saw only the best in people and would do anything not to make waves, taught Lucia to be thankful and good and to live without anyone noticing. She grew up feeling doted on and pretty much invisible outside her home. She was always the child who gave the nuns no trouble in school, who sat with her hands folded and her attention fixed on her teacher. She was the student whose grades were good and whose love of music, for her violin, gave her a path to college. To Lucia's astonishment, the Oberlin Conservatory of Music welcomed her with a scholarship. Her parents were equally flabbergasted. Yes, Lucia liked to play the violin. Yes, the music that poured out of it was sweet and often made her mother weep, but a scholarship? College, when neither of them had ever gone? This scholarship, this chance to go to college, it was a gift. And Lucia thought of it that way as well. Not as something she'd earned. Not as the logical conclusion to all the years of practice and praise. A gift, an unexpected turn in her life.

And now far away from home, in California, if she doesn't have the words to tell Richard why she's leaving, she certainly can't begin to explain this decision to her parents. In her family, you stayed married. In her family, you didn't inform your husband that you were leaving with a note propped up on the kitchen table, a note that explained pretty much nothing and that explicitly didn't give him any address where he could find you.

AS LUCIA'S CAR SPEEDS WEST ON the 60 Freeway, away from hot, steamy Riverside, she concentrates on her driving. Even though Richard has no idea that they are leaving, it somehow seems urgent to get as far away from the campus as quickly as possible. When the 60 merges with the Santa Monica Freeway, the 10 West, around Boyle Heights, Lucia finally allows herself to draw a breath. This freeway will take them to the ocean. They are on their way. She glances over to see Maggie looking out the passenger-side window, humming quietly to herself.

"Do you remember Bernadette?"

Maggie nods. She remembers that Bernadette laughs a lot and moves around quickly and isn't a restful kind of person. But she also remembers that when Bernadette would come for dinner, she would always bring a present for her. Once she brought Maggie a goldfish in a plump plastic bag tied with a striped ribbon. Another time it was a book about the animals that live at the North Pole. But the best present was a soft doll with long, black braids who was wearing a honey-colored dress embroidered with beads. She had tiny moccasins on her feet. Bernadette explained she was an Indian girl from the Lakota tribe. Later her mommy said that Bernadette taught anthropology classes where her daddy worked, sometimes about the Lakota, sometimes about other native people.

"Well . . ." Lucia continues as the 10 Freeway loops around the shiny, mirrored skyscrapers of downtown L.A., "Bernadette fell in love with a man named Max and she moved to his house in a part of Santa Monica called Ocean Park. She said we could live in their guesthouse for a while, so that's where we're going. We're going to be their guests."

Maggie doesn't like the sound of that. When you are a guest, you have to be on your best behavior and you can't act the way you really want to. She glances over at her mother, whose eyes are now on the road. Maggie knows that her mother doesn't like to drive the freeways. Whenever they went somewhere far away from home, somewhere that included freeway driving, her father always drove and sometimes her mother would grab hold of the front seat, where she was sitting, hold on tightly, and say, "How fast are you going, Richard?" Her daddy always answered with a wave of his hand toward the road, "The flow of traffic, Lucy."

Now, as her mother concentrates on getting them to Bernadette's, her tightly curled body hunched over the wheel, Maggie knows that if she said she didn't want to leave her bedroom with all her favorite books lined up in order of preference, and her best friend, Ashley, and her preschool teacher, Miss Julia, not one of those things would change her mother's mind because here they are, after all, in the car, on their way. As Maggie looks out the window and silently counts all the blue cars she sees, she wonders what her daddy did that was so bad that her mother had to pack their bags and leave.

She feels like she has two daddies—the during-the-week daddy who goes to work at the university and comes home talking about his work and doesn't really have time to play with her because he goes into the den after dinner and works some more. But then there is her Sunday daddy. Ever since she was just a baby, from lunchtime on Sunday till dinnertime, it was understood that it was their day. And as Maggie got older, Richard would let her set the agenda. "What do you want to do today, mouse?" he would ask her. And unless she said something silly like "Fly to the moon," Richard would find a way to make it happen. Sometimes they went to the beach. Lots of times they drove to different cities— Long Beach to see *The Queen Mary* or the Anza-Borrego desert to see the cactus. One Sunday he took her to Olvera Street in Los Angeles, the place where the city was born, he said, and there was mariachi music and Mexican food and tiny shops selling straw purses and embroidered shirts. Another Sunday they bundled up in parkas and went to Big Bear Mountain to play in the snow.

But even on the Sundays when they didn't do anything extra special, they still went to a restaurant to eat lunch, or to a park to watch the dogs play, or just drove to see where they would end up.

Those were the times Richard wasn't impatient or too busy to read her a story, which seemed to happen the rest of the week. It was their Sunday afternoons that Maggie would miss. It is the daddy who did those things with her that she's afraid she'll never see again.

LUCIA TAKES THE CLOVERFIELD BOULEVARD EXIT off the 10 Freeway and stops at the light. Immediately she turns off the air conditioning and opens the windows. It's like they've traveled

to another country. It was close to one hundred degrees in Riverside, and now the breeze coming through the window is cool and
smells like the ocean.

Lucia lets out a sigh that sounds like a long, drawn-out
"ahhhh." Maggie turns to her, a quizzical look on her face, and
Lucia laughs. "It just feels so much better here. We've dropped
thirty degrees."

As Lucia makes a left turn and travels south on Cloverfield,
her shoulders lower, her back gets straighter. So concerned has
she been with getting them here to Santa Monica that it hasn't
occurred to her that her daughter hasn't uttered a single word the
entire trip.

BERNADETTE IS GARDENING IN HER front yard as Lucia's Honda
Civic travels slowly down Sycamore Street, braking for the multiple speed bumps that run the length of it. She's a solid woman,
ample, in her forties, with freckled skin and hair that has gone
prematurely white and is swept back loosely into a ponytail. She's
wearing shorts, a T-shirt with a giant sunflower silkscreened on
the front, and a wide-brimmed straw hat as she kneels next to a
flower bed, pulling out weeds. When she spots Lucia's car, Bernadette stands and waves, wide, long sweeps of her arm, as if she
were calling in circulating aircraft.

The house she stands in front of is Max's house. It is a small
two-story, painted white, with a wide front porch punctuated
by square pillars. The trim on the house is black, and the shutters are a faded cinnamon. It looks like a miniature plantation,
someone's idea, way back in the forties when it was built, of an
homage to the South. Like most buildings in Ocean Park, it is far
from spruced up and a long way from new. Along with its nearest neighbor, Venice Beach, Ocean Park is proud of its California
casual air.

There's a long driveway to the right of the house, and, at the end of it, in the far right corner of the backyard, is a two-car garage with a small apartment sitting above, spilling over the sides like a muffin top. Maggie stares at it as Lucia parks their car in front of the garage. *Is this where we're going to live? For how long? Why?* These are the questions running through Maggie's head, but she doesn't ask them. She turns and watches her mother, waiting to see what Lucia is going to do.

RICHARD WEISS ARRIVES HOME AT five thirty. Today is the last day of student conferences to wrap up his senior seminar on the ethics of genetically modified foods. It's the one class he enjoyed teaching; the conversations were always lively. He's already turned in his grades for his freshman Introductory Chemistry and his upper-division Chemistry 240. Now, finally, this summer, he'll have time for his own research. He's struggling with a process called RNA interference, which has the potential to shut down an organism's ability to express a specific gene. Richard is interested in the gene that produces polyphenol oxidase, the enzyme responsible for browning in fruit. Richard's hope is that he can create an apple that doesn't discolor when cut.

The first thing he notices as he parks his car in its assigned space, behind the apartment building, is that Lucia's car isn't in her spot adjacent to his. She's almost always home when he gets there, but he figures she might have forgotten something and made a quick run to the store. Or maybe Maggie had a playdate that ran long. Always logical, he runs through these possible scenarios as he walks through the courtyard and makes his way to the front unit of the westernmost building. Although he often spends large swaths of his day impervious to his surroundings, this afternoon, perhaps because he's a bit more relaxed, he notices again how graceful their old apartment complex is—two buildings of three units each, forming a square around an open green space. Yes, it's old, probably built in the twenties, but the architecture is Spanish, the walls are thick, and the roof is half circles of weathered red tiles.

Once inside his apartment, he puts his briefcase and keys down on the small table by the front door and goes immediately into the bedroom to change. This is his routine. Whatever clothes he wears to teach in, even if it's only jeans and a button-down shirt, always feel too constricting when he's home. He sheds his shoes and socks, his confining long pants and long-sleeved shirt, and dons flip-flops, shorts, and a T-shirt with the faded Oberlin logo on it. *Ah, comfort, finally.*

Next he goes into the kitchen, as Lucia knew he would, and pours himself a cocktail of his own devising. One part lemonade, one part iced tea, and one part cranberry juice, mixed well with three ice cubes. It is as he's stirring his drink that he sees the note, but it sets off no alarm bells. His first thought is that Lucia, in her ever-considerate way, has written him a note telling him where she is and when she'll be home.

He opens it to read:

Richard,

I'm afraid you're going to be surprised when you read this. Looking back on the eight years we've been together, I can see now that I never managed to say what I needed to say. I realize that my failure makes this note that much harder.

I've known for a long while that we were never meant to be married. Instead of getting pregnant when we did, we should have broken up and each of us should have moved on, but that's not what happened.

I'm not saying I wish Maggie hadn't been born—oh no, just the opposite. She is a miracle and makes my life joyful every day. I guess what I'm saying is that I haven't been happy for a long time. Would I have had the courage to leave you if I hadn't gotten pregnant? Probably not. I honestly don't know. I just know that somehow, maybe through being Maggie's mother, I've found the courage to do what I should have done five years ago.

I'm sorry this is so long and unfocused. I'm sure you are reading it saying to yourself—will she please get to the point already?! Okay, the point is Maggie and I have moved away. I am sure of my decision. I've been thinking about it for more than five years. Please don't try to change my mind.

You know that I will take good care of Maggie and when we are settled, I will contact you.

Lucia

Richard stands in his tidy kitchen with a look of utter confusion on his face. Blindsided by Lucia's words, he really can't process what he just read. It makes no sense to him. Lucia unhappy? Their marriage a mistake? Neither of those things is true. They can't be. He has to read the note again.

He sits down at the table, lays the note flat in front of him, and starts from the beginning. When he's finished, his first thought is that something has happened to Lucia. You live with someone for eight years and you don't know they're unhappy, that they don't want to live with you? That's impossible. Something's wrong, very wrong. He has to find her and talk to her and bring her home. That will make everything all right again because when she was here, everything *was* all right. And once he decides that, he launches into goal-seeking mode. Not for another second does he stop to consider what Lucia has tried to say. He knows what has to be done and he will do it.

He calls her cell phone.

LUCIA AND MAGGIE ARE HAVING DINNER with Bernadette and Max in their house when Lucia's cell rings in her car, parked in front of the garage. She made sure to leave the phone behind.

The four of them are sitting at a banquette table in the large kitchen, which overlooks the backyard. Lucia and Maggie sit on the bench that is attached to the wall. The child, leaning against her mother's side, plays with her food. She's not used to what's on her plate—a lot of vegetables and grains. Across from them sit Bernadette and Max, someone neither Lucia nor Maggie has met before.

Lucia watches Maggie watch Max. He's such a different sort of man from her father. Where Richard is slender, precise, and exacting, Max is big and shambling. He has blond, bushy hair that is mixed with gray and in need of a cut. Every few minutes, without thinking it seems, Max has to flop the hair off his forehead and away from his eyes so he can see. As big as he is—and he's well over six feet tall and more than two hundred pounds—his presence at the table is soothing and quiet. Bernadette does most of the talking for both of them. And he appreciates her, it's obvious. He's either patting her shoulder or putting an arm around her or holding her hand in those few seconds when she's finished gesturing with it and places it on the table.

Max teaches history at Santa Monica City College, where he got Bernadette a job in the anthropology department. They drive to school together. They teach. They come home together and find very little reason to go anywhere else.

Bernadette told Lucia all about Max when she met and quickly fell in love with him, but seeing them together for herself is another thing altogether. *This is what love looks like,* Lucia is thinking as she watches them across the table—a delight in the other's presence, a need to be touching, a lightness of spirit just being close. It's how she feels about her daughter but not Richard. She's not asking the universe for validation that she did the right thing in leaving her husband, but the evidence is in front of her anyway. Bernadette and Max love each other. She and Richard do not.

Bernadette is talking to Maggie now, telling her how glad they are that she's visiting. That's how Bernadette explains why Lucia and Maggie are here—she says that they're visiting. Maggie presses closer to her mother, not really looking at Bernadette. "Are you feeling shy?" Lucia asks her as she raises her arm and fits Maggie snugly into her body like two puzzle pieces clicking into place.

"It's been quite a day," Lucia says to the adults in explanation.

"Yes," Bernadette agrees, struck again by how much mother and child look alike—both small and dark, each with an air of gentle patience. Neither looks very happy now, and then Bernadette has an idea. Her eyes light up. "Maggie, maybe you'd like to see what Max has in the backyard. It's pretty amazing. Would you like him to show you?"

Maggie wouldn't, but she sees her mother looking expectantly at her and she realizes she's supposed to say yes, and so she does.

"Come on, then," Max says as he gets up. He holds out his hand, and Maggie puts her very small one in his very large one. His hand is warm and gentle. Lucia and Bernadette watch the two of them walk through the kitchen, Max doing all the talking. "It's a project I've just started, so I'm not much of an expert, but still, it's pretty interesting, I think. . . . Well, you'll tell me if it is. . . ." And the back door opens and closes and it's quiet.

The two women look at each other, Bernadette waiting for Lucia to speak, and Lucia, having so much to say, doesn't know where to start.

Finally she tells the whole truth in one sentence. "I'm thrilled and terrified all in the same breath."

Bernadette nods. "He won't just let you go." She's known Richard for the five years they've been in Riverside, and she knows this about him—he never gives up.

"He doesn't know where we are."

"For now."

"That's all I can handle, Detta, the now."

And Bernadette believes her. She's frankly amazed that Lucia is sitting in her kitchen.

As much as she likes Lucia—and Richard, for that matter, although she'd never want to be married to him—she never thought Lucia would be able to leave her marriage.

She watches Lucia fiddle with the silverware, her eyes downcast, her shoulders creeping forward, her very posture apologetic. *Here is a smart woman,* Bernadette is thinking, *who doesn't think she's smart enough, who second-guesses herself constantly.* The woman she sees in front of her is a gifted mother, certainly, a kind woman, unfailingly kind, who always feels she's falling short. Bernadette has no idea how Lucia managed to actually put her escape plan into action.

"We wouldn't have been able to do it without you," Lucia says now as if reading Bernadette's thoughts. "If we didn't have you to come to . . ." Lucia breaks off, looks out the window to the backyard where Max and Maggie, hand in hand, are nearing the farthest corner of the yard. She shakes her head and doesn't finish her sentence. There's no need.

· · ·

OUTSIDE IN THE BACKYARD, at the opposite corner from the garage, Max brings Maggie close, but not too close, to a structure made up of three rectangular white boxes stacked on top of each other.

"Do you know what that is?" he asks her.

She shakes her head.

"Listen," Max says. "Shhh . . . be very quiet."

And they both stop talking and moving and there it is! In the hushed, dense air of the beach twilight Maggie hears a faint buzzing, and her face lights up. She turns to look up at Max and he's grinning. "You hear it, don't you? Those are the bees. Shall we open the hive and see what they're doing?"

"Yes, please," Maggie whispers and Max grins. He so hoped she'd be as entranced by the colony as he is.

"It's awesome. You'll see," he whispers back at her. "Come with me, we have to prepare."

He takes her hand again—and she's so glad that he has—and they walk to a small garden shed. It's made out of wood and looks a little like a playhouse with a short door in front that Max has to stoop to use, and a little window next to it. He comes out carrying a bunch of strange stuff—something that looks like the oil can that the Tin Man in *The Wizard of Oz* carries, long leather gloves attached to sleeves, and two white hats that look like pith helmets with trailing white netting attached to the brim of each.

Max squats on the grass and Maggie follows suit. He puts what Maggie thought was the oil can in front of them. Now she sees that there are two parts—the part that is a round canister with a spout on top and the part that looks like a partially opened book. Max begins by stuffing newspaper into the metal can. Then he lights the paper with a match and quickly layers pine needles on top of the paper, and then, when those are burning, he puts in wood chips and closes the top. When he squeezes what he tells Maggie is the bellows, smoke comes out of the cone-shaped spout.

"The smoke quiets the bees," Max tells her, and although Maggie isn't sure what that means, she can't wait to see what's inside the white boxes.

The both stand up and Max fits one of the white helmets on his head and settles the netting over his neck and shoulders and chest. When Maggie puts her helmet on, the netting flows from her hat and pools at her feet.

"Perfect," Max declares. "Now you're safe from head to toe. Let's go." This time they reach for each other's hand at the same time and walk to the hives.

The first thing Max does is remove the top box and place it on the ground. "That's where the honey is being made," he says, "but I want to show you something else." He squeezes the bellows, which squirts puffs of smoke around the top, the bottom, and the sides of the middle box. Then he gently lifts the hinged lid, and immediately the buzzing gets much louder.

"Come a little closer," he tells Maggie and she does. Then Max lifts out what looks like a drawer that's been set on its side. And there are the bees! Hundreds of them, maybe thousands! And they're very busy, moving around, bumping into each other, vibrating their wings.

"This is a brood frame," Max tells Maggie as he points to the five-sided wax structure the bees have built across the wooden border. "All the way through it, there are baby bees in different stages of growing up. They start out as eggs. . . ." and Max points to some tiny white cylinders, no bigger than the eye of a needle, attached to the walls of some of the cells, one egg per cell.

"And then the eggs turn into larvae." And here he points to some bigger creatures, translucent white and curved like a *C*. They are embryonic and grublike.

"Icky," Maggie says.

"Yes, icky," Max agrees.

Then Max points to some cells that have been sealed with wax caps. "And in there are the pupae."

Maggie is fascinated. Max can see it on her face, and he's glad he's able to show her this. He knows from what Bernadette has told him that Lucia and Maggie have a hard road ahead of them.

"It's called metamorphosis," Max tells her. "That's a big word, but what it means is to change."

Gently he takes the tip of a knife and peels away the wax cap from a pupa cell. "Here," he says, "take a look." Maggie peers inside to see an organism, also very white, with an enormous dark eye and incipient tendril-like legs and antennae. "This pupa will come out of its cell only when it has changed into a beautiful bee. It has to do this—to change three times—until it's finally where it's supposed to be," Max explains to her, and Maggie looks at him and nods. He has the uncanny feeling that she knows what he's trying to tell her.

BECAUSE IT'S JUNE AND THE OFFICIAL start of summer isn't far off, the days are long. Even though it's after eight o'clock as Lucia and Maggie climb the stairs to their apartment, it's not quite dark. There's a breeze and the tangy smell of the ocean and a few stars poking out through the nighttime overcast that is as much a part of the beach communities as the bright, sunny afternoons.

Lucia opens the door to their new home, turns on the light, and deposits her purse and their two duffel bags at her feet. Maggie takes off her backpack, which contains Raymond, her stuffed dachshund, and five favorite books Lucia said she could bring. And then the two of them stand just inside the door and look at where they've landed. The living room is small and takes up the front of the apartment. From the many windows, Lucia can see Max's backyard and the main house. Their kitchen is directly behind the living room and contains a tiny table, just big enough for the two of them.

Some of the furniture Lucia recognizes from Bernadette's house in Riverside—the blue denim couch with yellow piping, the flowered area rug underneath the coffee table. Bernadette's decorating is an extension of her gardening, primary colors and flowered patterns wherever possible. It's not Lucia's style, she much prefers a more neutral approach, but its exuberance makes her smile. It's why she adores Bernadette so much—her willingness to always dive headfirst into anything at all.

Maybe this is an appropriate place for them to have landed, Lucia thinks, because here they are, she and Maggie, diving headlong into whatever comes.

"Shall we go see the bedroom?" And Lucia takes Maggie's hand and they move down the narrow hallway and into the back of the apartment.

"Well," Lucia says as they stand in the doorway surveying the small room. Like the living room, it has three good-size windows along the outside wall. "It faces west, so maybe we can see the ocean from here."

They walk to the windows, but no luck—there are far too many buildings between where they stand and the Pacific Ocean for them to see it. Everything at the beach is so densely packed, each square foot of land so valuable, that they look out on a jumble of roofs and apartment buildings and telephone poles and wires and a few tall old palm trees that sway in the breeze, their fronds rustling in the night air like tiny mouse feet along a wooden floor.

A double bed takes up most of the space in the room. "We're going to have to share a bed, sweetheart. Okay?"

Maggie's face lights up—this part of the arrangements she likes. She can have her mother with her all night. And she manages to say softly, "We can cuddle."

"Yes!" Lucia says, grateful that Maggie has seen some positive in this exile she's arranged for them. "Every night."

"Until our visit is over" is said even more softly, but Lucia has heard her. There's a minute while she looks around the small room and decides what to say. Finally, she chooses the most comforting words she can honestly employ. "Yes," Lucia says, "until our visit is over."

RICHARD CALLS AGAIN. He's been hitting redial every ten minutes from the moment he found Lucia's note until now, more than two hours later. Suddenly, on the next try his call goes directly to voice mail. Lucia has turned off her phone. It's clear she has seen his many messages and made the decision to turn it off. All right, he gets it; she doesn't want to speak with him. So he'll have to figure out another way to find her.

He brings up his list of contacts, starts with the A's, and begins to call every person on it who ever met Lucia. He leaves off his colleagues from the lab who only know of her, but calls everyone whom Lucia might have met and certainly everyone who knew her, however well. That means explaining to each that she's left him, but he doesn't care. She's obviously had some kind of breakdown—her note made no sense to him. He needs to find her and bring her home.

AS MAGGIE SLEEPS IN THE BEDROOM, Lucia sits on the blue denim couch in the living room, scrolling down the seemingly endless list of calls Richard has made in the hours they've been gone. It panics her to see how relentless he's been, but she can't think about all that now. For the moment, he has no idea where she is. For the moment, she and Maggie are safe. When he calms down, she'll talk to him, she tells herself. She knows Richard; he wouldn't be able to hear a word out of her mouth right now. He'd just talk nonstop, making his case that she come home. If she has any chance at all of having him understand why she left, she'll have to wait.

She turns the light off in the living room but doesn't move. This is the first quiet moment she's had all day to consider what she's done, and the thrill of it all has receded and she's plainly terrified. Even though she shed her Catholic beliefs somewhere in the middle of college, she finds herself whispering in the dark room, "God help me." It's not clear to her to whom she's pleading, but it is very clear, as she sits in this unfamiliar room with nothing but uncertainty in front of her, that she is going to need a lot of help.

And so she gets up and moves silently to where the help is—to the bedroom, to Maggie. Her daughter will give her the strength she'll need. Lucia slips into bed beside Maggie, curving her body around the child's warm limbs, enclosing her smaller body with her own.

"Mommy?"

"Yes, sweetheart, go back to sleep."

But Maggie doesn't. She turns around so that she's looking at her mother, their faces inches apart. And then Maggie takes a small, warm hand and traces the planes and angles of her mother's face. Lucia closes her eyes and lets her do it. The language of touch. Lucia understands intuitively that Maggie is making sure she's there, that in the midst of all the upheaval, she is still the same. And she waits while tiny fingers flutter down her jawline and slide across the curve of her full bottom lip,

Maggie honing one skill, touch, as she prepares to give up another, speech.

IT IS THE NEXT DAY THAT MAGGIE stops speaking entirely. It isn't a conscious decision. Maggie does not wake up and tell herself—*Today I won't say a word.* She just slips into it.

The day starts with Bernadette knocking on the door early in the morning. Both Lucia and Maggie are still asleep, but Lucia slips quickly out of bed and pads into the living room.

"Off to school, lovey, we've got finals to give." She hands Lucia a wicker basket. "Blueberry muffins for breakfast."

"Oh, Detta, you don't have to worry about feeding us, too."

"Just this morning—there's not much in the kitchen."

"I'll do a shopping."

"There's a Vons about five blocks down, turn right on Lincoln. There's coffee right beside the stove and a French press on the counter."

Lucia puts a hand on Bernadette's forearm and says quietly, "You've saved my life."

"You'd better do that yourself," Bernadette answers, her voice light to take the sting off the imperative.

Lucia brings the basket of muffins back to bed and climbs in beside Maggie.

"Yummm, they smell good, don't they?"

Maggie holds out her hand and Lucia gives her one and oh, they're still warm! Mother and daughter lean back against the headboard and eat their muffins in companionable silence. Breakfast in bed, something Lucia would never have let Maggie do at home.

When the muffins are finished, Lucia needs her coffee, so Maggie follows her into the kitchen to watch her grind the beans and pour the boiling water into the French press. And here, too, Maggie doesn't need to say anything, because Lucia talks the whole time about all the fun things they'll be able to do now that they're there and how much better the weather will be and how they'll wake up each morning and figure out each day.

Then, instead of going grocery shopping, they go to the beach.

THE BEACH IS WINDY AND OVERCAST and Maggie has to wear a sweatshirt over her red bathing suit. But because it's early in the morning and because it isn't officially summer yet, they have the sand mostly to themselves.

Lucia takes an old blanket out of the trunk of her car along with a sand bucket, a shovel, and some plastic cups that always come out when they go to the beach, and they make their way to the waterline.

On the blanket, from several feet away, Lucia watches her daughter dig a hole, each shovelful carefully lifted out and the remaining sand patted in place, Maggie humming softly to herself as she works. And then suddenly it's as if something heavy, something Lucia's been carrying, slips from her grasp and she is overwhelmed with exhaustion. Now that they're here, now that they've made it to Bernadette's, she has no idea how to take the next step. Rationally, logically, she knows what to do—find a job, find an apartment, find a school for Maggie for the fall. But how to do all that? She's never been on her own, not really. Living in the dorms at Oberlin doesn't count. And then she met Richard and they began living together and the next eight years were spent listening to what he set out for them and agreeing.

"Maggie," Lucia calls out, "what are you building?"

Maggie looks up at her mother, frowns, shrugs her tiny shoulders, and goes back to her digging.

"Is it a swimming pool or a lake?"

Maggie turns around but doesn't answer.

"A bowl for spaghetti or a birdbath for the seagulls?"

This time Maggie doesn't even turn around. And Lucia gets up and walks to where her daughter kneels on the sand, deeply focused on the job in front of her, working carefully, in a rhythm.

Lucia sits beside her child and puts a hand on her small back. "Will you tell me what you're making?" Maggie shakes her head. "Because . . . ?" Lucia leaves the question open-ended, but Maggie doesn't bite.

Lucia takes a minute, looks out to the water, allows the waves to lull her into a slower rhythm. *Take notice of what's in front of you,* she reminds herself. *Watch.* She knows her child well enough to know she's upset. Well, why wouldn't she be? She needs more of an explanation.

"I love you with all my heart," she begins again. Maggie doesn't look at her, simply continues digging and patting. "And I know Daddy does, too. But when Daddy and I live in the same house, that doesn't make me happy anymore. And I know that you're happier when we're all together and that's what makes all this so much harder."

She waits to see how Maggie will react to what she's just said, but there's no change in her expression or body language.

Lucia sighs, thinks of what to say next, and then, "You must have some questions. You can ask me and I will tell you as much as I know." There's silence. "Maggie?" And her daughter looks up, her dark eyes clear and present, but that's all. No question follows and Lucia is getting annoyed.

"Maggie, I know you must have at least one question."

The child goes back to her digging.

"Oh, so today you're not talking. Is this a game?"

Maggie shakes her head, a tiny shake without looking at her mother.

Lucia backs off. Okay, she won't push. If this is what Maggie needs to process all the changes that she has thrust upon her, well then, Lucia can wait.

BUT MAGGIE DOESN'T TALK THE NEXT DAY and the day after that, and Lucia spends those days watching her intently. Suddenly there's nothing casual or easy about her interaction with her daughter. Now she must pay close attention at all times because Maggie volunteers nothing and will answer only with a shake or nod of her head.

Bernadette, who has never had children, tells her to give it a while. Max, who has two grown boys, agrees.

"Children go through phases," he tells Lucia on Sunday night as they sit in the backyard, late, Maggie asleep upstairs in the apartment, Bernadette and Lucia sharing a bottle of wine, Max drinking a beer.

He tells her about Noah, his youngest, who wouldn't eat anything that wasn't white for, oh, it must have been about two years. Pasta, butter, white bread, ranch dressing, potatoes—that was about it.

"What did you do?" Lucia asks him. "Weren't you frantic?"

Max shakes his head. "Our pediatrician said not to make a big deal about it. He was of the school that believes kids know what they need better than we do."

"Do you buy that?" Lucia asks him.

"Not really, but I didn't have a better answer. What was I going to do, hold him down and force-feed him?"

"And Janie, their mother, had just died," Bernadette adds to bring some context into the conversation.

"Oh, I didn't know. . . ." Lucia says quietly. "That must have been such a difficult time."

"Yes, that's why I'm telling you," he says. "Children find their own way of dealing with difficult times."

"She's not being willful," Lucia says, needing validation.

"Of course not," Bernadette agrees.

"She's waiting." This last judgment from Max.

AFTER LUCIA GOES UP TO BED and curves her body around her sleeping child, Bernadette and Max remain in the yard, talking in whispers.

"Did you tell her Richard's been calling?" Max asks.

"No. I thought about it, but no."

"Do you think he believes you—that you don't know where she is?"

"I don't know. I told him we don't have any room for them, that you have a small house. Luckily, he's never been here to see *that*." And she gestures toward the garage apartment, then puts her feet up on the chair Lucia vacated and changes her tack. "A lot of us do what Lucia did."

Max looks at her, puzzled.

"Oh, you know, commit to a starter marriage for all the wrong reasons."

"Such as?"

"Lucia had no idea what to do with herself after graduation, so she followed Richard out here. Problem solved." Bernadette sighs. "And a new one created. No one knows what they truly want when they're eighteen or twenty-two or even twenty-five."

"Speak for yourself."

"Okay, I was completely clueless." And then Bernadette reads Max's face. "But not you and Janie."

"No."

A moment and then Bernadette says, "And that made her death so much harder."

Max takes her hand, grateful she isn't jealous. "We need to stay out of this mess, Detta."

"I know," Bernadette agrees, but without much conviction in her voice.

IT'S SUNDAY NIGHT OF THE WEEK Lucia left, and Richard hasn't slept more than a few hours since the Thursday evening he came home to find the apartment empty. He's started smoking again, something he gave up when he started graduate school and began running. Now he sits at the kitchen table, Lucia's note permanently in front of him, unaware that he's rocking slightly back and forth as he smokes one cigarette after another. The ashtray overflows. He's staring at his laptop screen, trying to craft the perfect e-mail, the one that will bring her back. So far he has written, "I love you," and nothing else.

He deletes it. That's the wrong approach, he thinks. He needs a grand gesture, something that will wake her up, something that will make her see just *how much* he loves her. It seems an impossibility to get that into an e-mail. His heart is bursting with love for her. How can she be throwing all that away?

IT'S BEEN EXACTLY A WEEK SINCE Maggie stopped talking, a week in which Maggie and Lucia have spent every hour of every day together. And without consciously planning it, Lucia has stopped expecting Maggie to speak and has begun to speak for her. If asked, Lucia would have said that she was taking the pressure off her daughter, not demanding something—speech—that Maggie wasn't ready to give.

But what Bernadette sees as she watches them together is that already, in a week, any separation between mother and child has evaporated. Lucia reads Maggie's sighs and translates those into wants. She studies Maggie's shrugs and facial expressions and immediately knows, or thinks she does, when Maggie's anxious, or bored, or needy, all without a word being spoken.

Bernadette can see these two dark-haired and spritelike creatures begin to spin their own communication, to build a universe of only two. It feels so intimate that sometimes Bernadette has to turn away, as if she's witnessing something too private to be shared.

The only time Maggie leaves Lucia's side is when she goes to visit the bees with Max. And in those few minutes, on those nights when the four of them eat together or get together after dinner for coffee and homemade cookies in the backyard, it is then that Bernadette has an opportunity to talk to Lucia. But what to say—*Are you sure it's good for Maggie to spend so much time with you?* How can Bernadette say that to any mother, especially since she's raised no children of her own? No, it seems she must watch this drama play out from the sidelines. She must observe a child attach herself to her mother and begin to grow into her flesh. And say nothing.

Well then, isn't it fair for Bernadette to suggest that Lucia let Richard know where they are? Should she describe what his daily phone calls are like? How he sounds frantic and bewildered and furious, sometimes in the same sentence. How he goes on and on without needing Bernadette to say one word. Of course, Bernadette isn't surprised by any of this. She's always known that within Richard the precise, detail-oriented scientist is in tension with the extravagantly emotional man. That combustion is part of his charm and what makes him so exasperating.

Bernadette is mulling all this over as she parks her car in the college parking structure and begins walking to the anthropology department office, her briefcase stuffed with graded finals, her mind preoccupied with her concerns about Maggie and Lucia and Richard. That's why she doesn't see him until she's practically on top of him. He says nothing, simply stands alongside the path and watches her approach, smoking, looking like he's dropped fifteen pounds in the ten days his family has been gone.

"Oh, Richard," Bernadette says, and all resistance flees. He looks haunted, horrible. She has to tell him some version of the truth. "Let's sit somewhere." And Bernadette leads him to a bench tucked into a small green space, one of the many pocket parks that seemed to have sprung up around campus in the past year.

She sits. He doesn't. "They're with you, aren't they?"

Bernadette doesn't answer.

"At first I thought she'd gone home to Ohio and I tried her parents. When they said she hadn't contacted them, I thought they were lying, because, after all, they'd be protecting her, you know? But their story never changed—they didn't know where she was. They hadn't known anything was wrong. She told them nothing. Finally, it made sense to me. Her parents are the last people she'd tell. Leaving your husband isn't something you do in Lucia's family. She wouldn't go home to her parents. She wouldn't want to hear what they had to say, but you, Bernadette, you've left two husbands, so there you are—the logical person to support Lucia's insanity. That's how I figured out she's with you."

Bernadette takes all this in without rancor and says nothing. She watches him smoke and pace, head down, not looking at her, lost in his version of events, wound up to a degree she's never seen. She proceeds carefully.

"She seems quite clear and resolved to me, Richard. This isn't a whim."

"Are you kidding me? Are you fucking kidding me?! She walks out of an eight-year relationship with no explanation. She leaves a husband who loves her more than anyone ever will. That's sane?! That makes sense to you?!"

And before Bernadette can utter a word, Richard begins to weep. He turns his back to her, but his shoulders rock with sobs and strangled gasps of grief pour out of him.

Bernadette waits. She doesn't try to comfort him or interfere. It seems clear he has to do this, as if he needs to show her just how devastated he is. Finally he subsides and turns around, wiping his face with the sleeve of his T-shirt.

"I have to see her. Alone. You need to tell her that. Otherwise, I swear to God, Bernadette, I'll follow you day and night until you lead me to her."

Gently Bernadette says, "She has some rights here."

"NO!" explodes from Richard's mouth. "She owes me an explanation."

Bernadette nods. She agrees with that, if not with the way it is said. "I'll speak with her and I'll call you."

"She needs to see me, you tell her that" is put forth as a final threat.

It occurs to Bernadette as she continues on to the anthropology office that Richard didn't mention Maggie's name. Not once.

THAT NIGHT AFTER DINNER, after Lucia has put Maggie to bed and come back down to the backyard, she finds that Bernadette is the only one there. Max has made himself scarce and Lucia knows, even before Bernadette opens her mouth, that she's seen Richard.

"How did he find me?" Lucia says as she sets foot on the grass.

Bernadette sighs; this isn't a conversation she's eager to have. "Come sit with me."

And Lucia does, in the lawn chair next to Bernadette. The two women stare out over the backyard in silence, each bracing herself in her own way for the words to come. The light from the kitchen windows pools a warm yellow on the patio where they sit, but the rest of the yard is in darkness, the sky overcast again, no stars or moon this night.

Bernadette begins to speak. "He needs an explanation, Lucia. It's killing him not knowing why."

Lucia nods. She knows Richard well enough to know he has to understand. What she doesn't know is how to explain it all to him so he hears her. He's never been big on listening. He gets impatient with points of view that don't contain his own brand of logic.

"Why has all this come as such a surprise to him? Usually when couples separate, they leave behind a long trail of arguments and trips to the therapist's office."

"I know, but Richard really isn't interested in anything but his own point of view. I'd talk and he'd interrupt and tell me that none of what I was saying mattered because he loved me so much." She shrugs. "What I had to say seemed irrelevant."

"So you stopped talking," Bernadette says carefully.

"Yes," Lucia says, but Bernadette can tell that Lucia is too caught up with the appearance of Richard to catch her implication. Our children watch us.

"Well, now he says he wants to hear."

"I don't love him. Can I say that?" And before Bernadette can speak, Lucia answers her own question. "I can't. I can't say that. It's too painful."

"Well, you have to say something," Bernadette says with a trace of irritation. It's one of those moments when she wonders whatever has she done by inviting Lucia here. "Because if you don't talk to him he's going to show up here."

"You didn't tell him—?"

"Of course not, but you know Richard. All he has to do is hide out at school and follow me home."

"And he would."

They arrange to meet in a public place. On the bluffs above the Pacific is a narrow park with a path that runs north to south along the rim, high above Highway 1. There are benches situated along the cliff, placed straightforwardly ahead to maximize the ocean view.

Lucia gets there early and waits on one of them. She wants to be prepared. She doesn't want Richard catching her unawares. All morning as she gave Maggie breakfast and brushed her unruly hair into shining black curls and brought her to Max at the beehives, where they had plans to check on the Queen, she kept a running monologue in her head. She told herself to be strong, to be clear. To say what she felt. She promised herself she wouldn't let Richard do all the talking.

Richard, in his motel room at the Surfsider, rehearsed various opening sentences—"I love you more than my own life. . . . I can't live without you. . . . Whatever you want, I'll give it to you. . . ."

She sees him walking toward her and she's stunned by how he looks, as if he hasn't slept in the two weeks they've been gone, or eaten, or showered. Richard, who has always been so meticulous about his appearance, could have been mistaken for a homeless man. Rather than being overcome with sympathy, Lucia's suddenly furious by this kind of self-indulgent excess. This is exactly what she's run away from.

Richard looks up and sees her sitting there, small, composed, always that air of elegant calm about her, and he wants nothing more than to pick her up in his arms and spirit her away. It would be so easy. She's so much smaller than he is. She's weightless in his arms.

Lucia doesn't stand as he nears. She doesn't move from the bench, but there's no way Richard can sit down now. "Can we walk?" are the first words out of his mouth. His voice is raw, from smoking, from emotion.

She nods and they take the path north, the shallow waves of

the Pacific Ocean on their left, far below them. The morning overcast is beginning to lift, the sky brightening as they walk, the sun
burning through, a hazy circle now. Lucia says nothing. She's waiting to see whom she's dealing with here. Is he as out of control as
he appears?

Finally he says, "I need to know why you did this." Each word
sounds like it's being ripped from his throat.

"Because I've been unhappy for a long time."

"How can that be?!" explodes from his mouth. It's an accusa-
tion and an outrage. "I love you, Lucy, more than life itself."

She waits for the outburst to dissipate into the ocean breeze,
until there's a pool of quiet. What kind of love is he talking about?
To Lucia it feels like love as steamroller, a sort of love that destroys
everything in its path. She says quietly but firmly, without looking
at him, "That doesn't make everything all better."

"What do you want me to do? Anything. Just tell me."

"I want you to listen to me." She says it as clearly, as firmly, as
she can.

"I am. Just tell me what to do and I'll do anything you say. All I
want is for you to come back. Lucy, anything. Tell me."

They walk in silence, Lucia trying to figure out how they got
from her declaration of unhappiness to his demand that she come
up with tasks for him. Richard is watching her, holding on desperately to the slimmest hope that maybe, if he's good enough and
careful enough, she will come back.

"It feels like," she begins tentatively, "that your need to love me
has nothing to do with me."

"That makes no sense."

Again he doesn't understand or won't stop a minute to understand or refuses to try or . . . ? Lucia doesn't know anymore. All
right, she tries something more concrete. "I don't think we're well
matched."

"How can you say that?!" It's almost a scream.

Lucia ignores the tone and continues. "You're certain about everything. It used to be fine for you to be certain for both of us, but it isn't now."

"What the hell are you saying?"

Lucia winces and then pushes herself to try again. "I don't know anymore what I like or what I want or how I want to be in the world. All I know how to do is to agree with you."

Richard stops walking and so she does, too. "Just come home."

She looks at him in complete incredulity. "Do you hear one word I said? I'm trying to explain—"

But he cuts her off. He doesn't want any more explanations. "We'll work out everything we need to when we're home. I promise you."

She stares at him. She's a statue, turned to stone, a statue staring, then suddenly she turns and starts walking away from him.

"Lucy!" he screams.

And she whirls around and screams back at him, "I hate that! My name is Lucia, Lucia! Lucy is someone you made up!"

LUCIA DRIVES AROUND IN CIRCLES. She travels east on Wilshire and makes an angry left turn, north, on Fourteenth Street instead of south into Ocean Park. She checks her rearview mirror every ten seconds—*Is that Richard's car?* She makes a precipitous right turn onto Montana, checks again, drives all the way to Bundy. Another look. She knows he's capable of following her, and the possibility keeps her anger lit—how intrusive he is! It's more than an hour before she feels safe enough to drive to Max's. Finally, the need to be "home," the need to talk to Bernadette, propels her to Sycamore Street and the long driveway, where she leaves the car, almost tripping in her haste to get into the kitchen. *Let Bernadette be there alone.*

And her prayers are answered. Bernadette is sitting at the kitchen table, drinking a cup of tea, quietly reading the morning paper as Lucia rushes in.

"I feel like I've been mugged."

Bernadette sighs as she puts the newspaper aside—does she really want to hear about this? But she has no choice. And then she sees that Lucia's hands are shaking as she pulls out a chair and sits down across from her, and immediately Bernadette regrets her own lack of empathy.

"It's all about what he's feeling, Detta—'I love you, therefore everything's all right!' But it isn't. And he won't hear me. I tried, really Detta, I did."

Bernadette nods. She believes her. "Did he cry?"

"No. At least not that."

"He cried with me."

"Oh no, Detta. I'm so sorry, but then you saw—he revels in this excess. He keeps saying he loves me, but it's all about his *need* to love me. Him. Him. All about him!"

Bernadette shakes her head, a finger to her lips, her eyes over Lucia's head to the doorway where Max and Maggie stand, hand in hand. But Maggie has heard, at least some of it—her mother's angry tone, saying bad things about her daddy. And she doesn't want to hear any more of it. She launches herself across the kitchen into her mother's legs, pushing her head into Lucia's lap. If she were speaking she would be screaming, "Don't say that! Don't talk about my daddy that way!" but her actions speak loudly enough because Lucia gathers Maggie into her lap and the angry buzzing in the air settles at once. Better, now it's better, Maggie sees, and she didn't have to say anything. Words don't matter all that much because look—her mother is holding her and has quieted down and she's not talking about her daddy in that way now.

Lucia stands with Maggie clinging to her. She looks at Max

and Bernadette over Maggie's head, a condemnation of Richard in her eyes—*Do you see what he's wrought?* And with Maggie's legs circling her waist and the child's arms around her mother's neck now, Lucia walks out into the backyard and then up the steps to their apartment, murmuring words only the two of them can hear, soothing sounds that quiet them both.

RICHARD DOESN'T GO BACK TO RIVERSIDE. He can't manage to get into his car and drive east for an hour to the empty apartment that is waiting for him, so he stays at the Surfsider on the outskirts of Venice and calls Lucia nonstop. He leaves tangled, rambling messages that he fears don't help his cause, but he can't seem to stop himself.

At night, he walks. Long midnight hikes that take him from Venice Beach north to Santa Monica, then farther north to Pacific Palisades and then up the coast through Malibu, until his legs give out.

During the day he haunts the Santa Monica City College campus, hoping against all expectations that he'll see Bernadette again. And then, one day he does. She's walking hand in hand with a large man with a lot of bushy, blond hair who he figures must be Max. They're talking to each other in the way that people do when their relationship is new and they have lots to say, so Richard has to call out to her—"Bernadette!"—which stops them both. Bernadette finds him standing outside Drescher Hall, and something close to panic races across her face. Max sees it and tells her to stay put. Then he walks toward Richard.

"Max Weber," he says with his hand extended for a shake.

Richard ignores the gesture. Looking over Max's shoulder, he says, "I need to talk to Bernadette."

"No, you don't."

Max's words don't even register with Richard. He attempts to push past the larger man, to get to Bernadette, who takes two steps back instinctively. Max wraps his hand around Richard's upper arm and starts walking him away. "She's told you everything she's going to say."

Bernadette, watching, is so grateful to Max that she thinks seriously, for the first time, of marrying him.

"You need to go home," Max is telling Richard in a low voice.

"This is none of your goddamn business."

"Yes, it is, because you're upsetting Bernadette. When you love someone," Max says pointedly, "you don't want them upset."

"Don't you lecture me on—"

"Lucia and Maggie are upset, Maggie especially. It's Maggie I'm worried about."

Richard wrenches his arm free and stops walking. "What are you talking about?"

"She's stopped speaking. She won't utter a single word."

"To you, maybe."

"To anyone. Her mother included. Lucia didn't tell you?"

"No." Richard seems genuinely stunned. "For how long?"

"Weeks now."

"But she chatters away nonstop."

"Not now." Then, because Richard looks so puzzled: "It may be her way of dealing with all this stress."

"Stress that her mother created!"

"That you're making worse."

Richard shakes his head. "Don't put this on me. I'm not the one who left. I'm not the one who's ripping this family apart—"

"Richard!" Max overrides him, his voice harsh—*Pay attention to what I'm saying.* "You can't think all this stalking and drama is helping. You know it isn't."

Max puts a hand on the younger man's shoulder in sympathy.

What does Richard want but his wife, whom he loves, to come back to him?

"Go home," Max tells him. "Let them be for now. Let Lucia take care of your daughter. Be a mensch."

Richard lowers his eyes and stares at the sidewalk beneath his feet. "And then what?"

"I don't know. You'll wait and see."

If Max weren't so nice, Richard could get angry, but he can't. Instead he has to do the hardest thing for him—nothing. Instead he has to feel the pain that has turned his heart into a tiny, tight kernel of perpetual ache.

Now he knows he has to go home. Max is going to be the gate-keeper, he's made that clear, keeping him at bay. Richard leaves an explicit message on Lucia's voice mail saying he's leaving and making sure she understands that it doesn't mean he's given up or that her insanity makes sense to him.

Back in his lab at the university, Richard continues his research but finds himself, without warning, several times a week, hunched over his microscope, weeping. One of his lab assistants, Mei-ling, places a hand on his back in comfort and then goes back to her workstation when Richard's sobs subside. They don't speak about it.

IT IS BERNADETTE'S HOPE, WITH RICHARD GONE back to River-side, that Lucia can now take the next necessary steps—finding an apartment of her own, a job. They had all agreed in the weeks before Lucia and Maggie showed up, during the many phone calls leading to their flight, that Max's garage apartment would be a temporary refuge, "a way station," as Bernadette referred to it when speaking with both Max and Lucia. But Lucia has seemed to have forgotten that agreement, or worse yet, and this is Bernadette's fear—Lucia is stuck. It seems to Bernadette that all forward motion has stopped.

Max hasn't complained—he's generous and understanding that way—but Bernadette feels responsible for the disruption in what was an almost idyllic solitude that they both cherished.

BERNADETTE REALIZES SHE HAS TO do something. What she'd like to do is jolt Lucia into action, but she knows that probably isn't the best way of approaching the situation. *Change is hard,* she keeps reminding herself in order to bolster her compassion level. What she needs to do is guide Lucia to the first step. It's always the hardest, that first step.

With "guiding" in mind, with "easing" as her goal, Bernadette takes Lucia with her to the Santa Monica Farmers Market, the one she always goes to on Saturday mornings at Pico and Cloverfield, exactly across from the off-ramp Lucia and Maggie took when they got off the Santa Monica Freeway weeks ago. *Fitting, isn't it? Symbolic,* Bernadette thinks.

It's not the biggest of the farmers markets, but it's in their neighborhood and Bernadette knows most of the vendors now by name. Of course, she stops and chats every few feet as they make their way through, Lucia following along in Bernadette's wake, feeling like an afterthought.

And then there is the produce. Bernadette seems mesmerized by the varieties of heirloom tomatoes—yellow, pink, striped, blushing red. Huge tomatoes that must weigh more than a pound, tiny tomatoes that look like clusters of grapes. And the squash— zucchini in shades of green and black, crookneck squash in sun-bright yellow, pale green trombone squash that curves around itself almost three feet long. And eggplants in all colors—pink, lavender, white, deep purple that glows black. Bernadette is in her element. All the colors, the aromas! She picks up a bouquet of Thai basil and inhales its smell before putting it back. No one seems to mind.

As they walk, Bernadette chatters on about the "edible art," as she calls all the gorgeous vegetables, and tries to figure out how to bring up the issue of Lucia's unemployment. She can hardly say, "When are you going to do something about getting a job? How can you rent an apartment without any money?"

Instead she begins talking about Max's oldest son, Danny, who teaches first grade at a charter school in East Oakland. How much he's taken to teaching, how grateful Max is that his son has found what he loves to do.

"But the summers are hard," Bernadette tells Lucia as they approach a vendor selling a kaleidoscope of sweet peppers. "They pay beginning teachers so little that he has to find a summer job. Each summer. There's something wrong with that, don't you think?"

Lucia agrees, but Bernadette can tell she's not really listening. They've got to sit down and face each other so she can have all of Lucia's attention. She steers her to a little outdoor café—really just a coffee cart and a few tables set up under a tree—and brings two lattes back to the table.

"Richard must be calling you," Lucia says before Bernadette can even put their coffees down. "He's harassing you, isn't he?"

"Don't worry about that." Bernadette doesn't want to have yet another conversation about Richard.

"Because we both know he can be ruthless."

Bernadette needs to focus Lucia's attention on her own situation. "He's just venting—"

"He's taking advantage of you. That's what he does! He uses people—"

"Lucia, we don't need to talk about Richard. It's fine. . . . I wanted to tell you about Danny and this really interesting summer job he got."

"Danny?" Lucia is having trouble shifting gears.

"Max's oldest, who we were talking about."

"Oh, yes. The teacher."

"Right. And he got this research job with an educational think tank, something about different learning styles for different kids. Anyway, it dovetails beautifully with his real job and pays enough for him to get through the summer and he got it on Craigslist. Amazing, huh?"

"I've thought about Craigslist. . . ." Lucia says, a half sentence.

"Oh, it's a great resource." Bernadette tries to keep the relief out of her voice. "I think Danny met his partner on Craigslist, too, but he hasn't ever really said that. Max and I guessed it, but maybe we're wrong. And then Max found a lot of his beekeeping equipment there. You can find anything on Craigslist!" She puts a hand on Lucia's hand, to reinforce what she's about to say. "You know, Lucia, feel free to come in and use my computer whenever you want. There are just tons of jobs listed."

"Oh, I will, thank you, Detta," Lucia says.

And Bernadette lets it rest there, out on the table—*You need to come in and start checking Craigslist for a job.*

But Lucia doesn't. Each day, as Lucia watches her child retreat further into herself, she grows more and more concerned and less and less capable of any purposeful movement.

Maggie's eyes are usually downcast. She draws constantly or rereads the books Lucia has bought her since they've moved, flipping the pages over and over. Lucia's initial response to her daughter's speechlessness—her wait-and-see approach—no longer serves either of them.

She tries cajoling and bribes and pleading. Early in the morning when the two share the same pillow and look into each other's eyes, Lucia whispers, "Please, sweetheart, tell me one thing." But Maggie doesn't. Any of the things she wants to say to Lucia, her mother doesn't want to hear. Instead, Maggie chooses silence and her mother's total attention. Something will happen, she feels it, if she doesn't talk. She doesn't know what it will be, but she's betting that it will be better than what she's got.

FROM RIVERSIDE, RICHARD HAS SETTLED on text messages now as his communication of choice. He's able to send more carefully crafted diatribes, endless loops of accusations. Lucia's steadfast refusal to change her mind has finally provoked Richard's anger, and he focuses it where he knows it will hurt the most. Obviously, Lucia's selfish and precipitous decision has caused Maggie's problem; obviously, it's not normal for a five-year-old child to suddenly stop talking; obviously, Lucia must get some help for Maggie. If she doesn't, Richard will get a lawyer and force her to—it may be the one thing that Richard can make her do. Send me the bills, he texts her, but get Maggie some help. The message that she's being a terrible mother is delivered loud and clear.

That's how they end up at Dr. Greenstein's. The recommendation came from Max, no stranger to the idiosyncratic ways children have of dealing with life's vicissitudes. He enlisted Dr. Greenstein's help after the death of his wife.

Maggie doesn't resist going to the doctor's office. There are lots of things to do there, games and puzzles, new books to read, and large pads of creamy drawing paper next to cups full of thick Magic Markers and crayons, some in colors she's never seen before—fuzzy-wuzzy brown, atomic tangerine, screamin' green, and her favorite, razzle-dazzle rose. If she can draw here, she's fine. She can shut out the rest of the world. The doctor talks to her, and even though she knows she's supposed to talk back, nothing happens when she doesn't.

Dr. Greenstein seems like a nice enough lady, more like a grandmother than a doctor. She wears long skirts and loose blouses and thick, flat sandals. And her toenails are painted a shocking baby blue. Maggie can't stop looking at her feet. They seem to belong to another person, a younger person.

After Maggie has been seeing Dr. Greenstein for several weeks, two times a week, Lucia and the doctor have a session. Maggie stays with Max. They have a date to harvest the honey.

In Dr. Greenstein's corner office, part of a one-story brick medical building in Westwood, Lucia watches the older woman close the drapes against the afternoon glare and settle her heavy body into her leather desk chair. Lucia waits. Is this the woman who is going to unlock the mystery of her child?

"Maggie may be punishing you for leaving her father" is what the doctor says. No preamble, simply the diagnosis put forth as a suggestion.

"That's not in my daughter's nature."

"Do you have an alternative theory?" the doctor asks, her voice neutral, not a hint of impatience in it.

Lucia shakes her head. "This is all so out of character for her."

"Well then," the doctor says carefully, "could she be repeating behavior she's witnessed? Silence as coping mechanism?"

"I don't know" is said too quickly, but Lucia knows immediately without having to search for it, the moment when she decided just that.

She is seven months pregnant with Maggie and so proud of it. She and Richard are standing in the kitchen of their Riverside apartment. It is late afternoon and the setting sun lies in a wide stripe across the tile floor, turning it a glowing red. Richard is going on and on about the stupidity of "all those home-birthers" and how they don't realize that they put the baby at risk. He did some research, he tells her, since she raised the topic at dinner the night before and he holds several pieces of paper in his hand with columns of statistics spread across the pages and he is waving them around as he speaks. Facts, figures, numbers, and percentages—all that Richard deems holy.

Lucia remembers that she attempted to get a word in about how she felt. That she wanted more say in what happens during the birth. That if they were in a hospital, then their doctor, Dr. Roebuck, would be setting the rules and she is afraid that her wishes wouldn't be honored.

"Richard," she remembers saying as calmly as she could, "I'm here, too. Try to hear what I'm saying. I want to be present at our child's birth. I want you there, too. It's something we can do together—"

"Of course you'll be present. Who else is giving birth but you?"

"No . . . what I mean is—I want to participate in the choices and the decisions. I want it to be collaborative. You know Dr. Roebuck, he's so . . . definite, but if we had a midwife—"

And Richard interrupted her again. "No child of mine is going to be born at home with some medieval person called a 'midwife.' End of discussion. End of story." And he walked out of the room, leaving Lucia standing there in the empty kitchen. *He never listens. Ever. What's the point?*

Such a small moment, Lucia knows, but she remembers thinking—*That's it, it's useless.* It was the moment that crystallized all that went before, the years of not being heard, the attempts to say what she felt. And then, during all the years that followed when nothing changed, Lucia began to plan her early morning flight that ended up at Bernadette's.

"All right," Dr. Greenstein says now with a certain briskness as she recrosses her legs and pushes her body back in the chair, "then we must ask ourselves, what is your daughter getting from this behavior?"

Lucia shakes her head. "Everything's harder because she won't speak."

"For you or for her?"

"Both of us."

"What do you think she would say if she were still speaking?"

Lucia doesn't answer right away. This question she considers seriously. She looks around the crowded office, giving herself time to ponder it. If Lucia came here twice a week instead of Maggie, she knows she'd be hard-pressed not to tidy up. She's itching to put the toys away that are scattered throughout the play area, straighten the medical books that are pushed haphazardly into the bookshelves, or at least straighten up the piles of paper on Dr. Greenstein's desk so they don't look like they're ready to topple over. What does this kind of messiness say about Dr. Greenstein's skill as a therapist? Lucia has no idea.

The doctor waits as silence accumulates in the room. Finally, Lucia speaks. "She'd probably tell me she wants to go home, to her father."

Dr. Greenstein nods. "Most children, no matter how unhappy the home situation, want their family intact."

"I understand that." Then, "It's hard to explain to a five-year-old why I had to leave her father."

The doctor nods. She agrees.

"But I did." Lucia decides to say what she's told no one else. "I was certain I couldn't be the mother Maggie needs if I stayed."

"Ah . . ." Dr. Greenstein says as if she completely understands, and Lucia relaxes for the first time since she sat down in the very uncomfortable upholstered chair opposite the desk.

It is only then that Lucia can ask, "What can we do?"

"Don't speak for her," Dr. Greenstein says carefully.

"Oh, I don't," Lucia answers in a split second, telling Dr. Greenstein that she, in fact, does. Most mothers do without even realizing it.

"In selective mutism it often happens that the mother, unconsciously, becomes the child's voice in the world. She knows her child so well. She wants to facilitate her way, but speaking for your child makes it less and less necessary for her to speak for herself."

"All right."

"And don't so easily understand all her gestures and signs. Do you feel sometimes that you're having a conversation with her, only you're voicing both parts?"

"Yes."

"Don't. You're making it too easy for her."

After a moment, "I see."

"And never underestimate the courage it will take your child to begin speaking again. Not speaking reinforces itself with almost no effort. To break free and speak . . . well, that is an act of bravery."

"But she'll do it, won't she?"

"We certainly hope so."

That answer isn't at all satisfactory to Lucia.

MAGGIE WATCHES MAX TAKE A LARGE KNIFE and cut around the edges of the honeycomb frame. "We're using the crush-and-strain method," he tells her. They're standing in the backyard, both wearing their pith helmets with veil. Max is making sure as he cuts that the honeycomb falls into a large white bucket, the kind painters use.

He's already explained what the other white bucket, which they've washed and is now waiting, will be used for. It looks exactly like the first one, only it has a spigot at the bottom. And Max has placed a large, snug-fitting strainer across the top.

"There's something called an extractor," Max explains as he takes up the second frame and begins cutting through the waxy comb, "which is a big stainless-steel bucket with a crank on top.

You put the whole frame in and the extractor spins it around and flings the honey out, but I don't have one of those yet. It's probably a whole lot easier, but I think this will work fine." Maggie thinks whatever Max does will work out fine. Max has taken up residence in a small piece of her empty heart, aching for Richard's presence.

After Max has cut the comb from the third frame, he shows Maggie a tool that looks like a paint scraper and tells her it's her turn. "Here's the 'crush' part. We need to break up the comb we've got in the bucket so that the honey can get out. Do you think you can do it?" Maggie nods, eager to try. "Mash away. Like this." And Max shows her how to jab and press on the comb so that the lovely honey squirts out.

"And after you break it up as much as you can, we'll pour the whole mess into the strainer and slowly, without us having to do a thing, only the honey will seep out through the strainer and drain into the bucket. And then we turn on the spigot and eat it!" They grin at each other like the coconspirators they are, and Max hands her the scraper.

Tentatively at first, Maggie pushes the metal against the delicate comb and is amazed to see honey spurt out in a golden ribbon. She looks up at Max, who stands close by watching. There's wonderment on her face and he laughs. "Yep, pretty amazing. Keep on going. We've got a lot of honey to squeeze out."

The afternoon is gentle—a soft breeze, the sounds of traffic a distant hum, the house empty and waiting because Lucia is at Dr. Greenstein's and Bernadette is at the market. To Maggie it feels like she and Max are sharing something secret, something magical. Only them, only the two of them. This is as safe as she feels these days—out here in the backyard with Max and the bees. It is the kindness of Max and his complete lack of expectation. He doesn't need her to talk. He's fine with her just as she is, which is why Maggie is able to murmur, without looking at him, "Where's my daddy?" It's a whisper, just as Dr. Greenstein said, no more substantial than the air rustling the palm fronds, but Max hears it and he makes sure he doesn't startle.

Maggie's eyes are downcast. She concentrates on her task, her brow furrowed, pushing and poking at the combs and releasing the luscious honey. Did he really hear what he thought he heard? He answers it anyway.

"In Riverside, at the apartment there."

"Why doesn't he come?" And this time she looks up at Max, and her total bewilderment, her helplessness, breaks his heart. What can he say?

"Your mommy and daddy are working that out" is what he finally comes up with, even though he knows it's not satisfactory in the least. More evasion, he knows, and then a flicker of anger within him that he's being put in this situation—having to dish up half-truths to a desperate child.

Her eyes still searching his, Maggie pleads with him, "Don't tell. Promise." And he knows she means, *Don't tell about my talking,* and all he can do is promise. He nods solemnly and she is comforted. She believes him.

Later in the afternoon, as Max and Maggie are finishing up by carefully filling sterilized bottles with the strained honey, Lucia watches from the kitchen window. She's helping Bernadette prepare dinner, but her thoughts are on her child and the talk she had earlier with Dr. Greenstein.

"The only time she seems happy is when she's with Max."

Bernadette, stirring spaghetti sauce on the stove, shrugs. "He has the same effect on me." But Lucia hasn't heard her. She's still staring out the window, watching, the silverware in her hands forgotten.

"Do you want to put that on the table?" Bernadette says, hoping her voice doesn't betray the irritation she feels. Lucia is so passive. Lucia drifts. Lucia could be here for a very long time. And then, immediately, Bernadette feels guilty.

Lucia turns away from the window and begins to set the table. "That doctor basically told me I'm a terrible mother for taking Maggie away from her father."

"Oh, Lucia, I'm sure she didn't say that. Children survive when their parents split up."

"Apparently mine isn't."

Bernadette carries the heavy spaghetti pot to the sink and drains the pasta into a colander, the steam rising in a cloud to envelop her head. She has no idea what to say to that statement.

"Richard agrees with her. Every text is about what a bad mother I've become."

Bernadette is exhausted by it all. By the spikes of emotion, the endless conversations about Maggie, whom she's come to love, and Richard, who is driving her crazy because he won't stop calling, and now, here they are with Bernadette having to reassure Lucia that she's not a terrible mother. It's all too much. Nearly six weeks of it all with no end in sight.

And then Maggie and Max are in the kitchen, Maggie holding out a shining, golden jar of honey to place in Bernadette's hands with an equally shining smile on her tiny face, and Bernadette's heart melts. Anything, she'd do anything for this little girl.

MAX IS UNUSUALLY QUIET AT DINNER. He is wrestling with his conscience, with his pledge not to tell. Maggie watches his every move, reminding him with her steady gaze what he has promised.

Lucia is quiet also. There is so much she is trying to understand from her afternoon session with Dr. Greenstein.

So it is left to Bernadette to fill up the dead air. She babbles on about the honey and what she's going to make with it—chicken nuggets with a honey-mustard sauce, which she assures Maggie will be "nothing like those awful things you get at McDonald's. And maybe we'll have honey-cornbread muffins to go with them and then honey-glazed carrots on the side. How does that sound?"

No one answers but Max. "Sounds like a lot of honey."

"Well, in that case, we could have a honey-baked ham and honey-whipped sweet potatoes and a honey-vanilla pound cake for dessert." Bernadette rolls her eyes and clutches her chest. "Oh my God, honey overload," and she falls back in her chair as if she's been felled by honey and Maggie giggles.

There. That's what Bernadette was going for, and she and Max exchange a look. He's grateful to her and she's simply glad Maggie laughed. Lucia is lost in her own thoughts, Maggie pressed up against her, thigh to thigh, arm to arm.

WITH THE TURNING OF AUGUST, the heat comes. Usually the beach communities are spared the truly hot weather, but at least once a summer there's a period when the inland areas are in the hundreds and the beach communities get up into the nineties. Everyone complains. No one has air conditioning because, after all, they're at the beach and it's always cool there.

The first few days are manageable, but this particular heat wave extends into its second week. The hot air just sits there like a lid, in a holding pattern over the basin that is the Southland, no morning or evening overcast to cool things down. No winds to bring in the clouds. Just the pressure cooker of dry, scalding heat that cracks the skin and parches the throat. It's when people remember that the Los Angeles area was carved out of a desert and everyone is irritable.

Bernadette tries to chalk up her impatience to the weather,

but she knows better. Lucia hasn't made the slightest move. Now that Maggie is seeing Dr. Greenstein, it seems to have paralyzed Lucia further, as if Lucia has to wait until the doctor "fixes" Maggie before they can move on.

Bernadette doesn't think that's going to happen—either scenario. Dr. Greenstein isn't going to effect a miracle cure, and even if she did, Bernadette can't see Lucia marshaling the resources to get herself a job, an apartment, a school for Maggie who is supposed to be starting kindergarten at the beginning of September.

What to do? What would be helpful? What would be kind? What would get them out of Max's house? Bernadette lies awake for many hot August nights staring at the ceiling trying to answer those questions. Max lies next to her, awake as well. Bernadette assumes it's the heat, but Max is wrestling with an even harder question—should he tell?

Of course he promised Maggie he'd keep her secret, but she's a child in trouble. Doesn't his responsibility to help her supersede his promise? Shouldn't Lucia know how Maggie longs for Richard? But if he divulged her secret, what would that do to her sense of trust, rent as it has been by her parents' separation?

Max has waited, pinning his hopes on Dr. Greenstein, but it doesn't seem like she's been able to work her magic with this child.

Max gets up out of bed, repositions the box fan he found in the garage and hauled up to their bedroom. It helps a little to move it closer to the window, but not much. There's scant cool air to draw into the room.

He stands at the bedroom window and looks out over the yard to the darkened garage apartment. What goes on in there that keeps the two of them intertwined and motionless? He has no idea. He must have sighed, because he hears Bernadette say, "It's the heat, isn't it?"

And he goes back to her, to the bed, and lies on top of the sheet, spread-eagle; any body part touching any other body part is too much heat.

"Yes," he says, but Bernadette hears something in his voice.

"Something else, too?"

"Hmm," he murmurs.

"Max, we've got to find a way to get Lucia moving. I promised you 'a way station' and it's turning out to be 'a way-too-long station.'"

He grins in the dark room. She can't see it, but can feel his body relax beside her.

"It's Maggie. . . ." he says.

"Of course."

"She misses Richard."

"I would guess."

There's a silence. Max struggles with himself and then says, "I know."

And Bernadette understands immediately. She props herself up on one elbow and looks at him in the dark. "She talked to you?"

"Yes, but with a promise I wouldn't tell. She's desperate for him. . . . What should we do?"

"Jesus . . . I don't know." Then, "I'm so sorry I dragged you into this. . . ."

He takes her hand. "Shhhh."

"Things were so perfect before, just us . . . perfection."

Another grin in the dark. "I know," and he pulls her to him, the heat be damned.

Later, in the early morning hours when the outside air finally cools down, Bernadette, three-quarters asleep and languid with satisfaction, reaches for a sheet to pull over her. Max is still awake beside her.

"Bernadette . . . ?"

"Mmmmm . . ."

"You mustn't tell Lucia. I promised Maggie. Now you promise me."

There's a long silence. Bernadette isn't sure she agrees with him, but finally, she promises as well. "All right."

They reach for each other, find the right intermingling of legs and backs, stomachs and arms, and fall asleep.

IN THE LIGHT OF THE MORNING, Bernadette isn't at all sure she should have agreed to keep her tongue, but Max puts a premium on loyalty and discretion and so she has to honor her late-night promise. She can't tell Lucia about Maggie's words. But that's all she promised.

It seems like a beach day, hot already at ten a.m. She rounds up Lucia and Maggie, packs sandwiches for them all, and the three of them head to the ocean. Max is already at his office on campus. For years he's been trying to finish a book on the naval battles of the Civil War. Bernadette knows he'll spend all day there and come home frazzled and defeated by the writing process. That's why she's planned a special dinner and some peace and quiet.

Even this early in the day Santa Monica beach is crowded with people trying to take the edge off the heat, but Maggie is able to find a spot near the water, where she digs and builds. Lucia and Bernadette sit on their beach blanket, close enough to keep an eye on her but far enough away to have a conversation. Bernadette wears her large straw gardening hat. Her fair and freckled skin doesn't do well in the sun.

"I'm losing her," Lucia says, her eyes on her daughter.

Bernadette simply nods, an acknowledgment. Lately she has stopped trying to give Lucia either advice or reassurance. She feels certain now that neither makes any difference.

"She's disappearing in front of my eyes."

A little boy, around Maggie's age, maybe a little younger,

comes over and squats next to her, watching as she digs and pats the remaining sand into shape, forming the wide basin she's creating. He talks to her. They can see that but not hear what he says. Maggie says not a word but hands him the second shovel and the two of them set to work, side by side.

Bernadette is thinking how little we really need to talk. Wouldn't it be much more restful if we communicated primarily with touch and gestures? She smiles at herself, remembering the touch and gestures of last night with Max. Not a word was spoken. None were needed.

"I can't send her to kindergarten like this. No one would understand her."

Bernadette is worried about the same thing. How can Maggie go to school mute?

"If she's not talking, she'll have to stay home with me."

That's the last thing Maggie needs—to spend more time alone with Lucia. Bernadette almost says it, but instead takes a deep breath and spreads herself flat on the blanket. She puts her straw hat over her face and pretends to sleep.

Lucia sits with her arms around her shins, her head on her knees, her eyes on her child, watching, watching. Motionless.

They arrive back at Max's house at the end of the afternoon, Maggie's and Lucia's olive skins even more tanned, all three of them sandy and tired out from the sun. Bernadette parks her Volvo halfway up the driveway and Maggie sprints into the backyard to check on the bees. She knows she mustn't get too close without her pith helmet and veil.

Lucia is so exhausted she doesn't know how she'll manage the stairs to their apartment. These days everything is an effort. If she could make a decision about which direction to go in, she's not sure she'd have the energy to get there.

Bernadette sees it in her face and puts an arm around Lucia's shoulder, drawing her close. "This heat. We're all worn out by it."

Bernadette leads Lucia down the driveway. She wants to be with her when Lucia steps onto the grass.

"Maggie," Lucia calls out, "we need to get out of these wet bathing—" and she stops midsentence because there in the backyard, standing at the foot of the stairs, is Richard with Maggie in his arms, his eyes closed in what looks like rapture.

Lucia is stunned, caught completely off guard, and then she knows. She looks at Bernadette, who meets her gaze without flinching. If Lucia asks her, Bernadette will tell the truth—*I called him, I gave him the address*—but Lucia doesn't.

She looks back at her daughter in her husband's arms. Richard is swaying as he holds her, and Maggie's face is buried in his neck. No one speaks or moves. It's as if time has stopped and held its breath. Then Lucia shrugs as if what she sees was inevitable.

She walks slowly but deliberately across the lawn to her husband and child and the three of them take the stairs to the garage apartment, Maggie still in her father's arms.

Very soon, the Weiss family comes back down the stairs, Maggie walking now, her backpack on her shoulders, Raymond, the stuffed dachshund, in her arms. Richard carries the two duffel bags. Without a glance at the house, where Bernadette's face can be seen in the kitchen window, they walk down the driveway to the street, get into Richard's car, and drive back to Riverside.

AS THE SUN GOES DOWN, Bernadette sets the patio table with a batik tablecloth in shades of deep blue. She puts out two fat, red candles and lights them. She opens a bottle of wine and cuts shockingly pink and orange zinnias from the garden and installs them in a small white pitcher in the center of the table. She does not look up at the empty apartment, but she wrestles with her conscience.

Yes, she wanted her home back—the one she and Max were

beginning to build together. The quiet, the privacy, their intimacy. She readily admits that to herself. But there was more—Lucia wasn't capable of solving the dilemma she created for herself, so, ultimately, weren't Bernadette's actions an effort to save Maggie? Weren't they? Right now she honestly doesn't know. What she does know is that she can't wait for Max to get home and she won't let anything else, anything, get in the way of what they have.

YEARS LATER, WHEN SOMEONE brings up the summer Maggie spent in Ocean Park, she remembers it as the season of the bees when she fell a little bit in love with Max. Lucia remembers it as a time of shame. And Richard refuses to remember it at all.

 *Sweet Peas*

THE DAY AFTER HER HUSBAND'S FUNERAL,
Trudy gave away every piece of clothing he owned. She had heard
stories of widows who visited the hanging shirts and stacks of
sweaters for many months, even years, after their husbands'
deaths, unable to perform the simple task of grabbing and folding
and packing away that was required.

That wasn't her way. Brian was dead. She was under no illu-
sion that there was any other reality. She understood her task was
to find a way to live without him. The first thing to do was to get
rid of the clothes.

She suspected her grown son was appalled. He was. He knew
his mother so little that he attributed her behavior to hard-
heartedness when it was really the exact opposite. She ached for
Brian in a way that bowed her spine and hollowed her out, and
she knew she would feel this way for as long into the future as she
could see. The clothes were a reproach—*Remember when you used
to be happy?* they said to her. *Well, that's over now.*

So Trudy filled their bedroom with large cardboard boxes

bought especially for the job. Never in the past thirty years had she needed packing boxes of any kind. She and Brian had bought this small house when they were newly married and had stayed put. The town of Sierra Villa in the Southern California foothills felt like home the first time they saw it: a tiny business center with all the shops grouped within easy walking distance, one elementary school, one high school, a town library, where Trudy worked. It reminded them both of their Midwestern roots.

Trudy and Brian were people who were not easily dislodged. Neither saw any reason to change what was good enough decades ago—this two-bedroom house with green shutters on Lima Street or their commitment to love, honor, and cherish each other. Until Brian died, nothing had changed.

Now the boxes stood waiting, freshly creased and open-mouthed. There was no way Trudy was going to throw Brian's monochromatic sweaters, button-down shirts, and threadbare jeans into black garage bags as if they were junk to be picked up with the rest of the trash.

No. She folded and smoothed and lined up the creases in his suit pants, which he rarely wore, and rolled his black socks into tight balls, and evened out the shoelaces on his running shoes, which he laced up every Tuesday, Thursday, and Saturday rain or shine. And she packed each box tightly and secured the top with clear cellophane packing tape, also newly bought. She couldn't deny the satisfaction of zipping the tape across the top of each box, a tiny piece of the work completed even though the task was one that bit into her heart.

"Mother . . . ?" Her son, Carter, is standing in the doorway.

"What?!" she answers too sharply. He had startled her. With each garment her hands touch, another memory ambushes her, but she doesn't explain this and her son doesn't hide his sigh of exasperation.

He's so short, Trudy thinks again as she does at least once on every visit. *Why did he have to take after my mother's side of the family?* Trudy's maternal grandfather was barely five feet tall. Her maternal grandmother was not much bigger. She remembers them from her childhood as gnome people. Holding hands in their wedding picture her mother kept on the mantel, they looked like the illustrations in her fairy-tale books.

Brian had been tall. Tall and lanky. Angular. The sort of person who never seemed to be able to fold his body comfortably into conventional chairs. Definitely not the sort of person to have a fatal heart attack. Too many people expressed that same opinion to Trudy after the fact. But there it was—an undetected defect in his aorta biding its time, bulging and pressing and finally rupturing.

Carter shows Trudy his packed duffel bag. "I've got to go."

But Trudy doesn't answer. He's not sure she's heard him, because she's turned her back and is taking in the mounds of clothes, a lifetime of clothes, spread across the bedspread, the dresser, the chair where Brian sat every morning to lace up his shoes.

For his entire life, Carter has found talking to his mother difficult. He often wondered why his parents ever had a child. They seemed like such a self-contained unit, the two of them. Always, always he had felt like an interloper in someone else's world. Oh, it's not that they neglected him. Not at all. There were the requisite birthday parties when he was young, and carpooling to school and tennis practice, attendance at his matches when he was in high school, and visits to various potential colleges when the time was right.

It was just that when his parents were together, they were present with each other in a way that never worked itself into his relationship with either one of them.

It was hard to explain. With his first girlfriend, Sabrina, he had tried. "It's like they're going through the motions with me . . . but when they're together it's like the house and everything in it, including me, could go up in flame and they would just say, 'Is it getting warm in here?'"

They were naked at the time, and she ran her hand up the inside of his thigh, teasingly. "Oh, Carter's feeling neglected."

He shook his head—that wasn't it, but it was as close as he could come to explaining. No one was surprised when he chose a college as far from sunny California as he could get. It was in New Hampshire, with its brutal winters, that he began to feel less invisible.

"With all the security hassles . . ." is what he says now, standing in the doorway. He shrugs—an apology of sorts, for what he's long forgotten, probably his very presence. "They tell you to be at the airport at least an hour—"

She cuts him off. "Of course." Then, "I should have asked you. Do you want any of Dad's clothes? He'd want you to have whatever—"

"God, no." And then softer, "I couldn't, you know?"

He comes into the room then and awkwardly puts an arm around Trudy's shoulders. "You'll be all right." Trudy doesn't know if it's a question or a statement, but she nods. The last thing she wants is for him to worry about her.

As he gets into the waiting taxi, Carter looks up to see his mother's face in the living room window. *She's getting old,* he thinks, but really it's mostly the grief. Trudy is fifty-seven, but today she feels ancient.

She puts a hand up on the glass. He takes it as a wave and waves back before closing the car door.

And then she's alone in the house. She knows she should walk back into the bedroom and finish the job she started. Trudy prides herself on finishing jobs. But she can't. Instead she walks out into the backyard, and it's here, despite the oppressive heat of late September, that she can draw the first deep breath of the day.

It is here she still feels Brian's presence. While the house might be small, although it suited them fine, the backyard is enormous. She always called it "Brian's work of art." Now she sees it as a living testament to Brian's kindness because you can't garden without kindness. Brian taught her that.

The cosmos bloom because he seeded them. The wisteria climbs the arbor over the patio because he planted it more than twenty years ago. The camellia bushes, fifteen feet high now, thrive in the shade from the large oak tree.

The Costa Rican butterfly vines cover the back fence with purple-winged flowers set against dark green, heart-shaped leaves. Trudy remembers he had to special-order them and that it was touch and go before they took off.

The garden doesn't look its best, even Trudy can tell that. In the San Gabriel foothills the summer heat has done its work. The more tender plants are burned and shriveled, the astromerias beaten back into the relative cool of the soil, the sunflowers drooping and brown. The raised vegetables beds hold ripening peppers and eggplant—they love the heat—but the heirloom tomato plants, more delicate, are stalks of crackling brown shafts.

She sees Brian here—digging and weeding and amending and cutting back and turning with an enormous grin that could have graced the face of a seven-year-old who's just hit a home run to show her two arms full of peppers and tomatoes and trombone squash three feet long.

She remembers all the early evenings when she'd come home from work to find him planting the lettuce seedlings that would soon fill their salad bowl or pruning the bougainvillea before it brought down the trellis attached to the garage or spreading his homemade compost around the rosebushes. And she'd pour two glasses of wine and take a book and come out to the backyard.

He'd always turn with surprise—*Is it so late already?* And she'd take a chair and sit close to him and read to him as he finished whatever job he'd started. And the sun would go down and the light would turn purple and they would finish their wine and Brian would finally stand up, his gardening pants patched with mud, and they would be happy. Completely happy. Both of them.

She doesn't know what she's going to do about the garden— none of Brian's gardening knowledge has rubbed off on her—but she knows she must deal with the clothes. And so she walks back into the house to finish.

ON MONDAY, TRUDY GOES BACK to work. Clementine, the assistant librarian, is horrified to see her.

"Oh no, Trudy," pops out of her mouth before she thinks. "It's too soon."

"Who makes the rules, Clemmie? You?"

"But I thought you'd want to take maybe another week—"

"To do what? Mope around the house?"

"But you loved Brian" is what Clementine says.

Tears spring to Trudy's eyes. "That's not going to stop," she says crossly. "That's the problem, it doesn't stop with death."

Clementine doesn't know what to say. She's never managed to find a way to comfort Trudy about anything and especially not about anything this important, but she feels compelled to try. "You have all those wonderful memories—"

"That makes it worse, don't you see? I want what I had. Just exactly what I had. Thirty-two years wasn't enough, do you understand?"

Clemmie nods. She does. You could feel it when they were together—that they couldn't get enough of each other. She often pondered that. Brian was nice enough, but he could be daunting to talk to—small talk, pleasantries, seemed to make him even stiffer and more uncomfortable. And as much as Clementine has gotten used to, even found an affection for Trudy, she still can see that Trudy is not the easiest of people to be around.

"What happened to the blue beanbag chair?" is what Trudy says now, her tone accusatory as she makes a beeline to the children's section. She stands in the reading corner, where large floor pillows, a green and yellow rug, and small wooden chairs are set up in a loose semicircle.

Years ago Trudy divided the library's modest space into a children's section on the left and an adult section on the right. It escapes nobody's notice that the children's area is twice the size of the adults' and much more thoughtfully furnished with several small worktables and chairs, a play area with Legos, a wooden train set, and a table that holds picture books open to the most enticing illustrations. And, of course, the reading corner, where every Friday afternoon Trudy transforms into the Story Lady, complete with medieval costume and rhinestone tiara.

By contrast the adult section looks bereft. There are the stacks, a few large rectangular tables, and two old computers, back to back, set up against a wall.

The double glass doors of the entry open directly to the transaction desk where Clemmie now sits, and behind it is a small glassed-in cubicle with one desk for her and one for Trudy.

"The blue beanbag chair?" Trudy demands again. "The one Graham always likes to sit in?"

"It split, Trudy. We had stuffing all over. Really, there was no saving it."

"That's what I get for taking any time off whatsoever. You threw it out, didn't you?" And without waiting for an answer, "Perfectly good chair."

Clementine opens her mouth to respond, then quickly closes it.

Despite her youth—she's young enough to be Trudy's daughter—
Clemmie has learned not to argue with Trudy. Softly now, Clementine says only, "I'm glad you're back."

When Trudy's at the library, the hours go. They pass, and
somewhere inside Trudy the rhythm of it lulls her into thinking that maybe she can get through the days. But then she has to
go home. It is the stillness of the air in the house when she first
opens the front door that does her in—it is Brian's absence made
tangible. And it assaults her, like the reverberations of a bomb
detonated miles away but still terrifying. Her legs give out and she
grabs the nearest chair, the one in the living room that looks out
over the front garden. And she sits there, sometimes until the old-
fashioned streetlights (which she's always loved) go on and
the neighbors are finished walking their dogs for the evening and
the streets are still and dark.

It is only then that she can manage to stand up, walk into the
bedroom, and climb into her side of the bed. She sleeps near the
edge in the clothes she put on that morning, desperate not to roll
over and feel the emptiness where Brian's long body once lay.
She cannot, she simply cannot, confront the loss every night of
his arms, which enfolded her body and made her feel, if only for
those hours, as if the world were a safe and generous place.

They were an oddly matched pair, Trudy short and round,
Brian resembling a whooping crane with all the angles and odd
posturing that those birds employ. They never saw the mismatch.
Trudy found in Brian an unusual grace, and Brian was always
reassured that Trudy fit so easily into his embrace.

They were the sort of couple that most people didn't
understand—the attraction, the connection, the longevity. She's
so caustic, it was often said, such a brusque sort of person. He was
so quiet, that's the first thing people noticed. The sort of guy who
could sit in a crowded café—in fact could often be found at a window table at Sully's Coffee on Fremont Street—head down over

his laptop, oblivious to his surroundings, startling if you happened to say hello to him. A detail sort of guy, people would say, precise, as befit someone who restores historical buildings. Brian relished spending weeks matching replacement tile colors to the original hue, painstakingly uncovering crown moldings under decades of paint, preserving creaky window hinges that only he understood were beautiful.

This is where his architectural degree from the University of Southern California got him—a career in historical restoration. Instead of creating new buildings as he had once envisioned, he spent his days preserving and making beautiful what had been neglected and overlooked. He eventually made peace with the way things had worked out, never quite understanding why his own visions had never been enough.

He had struggled as a young architect, finding the give-and-take process of designing and reworking and adapting and redesigning a mystery. Clients complained to the head of his firm that he didn't seem to listen to them or that the new drawings had nothing to do with what they had discussed. Brian was always baffled by these comments. He had tried, he really had, to give them what they wanted, but collaboration was not his strong suit. He took their corrections and began to alter the blueprints, but somehow, during the rethinking and the redrawing, the concerns of the clients seemed to vaporize into thin air and the drawings took on a life of their own. Brian was frequently astonished at the finished product but usually also very pleased. It was as if he had been in a trance, a creative maelstrom, as he drew, and then, suddenly, here was an entirely new design. Wonderful, he always felt. His clients were more often than not bewildered.

Gradually he found his way into a field where he was more anchored. The building dictated its needs and Brian complied. And it was all right, limiting in a way that creating from wishes had not been, but comforting nonetheless. Brian found beauty and satisfaction in restoration and relief in not having to disappoint clients.

And he was not a man to complain. There was about him that sort of Midwestern stoicism, a practical quality that embraces what is and doesn't pine for what could have been. Trudy struggles with that now but finds nothing in her life worth embracing and everything worth pining for.

The only thing that propels her out of the house in the morning is the certainty that staying home would be worse. She has nowhere free of pain, but at least at the library she has to pretend, and that pretense carries her through the majority of the day. People marvel at how she's coping, really, since she and Brian were so close. It's amazing, they say, that she's doing so well. But none of those people follow her home and almost none of them call to see how she is, and even neighbors on Lima Street hesitate to ring her bell or bring over a newly baked banana bread or cookies. Trudy has never invited those sorts of easy neighborly exchanges. She's not one to stop on the street and ask after children or comment on the beauty of the first roses of the season in someone's yard or exchange gossip about the new restaurant filling the vacant spot on Banyon Street.

And so she is left alone. Carter calls dutifully every Sunday afternoon. And Trudy assures him that she's fine. And since he wouldn't know what to do if she weren't, he gratefully gets off the phone after five uncomfortable minutes of descriptions of the amount of snow they've had that week or the fall in temperatures predicted to be below the freezing mark. Trudy thinks of those weekly calls as "the weather report." She has no idea what the weather is going to be in Southern California, but she's up to date on New Hampshire.

. . .

FALL FINALLY COMES AFTER A SCORCHING September and October. It took Trudy quite a while to realize that in Southern California, October can be as hot as July, only with the near certainty of wildfires breaking out on the hillsides from Santa Barbara to San Diego, thickening the air with mustard-yellow clouds of ash, making it painful to draw a deep breath.

But November brings fall, with crisp nights that can dip into the forties or even the thirties and sparkling crystalline days of sun and bright, clean air. For the first time since last winter, Trudy reaches for a jacket in the front coat closet and finds Brian's gardening windbreaker instead. She forgot about that closet when she was packing up his things back in September, and so here it is—blue, well worn, streaked with dirt down one sleeve. She puts it on—it comes to her knees—and zips it up. Her hands in the pockets find his gardening gloves, and she takes them out and stares at them. Caked with mud, they hold the curve of Brian's fingers.

One in each hand, she puts them back in the two jacket pockets and holds the right glove with her right hand and the left one with her left. As she leaves the house for the short walk to the library, she feels she's carrying a secret. Arms in Brian's jacket, hands holding the imprint of his hands, she feels lighter. She also wonders, not for the first time since his death, if she's going slightly crazy. But she wears the jacket every day, and Clementine manages not to comment on it.

When the rains come, it's the holiday season. Carter doesn't come home for any of it. Not for Thanksgiving—too short a time, the airfare's too expensive—or Christmas—he's going skiing. Trudy thinks he should have offered to even though she's not sure she'd want him there, but she says nothing.

"Will you be all right?" he asks her on one of his punctual Sunday calls.

"I'm going to Clementine and David's," she says even though it's a lie. She's told Clementine she was meeting Carter in San Diego where her sister lives, that she's driving down on Thursday night after they close the library for the long weekend—Christmas being on a Saturday this year—and that she won't be back until late Sunday.

There's nothing to do but hide her car in the garage, pull the drapes on the house windows that face the street, and lie low for the three days. She can't have someone see her—Sierra Villa is just the sort of small town where somebody would—and report back to Clemmie that she lied about having somewhere to go for Christmas. Clementine has a readily available look of pity. "Oh, the poor thing" is her standard response to a child whose mother speaks harshly to him, or to a toddler who sports a large bandage over a skinned knee. The last thing Trudy wants is for that solicitude to be directed her way.

On Friday morning when she awakes, she sees no reason to get out of bed. She can't leave the house. She can't even walk down her front path to pick up her copy of the *L.A. Times,* lying there in its plastic sleeve. She turns over and goes back to sleep. If she could, she'd sleep away the three days until it was time to get dressed and walk the four blocks to the library and begin her pretend life, which at this point is far better than her real one.

It's the drone of the leaf blower that wakes her. *Aren't those things illegal yet?* is her first conscious thought. She slaps the pillow over her head, but the whine insists on continuing. Even with all the windows shut, the noise is assaultive. *Is this what happens every Friday?* She's always at the library.

Groaning, she gets out of bed, her body resisting this upright position. It wants nothing more than to dissolve back into the sheets, but the noise is like a prod. It forces her to the bedroom window. What she sees is not the gardener operating that noisy contraption but, instead, a quiet man, bent over the soil. He's kneeling, his back to her, but she can see that he cups tiny seedlings in his large hands and lays them gently into the soil of the planting bed next to the garage.

Brian's planting the sweet peas is her first thought, and she grabs the windowsill for support. *Of course it's not Brian, idiot,* she tells herself. *This man looks nothing like Brian.* He is much shorter, his back is broader, and his skin is darker. And yet, there's a whisper of Brian in the way he carefully unmolds the seedlings from their black plastic and places each tenderly, yes, tenderly, in the prepared soil, firming the dirt around the slender stem of each young plant with two fingers.

Trudy opens the back door and walks out. The man doesn't hear her because the damned blower is still going somewhere in the front of the house. Trudy has to walk farther into the garden, and it's then that she sees he's fastened columns of white string to the garage wall, from soil to roof as Brian did every December—a place for the sweet peas to go is how Brian explained it. "They like to know what's ahead for them," he always said with a grin. "Don't we all?"

"What are you doing!?" She tries to raise her voice over the mechanical drone, but the man doesn't hear her. "Hello!" She doesn't know his name. She's never seen him before. Or she's never noticed him. As she walks farther into the yard she sees that he's young, probably in his thirties, and he wears a red sweatshirt that says ARMANDO'S HOME GARDENS across the back.

"Armando!" By now she's yelling and then, suddenly, the whine from the leaf blower cuts off and she finds herself standing two feet from this strange man screaming his name.

He scrambles to his feet. "Mrs. Dugan . . ." And they look at each other. He sees a small, middle-aged woman with salt-and-pepper hair flying every which way as if she's just gotten out of bed and rumpled clothes as if she had slept in them and a face full of sorrow. That's what he notices first—the sorrow.

She sees a broad, open face and thick, straight black hair cut short. Hispanic, Latino, she's not sure which is the proper term these days. But it's his eyes that hold her—they're full of concern.

"I was sorry to hear about Mr. Brian. I haven't seen you before to tell you."

"You speak perfect English."

He shrugs—it's not quite true, he worries about his English still—and she wonders if she offended him. "Were you born here?"

"No, Mexico. I came when I was thirteen."

Trudy looks at the garage wall, the sweet pea seedlings in the rich, brown dirt. "Brian always . . ." she starts and then can't continue.

"I thought I would plant the sweet peas this year," Armando says to her. "I thought, maybe, you'd want to see them cover the wall."

"Yes," she tells him. She realizes she wants very much to see the sweet peas blooming.

"I would have used netting, you know, plastic netting across the wall," Armando tells her, comfortable, it now seems, with a lengthy conversation, "but Mr. Brian always liked to stretch the strings. It takes more time, but it's the way he would have done it." Another shrug. "I thought—he can't do it, I'll do it his way."

All she can manage is a "thank you" even as it catches in the back of her throat. She has to get back to the house. She can't have this conversation. She can't discuss Brian with this young man.

Armando watches her walk across the yard. *How does a woman live with so much pain?* is what he thinks.

. . .

SPRING ARRIVES IN FEBRUARY. When Brian used to tell his mother back in Ohio that bulbs begin to push up in February, that roses break out with their first red leaves, that fruit trees blossom white and pink popcorn in February, she refused to believe it. While the rest of the country is miserable in winter, Southern California sashays its way right into spring.

Across the backyard and the front planting beds daffodils, anemones, ranunculus, and narcissus seem to appear overnight where there was nothing but empty space. By March, the sweet peas are halfway up the garage wall. Trudy gets up every morning, puts on Brian's windbreaker, holds her hands around his curved gloves, and walks the four blocks to the library. Nothing's changed. All around her the natural world screams renewal, but she doesn't notice it.

The only thing she looks forward to is her Friday afternoon turn as the Story Lady. She gets to pretend on top of the pretense of her whole life now. It's the highlight of the week for Trudy and for many of the exhausted mothers of Sierra Villa who have preschool children and crave an hour off.

By three o'clock the library has filled up with children aged two to six. Usually once the kids hit seven, they won't be caught dead listening to the Story Lady.

Trudy makes a production out of it. The costume she found at the Rose Bowl Flea Market. It must have been made for some movie, she thinks, because it's intricately embroidered with silver thread, and fake pearls, and yards of flowing chiffon. The tiara Trudy wears she found at Walgreens, but the cachet of the dress extends to the insubstantial crown and makes it look like the real thing.

All the children are seated on one of the tiny chairs or big, floppy pillows arranged around a brightly painted big chair that Brian created for the Story Lady one Sunday. It almost looks like a throne, but right now it is empty, waiting for the children to settle so that Trudy can make her big entrance.

Clemmie manages to hush the last few whispers and then announces to the audience, "And now, straight from Fairy Tale Lane, our own Story Lady!" And she turns with a flourish and a sweep of her hand in the direction of the library's bathroom— where else could Trudy transform herself?—and there are "ooh's" and "aah's" as Trudy floats in her floor-length gown and diamond tiara to the reading circle.

"Today," Trudy tells the children, who gaze up at her with expectant faces, "I'm going to read you a story called *Wylie Makes a Wish.*"

The mothers, sitting at the wooden tables in back of the story circle, lean back, take out their cell phones or iPads, make grocery lists, sip their Starbucks. All heave a sigh—a free hour while Trudy works her magic.

"'Wylie wanted many things. He wanted a baseball mitt and chocolate-chip cookies for breakfast and swimming lessons in the summer. But most of all, he wanted a grandpa.'" Trudy turns the book toward the children so they can see the picture of Wylie. He's about five and has freckles and a thatch of red hair across his forehead. Above his head spin pictures of a glove, the cookies, and an outdoor pool.

"Sometimes my mommy lets me eat cookies for breakfast," pipes up one four-year-old with a mass of tiny black ringlets haloing her face, and a woman with the identical hair slides down in her undersize chair, her face blooming beet red. "Once," she murmurs, "I let her once." Clemmie, patrolling the perimeter of the reading circle, pats the woman on the shoulder.

"'Wylie had two grandmas,'" Trudy continues. "'One he called Nana and the other he called Toots because she didn't think she was old enough to be a grandma, and they were both very nice. But they weren't grandpas. It wasn't the same. Not at all!'"

The next picture shows a very stubborn Wylie with his arms crossed against his chest and his jaw set with indignation.

"'"Why don't you make a wish for one?" his mother said as a last resort since no amount of reasoning seemed to make a difference. "Yes!" Wylie yelled. "That will do the trick!" And so that night when his father was putting him to bed and he saw the first shining star, Wylie wished for a grandpa.'"

Now Trudy rests her forearms on her knees and turns the book so the children can see Wylie wishing on his star. "'Wylie believed that wishes come true . . .'"

Trudy pauses for a fraction of a second—*if only* is what she hears romping through her brain—and then continues. "'. . . and that because he wanted a grandpa more than anything, he would get one.'"

"That's right," says a very serious child, nodding as he speaks. "If you wish hard enough, you get it."

Fat chance! Trudy wants to scream but, of course, she doesn't. She starts the next page. "'Wylie worked very hard at his wishing,'" only now tears are falling from Trudy's eyes, straight from her eyes into her lap. She doesn't seem to know that this is happening. The little boy with the serious eyes sitting near her puts a hand on Trudy's leg in comfort.

"'And he kept opening the front door to see if a grandpa had arrived,'" Trudy manages to get out, though her voice is trembling. "'But the front step was always empty. No one was there.'"

And Trudy puts the book down on her lap, her face in her hands, and begins to sob. Huge, breath-shattering sobs that thunder from her clenched body as if propelled by an avalanche—an avalanche of grief.

The mothers stir, sit up straighter, punch off their cell phones.

What's happening here? They weren't really paying attention. But some of their children are crying now as well. *This is a disaster* runs through Clemmie's mind as she moves to stand in front of Trudy.

"The Story Lady . . ." she begins to explain, but Trudy stands up, hiccuping now with more sobs, and rushes out of the library, through the glass front doors and out onto the street. The children watch her with open mouths of astonishment.

Trudy is mortified, terrified. *What is happening to me?* is the only coherent thought she's able to manage before the sobbing picks up again, another round of anguished sounds escape from her throat as she runs down La Cruza Street, desperate to get away from the scene of her humiliation. She gasps for breath as she runs. Maybe she's having a heart attack. Maybe's she dying. She runs anyway.

By the time she reaches her front door, the sobs have become whimpers and it feels as though her body has cracked open. Everything is shaking—her legs, her hands as she tries to turn the key in the front door lock, her chest as it searches for air.

She manages to make it to the living room easy chair and pull herself into it. And she sits, staring at nothing, waiting for she doesn't know what. She's emptied out and stone cold and incapable of forming a thought or action.

She has no idea how long she's been sitting there when she sees the flatbed truck pull into her driveway and a man she doesn't recognize begins to wrestle a bulky electric mower down onto the pavement. And then Armando gets out of the driver's seat and goes to help.

Trudy watches because she doesn't believe she can stand up and move away from the window. She knows she can be seen, but she also doesn't have the will to do anything about it.

When the mower is on the grass and the other man has begun

the back-and-forth trudging across the lawn with the machine,
Armando looks up and sees her in the front window.

The sounds of the two gardeners continue to wash over her—
the lawn mower, the tinny scrape of the rake across the brick
of the front path, one of them yelling in Spanish to the other. And
then it's quiet and Trudy thinks they may have left, but no, she
hears the lawn mower start up again in the backyard and then she
hears a loud rapping on the back door. She ignores it. It starts up
again.

Armando is standing on the back door stoop, knocking as
loudly as he can over the lawn mower's engine. *Maybe she doesn't
hear me,* he thinks, *over the noise.* Maybe he should try the front
door, although he always used the back when he needed to ask Mr.
Brian something.

Trudy sees him come around the side of the house and take
the straight brick path to the front door. He knocks. Waits. Knocks
again. He knows she's there and debates whether he should just
leave her alone, but the picture of her sitting there, in that costume, staring at nothing, worries him.

"Mrs. Dugan," he says loudly as he knocks again, "could I just
speak with you for a minute?"

Trudy uses her arms to push her body from the chair. It may
be one of the hardest things she's ever done. Her body feels as
if all the bones have drained away and she's left with flesh that
won't sustain her weight.

"Mrs. Dugan?"

And Trudy opens the front door.

"I'm so sorry to bother you . . ." Armando starts, waiting for her
to say something, but she doesn't. She doesn't know how to form
the words right now.

"Could you come out into the backyard, please?" he asks.

She nods and closes the door. He waits for her on the back

lawn, not at all sure she heard him or that she will come, but no, the back door opens and Trudy walks out, comes over to him where he stands, two square, four-inch plastic pots in his hands.

"This one," he says, pointing to one pot, "is a Caspian Pink, and the other is something called Eva's Purple Ball. I plant this one because of my mother. Her name is Eva." He pronounces it "Ava."

She looks at him without comprehension.

"They're tomato seedlings. Heirloom tomatoes that I grow on my kitchen windowsill. Every year I would give Mr. Brian five or six and he would plant them, but I thought, maybe this year, you would want only one or two."

Trudy raises her hands in a gesture of helplessness. "But I wouldn't know . . ."

"I can plant them or I can show you how to plant them. There." He gestures to the raised beds Brian built so many years ago. "Come," he says, and he walks to the earth he has already prepared and kneels down, his back to her as it was the first time she saw him through her bedroom window.

"I added compost and tomato food so all you have to do is transfer the plants into the dirt. I'll show you," he says, and Trudy finds herself moving toward him and kneeling, in her Story Lady gown, beside Armando.

"This will be simple for you," he says. "And then you will have some tomatoes in the summer. I thought that if I didn't bring you some plants, you would have to eat those cardboard ones from the grocery store."

He digs a small hole in the pliable earth, turns the plastic pot over in his hand, the stem of the seedling sheltered between his first and second fingers so that the plant slips easily from its container. Trudy watches his hands as he lays the plant deeply into the hole and smoothes the earth back around the stem so that only the top leaves are visible.

"They like to be buried deep," he tells her, "because all along the trunk new roots grow and they make the plant stronger. You would think if so much of the plant is buried under the dirt, it wouldn't be good, but for tomatoes that's not true. The deeper you plant them, the stronger they get and the more they blossom. Now, you do the other one so you will know."

He places the Caspian Pink seedling in her hand. "Turn it over carefully," he says, "with the stem between your fingers." She does and the seedling pulls free of the plastic pot. "Good. You have gentle hands. Now into the earth. Deep, and pull up the covers to its chin." He smiles at her to let her know it's a small joke.

The dirt feels warm to her touch and damp as she nestles the seedling into the hole Armando has created for it. For the first time she realizes the sun is particularly bright and the day has a wisp of a breeze.

"Perfect," he tells her, "you will have gorgeous pink tomatoes in July. Lots of them to eat. Now we water."

He stands and waits for her but she doesn't move. "Mrs. Dugan?" He places his hand on her back—a soft gesture of concern—and it's the gentleness of the touch, the warmth of his hand that she can feel through the thin fabric of her dress. Dimly she's aware that his is the first human touch she's had since last September 16, the day that Brian died.

She turns to look at him, at the concern on his face, at the goodness she sees in it. She gives him her hand—to steady her as she bunches the flowing gown up around her legs. He takes her hand and helps her up.

 *What We Give*

THE FIRST TIME CLEMENTINE REALIZED
something was up was when Trudy moved the Story Lady to
Thursday afternoons from Fridays, where it had been for decades.
Clemmie hadn't been at the library for all those years, only four
of them, but Trudy often made a point of reminding her that the
Story Lady had been appearing in front of the preschoolers of
Sierra Villa for almost as long as Clemmie had been alive, every
Friday, three o'clock.

Trudy was nothing if not a model of consistency. Repetition
seemed to fuel her soul instead of dampen it. Newness for newness's sake made no sense to Trudy. Clementine had seen articles
of clothing Trudy must have bought well before she even moved
to California. They were neat and clean but also thirty years out of
style. Trudy didn't seem to notice. And Clementine knew exactly
what she would have said if Clemmie had been foolish enough to
point that fact out to her—*So what?*

Because Trudy had never seen the value of most change and
certainly not precipitous change, life, with its appetite for irony,

meted out exactly that seismic shift. At least that was Trudy's
bitter reasoning as she trekked through the mire of her particular
sadness. Brian, her husband of thirty-two years, went out for his
customary run one Thursday morning last September, calling
back to her as he always did before he shut the kitchen door that
he'd be "back in forty-five," but this time it wasn't so. One of their
neighbors, Peggy Coopersmith, walking her chocolate Lab before
work, found Brian sprawled across Madia Lane. Dead before
the paramedics could get there and ascertain that his aorta had
ruptured. Dead before Trudy could tell him she loved him one last
time. Dead, alone. That last part—that he died without her there
to comfort him—never stopped tormenting her.

Trudy coped with Brian's death the only way she knew how, by
continuing to put one foot in front of another. She couldn't think
of anything else to do. She went to work every day, walking the
four blocks back and forth from her house to the library, presenting to the world the same slightly irascible manner, only more so.
And holding close to her heart the devastating pain she felt every
day at the loss of the man she had known and loved quietly, but
oh so overwhelmingly, for all her adult life.

It was only at the end of the day when she closed the front
door of their neat house with the green shutters on Lima Street
that the loss of her sweet and gentle Brian walloped her into near
catatonia. No one knew—not Clemmie, whom she saw five days
a week at the library, or her son, Carter, who called every Sunday
for his five minutes of small talk and weather report from New
Hampshire, or her sister in San Diego who checked in with her
once a month. None of the neighbors, who nodded and smiled at
her but never intruded, suspected. None of them had any idea of
the countless hours she sat in her living room armchair, staring
out the large picture window and seeing nothing but the bleak-
ness of her life without Brian. Seven months went by like that, in

a blur of misery, until the day Armando noticed and rang the bell, two tomato seedlings in his hand.

Armando had never lost a spouse, being too young for that particular tragedy, but his father, Juan, had died after a long illness. From the day Armando finished high school—and his father had insisted he finish—father and son had worked side by side for thirteen years in the gardening business Juan had started. It was only then that Armando had come to truly know the taciturn man that his father had been and to admire his resolve as well as his stoicism that he had mistaken for indifference when he was a young child.

From the months and months of watching his father diminish and then suffer too much for too long, Armando understood loss. It wasn't the last patch of his dying that had been the hardest to bear. It had been the months right before when Juan was too ill to get out of the truck but still insisted on coming with Armando every day. His father had to be helped into the passenger seat and he would sit there, staring straight ahead, staring at his own death, Armando often felt, although his father never said a word. Juan didn't move from the truck as Armando mowed the various lawns, raked the leaves of other, more fortunate people's houses, but his father always knew what had been left undone or not done well enough.

"Did you spread Mrs. Marston's grass clippings in the compost pile?" he would ask as Armando climbed back into the cab. And Armando would shake his head, climb back out, and spread the grass clippings.

"The front border needs to be weeded," Juan would say as Armando began loading up their equipment at another house, the afternoon light beginning to fade.

"Next week, Papa," Armando would say, "we're late today."

"Next week they will be bigger."

And Armando would sigh—he was very tired. Doing the work of two men—his job and his father's—was wearing him down. But he would go and weed the front border before they moved on to the next house.

Once his father became too ill to sit in the truck, then his mother took over, nursing him through the long, last month herself until he died at home, surrounded by his ten children.

From then on, as he drove his father's truck and walked in his footsteps, Armando understood about continuation and honoring the dead.

ON THAT MARCH AFTERNOON, as Armando helped Trudy plant her tomato seedling, kneeling by her side, he felt something shift within her, something tiny to be sure, but he heard a small sigh escape from her body, and with it, he was certain, came some measure of the sadness that seemed to weigh her down so. For all that he was grateful and very pleased with himself that he had thought to bring the tomatoes.

For Trudy, to her amazement, those few quiet moments in the garden, cupping the tender seedling in her hands and firming the earth around it to ensure its growth, Armando at her elbow coaching and encouraging her, meant more to her than anything that had happened to her since Brian's death. She was astonished to realize that the weight of pain she had carried in her heart for seven months had lifted a little. She could draw a deep breath. She could feel the spring sunshine across her back as she knelt.

The next Monday morning she walked into the library and told Clementine that she was changing the Story Lady time from Fridays to Thursdays because so many families now went away for the weekend and too many children would miss the stories.

Clementine looked at her in puzzlement. "But, Trudy, the

library is always packed. We couldn't hold any more children than we do."

"I read an article in the paper over the weekend." Trudy is dogged about her logic because she is building a case against the truth. "It said there's a definite trend of families taking three-day holidays on weekends. Didn't you see it?"

Clemmie shook her head.

"Summer vacation is coming and there'll be more and more of that."

"We've got three months before the schools are out," Clementine is foolish enough to say.

"So what," Trudy snapped, irritated she was being forced to defend her decision. "We have to get people used to a new schedule."

"But, Trudy, don't you think if we waited until the summer—"

"What's the big deal about changing the Story Lady day?" Trudy definitely does not want this conversation to continue. "If it doesn't bother me, why should it bother you?"

Clementine is nonplussed. She shrugs and says, "Fine . . . I'll make a sign to put out front."

"Make sure it says starting this Thursday."

NOW THAT THE STORY LADY APPEARS on Thursdays, Trudy starts to leave the library early on Friday afternoons. Instead of staying to close up at five, she begins eyeing the clock at about three and manages to leave by three thirty at the latest. Clemmie raises an eyebrow the first few times but knows enough not to say anything. Each Friday's early exit is accompanied by an excuse Trudy has tried out that morning in front of her bathroom mirror— "I have a dentist's appointment," she tells her image to see if it sounds credible, or "I need to get to the post office before it closes."

Some Fridays when she walks from the library to her house
and turns right onto Lima Street, she finds her heart sinking
because she can tell by the neatly mowed lawn and the trash cans
lined up at the curb that Armando has come and gone. It is on one
of those days when she sits in her empty kitchen and looks out
over the empty backyard that Trudy thinks that, maybe, it would
have been better if she had made more friends during all those
years she lived on Lima Street. This thought had never occurred
to her while Brian was alive because Brian was all she needed. But
now she wonders if she should have tried to navigate through all
those female rituals that always mystified her—gossiping on the
phone or shopping together for clothes she didn't need or sitting
through those ladies' lunches she always thought were worthless
wastes of time.

But on those Fridays when she can hear the drone of the leaf
blower well down the block, her step brightens and her back
straightens and she makes her way home with something like
expectation.

Often on those Fridays she and Armando will exchange only
a few words. "How are you, Mrs. Dugan?" he will ask, or he will
tell her "The tomatoes are doing nicely. You are watering them
just right." Then she will sit at her kitchen table and watch him
work in the backyard, hoeing and weeding and cutting back the
lemon tree so it doesn't shade the raised beds—all things she had
watched Brian do for all those years. If Armando stands up and
catches Trudy watching him, he will wave and smile and she will
wave and smile back and that is enough. For now it is enough.

ARMANDO WONDERS WHY she sits by herself every Friday. He
has never seen her with friends or visitors. She never seems to
be talking on the phone. There are never young children run-

ning around, nieces and nephews perhaps. He wonders why her mother doesn't sit with her in the kitchen, drinking coffee or cooking Friday night dinner, anything to help her through this difficult time. The solitude that comes from that house is so unlike his own large, messy family.

His mother, Eva, lives nearby in the house they were raised in—all ten of them. Two brothers live at home with her. A sister, Jessenia, lives around the corner, next street over. Sunday dinners at his mother's start at four and continue until the last brother carries the last sleeping child to his car and the last sister washes the last platter and puts it away. Even in his own home there are his three children, his wife's relatives coming and going, his own brothers, who drop by whenever they want, the friends of his children, the two dogs—activity, people, noise, energy.

In the days and weeks and even months after his father died, his mother was never alone. They all made sure that the kitchen was filled with women cooking and talking, the backyard crowded with young children racing back and forth, the living room overloaded with Eva's sons yelling at the television screen as they watched football or basketball or baseball in the summer.

It makes Armando uneasy to see Trudy sitting alone week after week, and so one Friday he knocks on the back door and she comes immediately to open it.

"Mrs. Dugan," he says, "could you come around the side of the house with me? We have a problem."

"Serious?"

"We can fix it," he tells her. And she knows it's not too bad because he's smiling as he says it.

Along the driveway, between the paving and the fence, is a line of westringia, feathery shrubs with thin, arching branches and tiny lavender flowers. Trudy remembers when Brian put them in years ago. Right in the middle of the row, one plant is brown and wrinkled.

"You see"—Armando points to it—"I must take this one out."

"It looks dead."

"It is, but it can be replaced. If you buy another, I will plant it for you."

"Oh, I wouldn't know where to—"

"At the Home Depot. It's not far. You take the 210 Freeway and when you see the sign for Mountain Avenue, you get off and you are there. Ask for westringia."

"Westringia," she repeats.

He can tell she doesn't want to go. He doesn't know that she avoids freeway driving whenever possible.

"Won't the others just fill in?"

"No," he says, "it will always look like a line of teeth with one missing. You must buy a new one." *You must get out of the house* is what he really wants to say to her. *You must try.* But, of course, he has no right to say either, so he tells her to buy the westringia when he could very easily get it for her. He's at the Home Depot Garden Center several times a week.

"We must put a new plant in here or there will be an empty space always."

She nods. Somehow, maybe because he is so unequivocal, she agrees to do what she has no interest in doing.

TRUDY FOLLOWS ARMANDO'S DIRECTIONS exactly. The 210 Freeway is close to her house. She takes it going east and is soon at the Mountain Avenue exit. As she gets off the freeway, Trudy sees the large orange Home Depot sign on her right. So far, so good. She's a bit surprised at how well she managed to navigate the 210.

Once she's parked the car, Trudy enters the Garden Center through large open wire gates and stops in her tracks. In front of her, displayed on waist-high tables, are the most gorgeous colors she has ever seen gathered in one place. Pinks and purples and the deep red of roses, pristine white flowers whose name she doesn't know. Shocking magenta bougainvillea vines. Lavender and sage she recognizes from Brian's herb garden. Yards and yards of flowers and shrubs and vegetables neatly arranged in rows and ready for spring planting. Far from the entrance, in the back, are the citrus trees, palms, and flowering maples.

This is what Brian saw, she realizes. This beauty. These luminous colors and scents. This bounty of choices. Like entering a library, it occurs to her suddenly, with all the possible books laid out on their shelves and the excitement of any choice taking her somewhere she's never been.

Here she is lost in the possibilities. There doesn't seem to be anyone around to help her, so she wanders and reads the small plastic tags stuck into the pots and tiny six-packs. Nowhere does she see the name "westringia."

In the middle of the last aisle, with a dense jumble of plants in front of her, she stops, dismayed. How will she ever find the right plant, the one Armando has sent her to buy?

"This place can be overwhelming, can't it?" A woman about her age, pushing a large orange shopping cart filled with all sorts of plants, stops beside Trudy.

Eyeing her cart, Trudy says, "You seem to have found your way." Often she doesn't realize how abrupt she sounds, but the other woman simply shrugs. She's good-natured, a large woman, nearly six feet tall and broad rather than fat. She's wearing jeans and an oversize pink sweatshirt that reads GRANDMA'S JOB IS TO SPOIL ROTTEN.

"I just pick up what calls to me, you know." The woman surveys her crowded cart with a bit of wonder as to how she managed to accumulate so many plants. "It seems I just have to have all of these." She shrugs. "Even though I have no idea where I'm putting any of them."

"But you're buying them anyway?"

"Oh, they'll go somewhere. . . ." The woman waves her hand to indicate that the "somewhere" is amorphous.

"Not a very efficient system, is it?" Trudy can't help but say.

The woman just laughs. "Nope, but this is gardening, not running a Fortune Five Hundred company. Half the fun is experimenting, don't you think?"

"I don't know. I'm new at this."

"Well then," the woman says, "you've got so much good stuff ahead of you."

Trudy shakes her head. This woman has no idea what's ahead of her, but Trudy would never classify it as "good stuff." "Do you know where I could find a 'westringia'?"

"Oh, what a beautiful shrub," the woman gushes, "so delicate."

"Yes, well . . . I need one and there's just too many plants here for me to . . ." Trudy looks around, at a loss, and the woman sees it.

"You wait right here, honey," she says and takes off for the middle aisle.

Honey?! Trudy thinks to herself. Why do people use endearments when they barely know you? What is that? Sloppy language, Trudy concludes.

"There you go," the woman says as she comes back with a tiny westringia plant in a gallon container and hands it over. As she begins pushing her shopping cart forward, down the aisle toward the back of the nursery, the woman says over her shoulder, "I've decided I just have to have an apricot tree," and waves as she goes.

Walking back to her car, westringia plant tucked in her arm, Trudy feels as though she's accomplished something. She's managed the freeway, a task that was always Brian's responsibility. She's been bowled over by the colors of the flowers. She has bought the right plant.

When she gets home she places the plant in the empty space

in the line of westringia, where it already looks like it belongs. She knows Armando will plant it next Friday.

Without really thinking about it, on those Fridays when Armando has come and gone by the time she gets home, Trudy finds herself driving to Home Depot and buying a plant . . . or two . . . or more. Plants she doesn't know the names of. Plants she doesn't need. It doesn't escape the rational part of her mind that she may well be turning into the woman with the extra-large grandma sweatshirt—*Oh, please,* she begs herself, *no clothes with writing on them*—but she brings the plants home anyway.

When Armando arrives the next Friday afternoon there sits a pot or two or three on the backyard patio table. He has to knock on Trudy's back door and they have to have a discussion about where these plants might go in the garden. Some days that discussion is lengthy because Trudy hasn't thought through any of these purchases, but Armando never questions her choices. Together they figure it out. It makes his workday longer—he's often late for his next house—but he doesn't mind. He thinks of these spontaneously appearing plants as gifts, and Trudy, if she were honest with herself, would say the same about the conversations.

IN JUNE, WHEN SCHOOL IS OUT for the summer, things change. One Friday afternoon, Trudy comes home to find a small boy raking up the grass clippings from her front path. He looks to be about seven or eight, she thinks, dark skinned with thick black hair like a curtain across his forehead. He's skinny and quiet. Trudy is incensed.

"Who do you belong to?" is what she says to him. The boy stops what he's doing and considers the question, almost as if he's pondering the philosophical underpinnings of it.

"Maybe God," he says, but not with any attitude, simply his evaluation of the right answer, and it disarms Trudy. She puts her hands on her hips and shakes her head.

"No," she says, "are you here with your dad?"

"Uh-huh," and he points to Armando, who is just coming around the house from the backyard.

"Armando, what is your son doing working on my property?!" This is not said sweetly.

Armando puts a calming hand on his son's shoulder before he answers, "Did he do something wrong, Mrs. Dugan?"

"Not him. *You.* A child this age—how old are you?" she asks the boy.

"Eight and a half," he says.

"Exactly!" Trudy snaps. "What is an eight-year-old child doing *working*?! He should be at camp or riding his bike or just playing! Not raking my front path!"

"Mrs. Dugan," Armando says quietly, "there are days he does these things, but my wife works and today my sister can't take care of him and so he spends the day with me. There are worse things, don't you think, than spending a whole day with your father?"

The boy moves closer to Armando and leans back against his legs.

"What's your name?" Trudy asks him.

"Ricky," the boy says.

"Enrique," Armando says at the same time and then laughs. "Okay, Ricky." He explains to Trudy, "That's what the kids at school call him."

"Do you like stories?" Trudy asks the boy and Ricky shrugs. "Come on"—she holds out a hand—"let's go get you some books with really cool stories in them."

Armando grins at the "really cool" reference, and Trudy understands immediately what he's grinning at. "I can't be around kids all day without picking up some of their rotten language."

"Go on with Mrs. Dugan," he tells his son, "she knows everything about books," and reluctantly the boy takes the two steps to move closer to Trudy.

"We'll be back in a few minutes," Trudy tells Armando before she puts a hand around Ricky's wrist and begins walking briskly back to the library with him. "Really, Armando," is her parting shot, "there has to be a better way. An eight-year-old working?!"

But Armando just smiles as he watches the tiny, round lady and his skinny and adored youngest son walk side by side down Lima Street. To the library! Only good can come of that.

"What do you like to read about?" Trudy asks the child as they walk.

Ricky shrugs. "I don't know."

"Well, what do you like to do?"

"Play soccer."

"Good," she says, "so we'll get you some books about soccer."

When she walks back into the library with Ricky in tow, both Clementine's eyebrows rise. Trudy marches Ricky past her, explaining, "That's Clementine, she pays far too much attention to everything that happens around here."

"Find a seat," she says to Ricky as they approach the children's section, "and I'll bring you some books about soccer." With that, Trudy disappears behind some tall bookcases and reappears two minutes later with an armful of books.

She takes the child-size seat next to him, which seems to serve her small body well, and lays the books out on the table in front of them like a fan.

"Did you just finish second grade?"

"Uh-huh."

"Then this one—*Brendan Wins the Game*—should be right at your level."

Ricky takes the book, head down, and opens it to the first page—a simple drawing of a boy about his age kicking a soccer ball. The narrative starts, "Brendan loved his soccer ball." The boy stares at the picture, then the words, but only for a split second, and then he turns the page. On page two he examines the picture and ignores the words.

Trudy watches him go through the book, sleuthing out the story from the illustrations and skimming over all the words. Having sat with children in this library for over thirty years, she knows exactly what's going on.

She watches him go through the second book the same way, his eyes glued to the pictures.

"I'm going to let you take these books home," she tells him. "Your dad should read these with you. I'll tell him."

The boy shrugs. "Okay."

On the walk back to her house, Trudy watches the boy. He walks with his eyes on his feet.

"Do you like school?" she asks him.

He shakes his head.

"Do you have a rotten teacher?"

He looks up at her, surprised that an adult has made that kind of judgment about a teacher. In his house, no one would say that.

"She's okay."

"Then what don't you like about it?"

Ricky shrugs again, hoping that if he doesn't say much, she'll stop asking him questions.

"That doesn't tell me anything, a shrug. Tell me one thing you don't like about it."

"It's boring."

"Okay, I get that. Tell me one more thing you don't like."

Ricky doesn't know what this lady wants him to say, why she keeps asking him questions, but he figures he has to come up with something to tell her. "The boys' bathroom smells stinky."

And Trudy laughs. "I bet it does. But I have a hunch there's something else about school that you don't like."

Jeez, this lady won't leave it alone. Ricky risks a glance up at her and she's looking straight at him. She's not letting him off the hook anytime soon, it's obvious, and so he tells her, "I'm in the dumb kids' reading group and everybody knows it."

"Ahhh," says Trudy, "I see."

They walk together in silence. That answer seemed to satisfy her. Maybe now she'll stop asking him things. But when they get to the intersection, she starts talking again. "I have a secret for you."

He gives his all-purpose shrug again. He doesn't think this lady can tell him anything he'd like to hear.

"Being able to read right away and being smart have nothing to do with each other. Smart kids can have trouble reading."

After they cross the intersection, eyes down again, Ricky begins kicking a small stone as they walk. Trudy watches him. She wants to tell him to stop that, it's annoying her, but she doesn't. She walks and waits. Finally, he says without looking at her, "Is that true?"

"What do you think I do every day?" she asks him and then continues on without waiting for his answer. "I help kids read books and I've been doing it for almost as long as your mother and father have been alive, so I know it's true."

He doesn't look at her as she explains and he doesn't ask anything as they continue their walk. She watches the boy. She's not sure he believes her.

. . .

WHEN THEY GET BACK TO HER HOUSE, Armando and his helper, Faustino, are just finishing up, loading the heavy mower back into the truck bed.

"Armando," she says, "I need to show you something in the backyard," and she hands Ricky the three books she chose for him. "You bring these back next Friday and we'll get three more."

The boy takes the books but doesn't seem happy about it.

"Say thank-you to Mrs. Dugan," Armando tells his son. The boy mumbles something, but Trudy isn't interested in gratitude.

In the backyard, away from Ricky and Faustino, Trudy tells Armando what she suspects he doesn't know. "Your son can't read, Armando. He doesn't understand the first thing about letters and sounds and how they make words."

"Mrs. Dugan, he's only eight. He has time to learn all these things."

"No, what I'm telling you is that he's not going to learn these things without some help. Can you help him with that, or your wife?"

Armando shakes his head. "Maybe if he was learning to read in Spanish, then—"

"Bring him with you every Friday. We have the summer. Every Friday. All summer."

"No, Mrs. Dugan, I couldn't—"

"You want him to fail in school? You want him to drop out? Because that's what happens to kids who can't read."

"No, of course not, but I couldn't ask—"

"You're not asking. I'm telling you—bring him to me."

And they look at each other in silence. Trudy's gaze is clear and determined and, Armando suddenly sees, eager. He understands she wants to do this for him, for his son. For herself as well.

"Thank you" is what he says.

So now, on Friday afternoons when he looks into Trudy's

kitchen window, he sees she's not alone. She's sitting at the
kitchen table, head bent over a book, busy teaching Enrique how
to read. His son squirms and rests his head in his hand and sighs
a lot—Armando can tell he is anything but pleased to be there—
but Trudy pushes ahead and Armando knows that this is the summer that his son will learn something new. He will learn to read.

 *The Neighbor*

IT IS NOT A NOBLE SENTIMENT TO DETEST
one's neighbor—the rational part of Trudy's mind knows this.
Hatred leads to no good. Unfortunately, these days rationality
holds little sway on Trudy's emotions.

Until a year ago, Trudy would have described herself as the
most sensible of people. *Just look at my life,* she would have
argued a little too proudly—a practical job as head librarian, a
thirty-two-year marriage to her first and only love in which she
was faithful and happy, and she would have bet her last dime
that Brian, her husband, would have said the same. Together they
crafted the life that they, and in Trudy's exacting opinion every
sane person, would have wanted—a judicious, measured life.

And then all that changed in the beat of a heart. One September morning, when the Santa Ana winds were leaching all the
moisture out of the air, Brian went out for his regular three-times-
a-week jog and didn't come back.

In the early months of her widowhood, during those brutally
hot September and October days, Trudy was barely functional,

managing only to get herself to the library each day and back home late each afternoon. Then, once the front door was closed and no one could see her, she would collapse into her living room armchair and stare out the front window until it was dark enough to climb into bed.

Through those awful autumn and winter months, sitting in the dark, in the living room, evening after evening, playing back in her mind every kind and dear thing Brian ever did for her, Trudy got an eyeful of the new neighbor who had moved his family into the house next door only months before Brian died. And an earful. She learned right away that he is a yeller, a screamer of ugly words, and that she is in for an entirely unpleasant experience living next door to this man.

When Brian was alive she had easily ignored the commotion next door because what she and Brian had built together in their green-shuttered house didn't leave any room for animosity. She didn't have the energy or the inclination or the taste for it.

But now, more than a year after Brian's death, she's found that life is just chockful of things to rail against. Take the park situation. Even Trudy, who disdains the word "beautiful"— "Rendered meaningless by overuse," she complains—has been heard to admit that the park adjacent to her library is "beautiful." Set back from the street so it seems slightly hidden, ringed by hundred-year-old trees that keep the park cool and dappled in sunlight, Sierra Villa Park is an oasis of calm. And so, when the city council raised the question of selling the land to developers, there was a hue and cry in the neighborhood. Condos where neighborhood children now play soccer?! Concrete where the dignity of ancient oaks provides shelter for toddlers to play and for weary mothers to grab a few minutes of respite?! Trudy is incensed! She's seen the architect's drawing of the proposed complex. It makes her blood boil.

Pushing aside her natural reluctance to get involved, Trudy

decides to draw up a petition. If Brian were alive, he'd tell her to let the politicians handle it. Maybe, if she pressed him, he would have made a call to their city councilman, Scott Thurston, who lives around the corner, and registered his mild objection. But Brian is not here. He has left her to her own devices, and her own device is a neighborhood petition. That's how her disdain for her neighbor, acquired during those months after Brian's death, turns into full-fledged, lip-licking fury.

Brian had been fond of the ancient Russian woman who had lived next door to the Dugans since the day they moved in, her small ranch house's driveway abutting theirs. When Vivianna reached her late eighties and slowed down quite a bit, Brian added chauffeur duties to the list of tasks he did for her, a list that included grocery shopping, lugging the trash cans back and forth from the curb on garbage day, and watering her patchy lawn. Her grown children had been making noise for some time about how their mother couldn't take care of herself anymore, a sentiment Vivianna disdained. She told Brian that she planned to lock all the doors and windows if they ever came for her.

And they did. The night Vivianna started a fire in her kitchen, locked doors were no impediment to the firemen who burst through to put out the flames. Behind them came Russell, Vivianna's son, who used the opportunity to take her away. Too quickly, it seemed to Trudy, he rented an industrial Dumpster, parked it in her driveway, and filled it with a lifetime's worth of memories and debris, indiscriminately tossing out photo albums alongside mountains of saved plastic bags, gorgeous beaded gowns long out of style along with broken furniture. Both Brian and Trudy had to turn away as the workmen piled up Vivianna's life, higher and higher in the Dumpster. "Sadder and sadder," Brian said, and he was right.

The son and daughter had the house cleaned and painted and

then sold it to the Yeller who lives there now. His name is Kevin. Trudy sometimes hears the wife calling him, "Kevin Doyle!"

"He looks like a giant rodent," Trudy tells her son, Carter, during his dutiful Sunday afternoon phone call. "This guy who moved into Vivianna's house. Pointed nose, beady eyes, and an overbite."

"Now, Mother . . ." Carter says. Although he restrains himself, she can hear the *tsk-tsk* he's desperate to make. She knew he would admonish her. Since Brian's death, their weekly phone calls consist of her complaining and his admonitions. The interaction is satisfactory to neither but familiar by now and thankfully, Trudy thinks, short.

But when did they ever have satisfactory conversations? Maybe when Carter was three or four and Trudy began to introduce him to the children's books she had always loved. He loved them, too, and would ask her to read them to him over and over, and that bond lasted until he started first grade and began a life apart from her—friends, sports, the technology that boys seem to inhale into their pores. Every year after that, the distance between them grew wider and wider until finally, when Carter was able to make a choice of his own, he insisted on moving all the way across the country to attend Franklin Pierce University in Rindge, New Hampshire. *Ridiculous place to go to school,* Trudy has often thought but never said outright to anyone but Brian. "Freezing, in the middle of nowhere," Trudy would complain to Brian. "Yes, but so far away," Brian would say because he understood what Trudy didn't—that Carter was never comfortable with them.

She gets off the phone with him every Sunday afternoon dissatisfied and cranky. And misses Brian even more. Gentle, patient Brian would listen to her rants, shake his head at whatever unfairness she was railing against, and get on with whatever he had been doing, usually gardening, before Trudy had sought him out and unloaded her latest diatribe. The listening and the moving on—both brought Trudy comfort.

Now she has no avenue but action to displace her anger, and so she finds herself, petition in hand, ringing her neighbors' doorbells. The fact that she knows none of them, not a one, despite her thirty-plus years on the block doesn't seem unusual to Trudy. She's never been the sort of woman who stands and chitchats at the curb or makes small talk when out walking the dog. They've never owned a dog. In truth, Trudy didn't feel the need to know her neighbors while Brian was alive. He was the one who would say hello as he gardened out front. He knew them by sight. He waved as they drove by. That was sufficient.

So now Trudy has to introduce herself to her neighbors. At the first house, the woman who answers the door of the small Craftsman, way down at the end of the block, quickly signs the petition. She's young, maybe thirty, and has the distracted look of a mother of too many young children. Trudy can see at least three running around the living room, carrying on, as the woman, Susannah, as Trudy can see from her signature, tells Trudy how important the park is to them.

"Well, I can't imagine not having the park."

Trudy nods. She feels the same way. Good, a supporter.

"Where would the kids play?" and then she shrugs self-consciously and turns her shoulder to indicate the activity behind her. "And how much of *that* in the house could any one person take?"

As she hands the petition back to Trudy, she says, "You're so good to do this," and a fair-haired little girl of maybe four slips in beside her mother, holding on to one of her legs.

"You're the Story Lady," the child says, a thumb going into her mouth.

"You're right. Good remembering. And I remember you from when I read *If You Give a Mouse a Cookie. . . .*"

The child nods, pleased, and the mother takes the opportunity to say, "We're so sorry about your husband" and what has been a fine interaction, a moment that feels almost normal, suddenly stabs Trudy in the heart. She doesn't want to, she can't, share her grief with strangers, however well meaning. *That's the only trouble with living in Sierra Villa,* Trudy thinks as she says good-bye and moves on to the next house, *everyone knows your business.*

To her relief, the rest of the block goes smoothly and everyone on her side of the street signs. Trudy is fierce in her advocacy and people quickly agree that they must keep the park, that condos on that land would be horrible. To Trudy's great relief, no one else mentions Brian. And then, there's only one house left—the Yeller's, at the corner. Trudy could skip his house and head to the opposite side of the street. She's tempted to, but she won't allow herself this weakness. She knocks on what she will always consider Vivianna's door and a little boy of maybe six opens it for her. He's blond and solemn, the sort of child whose features seem to have migrated to the middle of his face, leaving lots of cheek and forehead.

"Is your mother home?" Trudy asks him. Far better to speak with the mother than the rodent father. Not that she's ever exchanged a word with the woman, but she seems more reasonable than the screamer. Trudy hears her speak nicely to the two boys.

But the child shakes his head no to her question; his mother isn't at home. And then she hears the voice from somewhere inside the house, that ugly voice which disrupts the daily quiet of her house. "Never open the door! WHO DO YOU THINK YOU ARE?!" And Trudy sees the little boy flinch and then his father is there. "Get away from here," he tells his son, who flees back into the house. And it is only Trudy and this man, this Kevin person, facing each other across the threshold. It's the first time she's ever been face-to-face with him and she's surprised at how tall he is. Tall and white skinned and just as menacing as his words.

Trudy chooses to ignore the interaction she just witnessed—
the ugliness of it, the evident fear the child has of his father's
anger—and presents the petition. "The city council is contemplat-
ing selling the library park to developers," she begins. He says
nothing. "If we get enough signatures on this petition, we may be
able to save the park."

She holds the clipboard with the petition out to him, but he
doesn't take it. Instead he says, "I don't sign anything. You never
know where your signature ends up."

Trudy can feel anger rising in her like a flush, but she attempts
civility. "I can guarantee you it will end up at the city council
meeting on the first Tuesday of next month."

"And then where? Can you guarantee me that it won't go any
further?"

Trudy is nonplussed. She has no idea what he means. But it's
immediately clear to her that he lives as if under siege. "Do you
want to save the park or not? You have kids, don't you want them
to have a place to play?"

"My kids play in the backyard."

"So you don't care what happens to the park?"

"You got it, lady."

"How civic-minded of you." Trudy can't help it. Her allotment
of civility has been used up and he's not stupid, although she
wishes he were, and he immediately gets the sarcasm.

"Get off my property. Do-gooders like you just gum up the system." And he closes the door in her face. It feels like a slap.

She crosses his driveway to hers—no fence in between, no line
of shrubbery. *Dammit!* They never needed any demarcation when
Vivianna was there, and now she regrets the open space with
every particle of her being.

In the kitchen she gets herself a glass of water, furious and
agitated, shaken really, but she refuses to call it that. That man

makes her so angry she could spit! She glares out her kitchen window directly into his, across their two driveways. When Vivianna was alive Trudy never minded the proximity. It was a way to keep tabs on the older woman, making sure she was moving about and everything seemed all right. Now, with the Yeller next door, it feels like the privacy of her kitchen is being violated every single day. Curtains, those frilly things Trudy has always hated, she needs to get curtains! And then she argues with herself, *No, I will not give him the satisfaction!*

The petition lies on the kitchen table and the first page isn't even completely filled. Trudy knows she has to go back out there. There's the whole other side of the street. Seven more doorbells to ring. Oh, how she'd love to just stop. Forget it. But then there's the park. And the principle of the thing. And the fact that she's not a quitter. And the fact that she has nothing else to do on this Sunday afternoon.

Sundays were always gardening days when Brian was alive. Not that Trudy gardened. No, that was Brian's domain, and over the years he made of their spacious backyard an Eden. That's the way Trudy thinks about it. She couldn't name more than a few of the shrubs and vines that Brian planted, but that never stopped her from appreciating the way they enclose the backyard in a circle of green, splashed with the vivid colors of their flowers, coral, deep purple, pristine white, and in the summer, the ruby red of the bougainvillea. And years ago, when Brian decided to grow tomatoes, then squash and peppers and eggplant in the summer and lettuce and snap peas and broccoli and cabbage in the winter—they had their own urban farm.

The garden misses Brian, even she can tell. Armando, their gardener, does his best to keep things growing, but he comes just once a week and his job is really only to cut the lawn and tidy up. The extra he does—cutting back leggy shrubbery, watering when she has forgotten to, fertilizing the plants just when they need it—

Trudy is grateful for but she truly feels she can't ask more of him. And so the garden mourns Brian's absence in its own way.

Enough, Trudy tells herself. Maybe she says it out loud. She's doesn't know these days when she speaks her thoughts and when she doesn't. There's nobody there to hear her, so she's not sure.

She takes the petition off the table and heads out the front door. The house on the corner, the opposite side of the street, has a white picket fence. The gate is painted yellow and has a heart-shaped cutout atop it. *Too precious,* Trudy immediately thinks, *where are we, Mayberry RFD?* There's a tiny bench on the small front porch with a matching heart-shaped pillow on it. Trudy almost turns around. *These people aren't going to sign my petition,* but they do. A white-haired couple in their seventies is as nice as can be. Neither needs to hear Trudy explain the whole problem. The man simply says to her, "You have honest eyes. Of course I'll sign." And then, as Trudy starts to turn away, step down off the little porch, he throws her the curve. "I liked your husband very much."

Trudy is stopped. "So did I," she says, "and thirty-two years wasn't enough."

"You poor dear" is what the woman says, and Trudy shoots back before she can stop herself, "I'm just fine!"

And then, once the couple has closed their door Trudy has to sit down on the curb, her legs not steady enough to take her to the next house. Those white-haired people, that was supposed to be her future, Brian's and hers. Growing old together, tottering around in their little house until they were well into their nineties. Trudy would never have admitted it to anyone, but that was her plan for the future. Now all she sees is an empty space where loss is a daily companion. Despite herself, she sighs, then pushes herself to stand and finish the task. She takes a measure of this side of the street. There are six more houses to go.

At the house next to the older couple, a wood-shingled bun-

galow directly opposite her own, no one is home. She tries the
one next to that, a beige, nondescript ranch. And again, no one
answers the bell, but there's a truck in the driveway and Trudy
hears muffled music from somewhere inside the house. She tries
to remember who lives there but can't.

She rings the bell again and then knocks smartly on the door.
No one appears, but she sees the closed living room drapes move
on the large window, as if someone was peeking out. Trudy is sure
now that someone is home and it makes her inordinately furious.
She's not some religious proselytizer who will talk endlessly about
soul saving. Is that what she looks like?! She isn't even a Girl
Scout with disgusting cookies to sell. She's a respectable woman,
here about a park. Someone should have the decency to answer
the door!

She tramps off the porch, elbows the shrubbery aside in order
to sidle close to the house, and makes it to the front window. She
knocks quickly and loudly and is startled to see a similarly startled
male Asian face pop up not three inches from her own. The faces
stare at each other through the plate glass until the man disappears and the curtains close and Trudy is further incensed. He is
home. He needs to sign the petition.

She marches to the front door and knocks again. In fact, she
continues knocking until he finally opens the door and they
assess each other. Trudy sees a short man, probably in his late
sixties, with steel gray hair neatly combed and parted, wearing
a plaid, short-sleeved shirt and well-worn jeans that sag off his
skinny frame. His face is impassive as he surveys the chubby little
woman with the determined stance who is holding a clipboard.
Anger radiates out of her like heat waves. Could she be so angry
simply because he didn't want to open the door? he wonders. But
he says nothing. She rang the bell. Let her speak.

And Trudy plunges in. "I have a petition here stating the neighborhood's opposition to turning Sierra Villa Park into condo units. Our position is stronger the more signatures we have." She holds the clipboard out to him. He turns his eyes from her face, which he finds mesmerizing in its intensity, to the petition but makes no move to pick up the pen attached by a string to the clipboard. He does nothing. Doesn't read it. Doesn't close the door. Simply looks at the piece of paper as if he were waiting for it to do something interesting. He has learned from years of working for irrational people that the best course of action when facing anger is not to engage.

Trudy is now beyond exasperated. "Do you speak English?" she demands of him. "Is that the problem here?"

"You, I think, are the problem."

"How rude."

"Yes, rude," he says, but he doesn't close the door.

"I live on this street," Trudy finds herself saying. She has no idea why.

He nods.

"And I work at the library." Why is she telling him this? His silence is unnerving, maybe that's it. "That's why the park matters to me."

The man picks up the pen and signs his name, Fred Murakami.

"Thank you." Trudy has to say it.

"You are welcome." But he doesn't close the door, and Trudy can't quite figure out how to get off his porch gracefully.

"That's it," she tells him.

"Yes."

And finally she turns and makes her way down his front path, turning right at the sidewalk and moving to the next house. She can feel his eyes on her back the whole way.

She gets signatures from three of the last four houses and feels, as she walks home, as if she's climbed Mount Everest. Later that evening, as she eats a bowl of cereal for dinner, she reviews her afternoon's work and sees that he has signed, "Fred Murakami, Handyman," even though the petition didn't ask for the signer's occupation.

TRUDY BRINGS THE PETITION into the library the next morning and Clemmie looks askance at it.

"I know what you're going to say and I'm going to ignore it," Trudy says before Clementine can get her mouth in gear.

"Well then"—and here Clemmie chooses her words carefully—"I was only thinking what would happen if a city official came into the library?"

"You mean like Scott Thurston?"

"Yes, maybe Scott."

"He'd tell us to put the petition away. He'd say this library is a city service and not a place for a personal agenda."

"Exactly!" Clemmie feels vindicated.

"And I'd ignore him as soon as he walked out the door."

They are at an impasse and that is where things are going to stay, Clemmie knows by now. Four years working under Trudy is more than enough time to understand that Trudy doesn't budge. Truthfully, four months was enough to pick up that predominant character trait—inflexibility.

The fact that she's young enough to be Trudy's daughter undermines Clementine's position even more. And the fact that she looks like Ramona in the *Ramona and Beezus* books. And the fact that there's an unquenchable optimism about her. All that makes equal footing with Trudy an impossibility.

But they have worked out a way to be together, these two women. Clementine has carved out areas of responsibility that border Trudy's but don't overlap. She greets the public. She remembers the children's names. She loves to spend however long it takes helping people find exactly the right book. She reads everything new that comes into the library. And Clementine, thankfully, takes care of the two computers they have in the adult section.

Trudy does all the administrative work, usually spending her day in the glass-enclosed office that faces the front door. From her desk Trudy can observe what goes on in the library but not necessarily engage. Only on Thursdays when she transforms herself into the Story Lady, does she mingle with the patrons, and those are mainly children, Trudy's humans of choice.

But Trudy likes Clemmie, even if she isn't demonstrative in that regard, and Clemmie has figured that out. When she first started working at the library, fresh out of graduate school, Trudy intimidated her—so curt, nothing soft or yielding about her. But Clementine has learned that's not entirely true. All the soft places were saved for Brian, and now that he's gone, Clementine wonders these days whether those same tender spots have hardened off and begun to die.

For her part, Trudy considers Clementine pretty near perfect. Oh, of course, she's too emotional. And she drives Trudy crazy with her solicitousness, but Trudy sees her goodness and her trustworthiness and her work ethic and her genuine love of books. The whole package, you have to take people as the whole package, Trudy knows by now in her life, and with Clemmie that's easy to do.

Now Clemmie watches as Trudy takes the clipboard with the petition on it and places it at the far end of the front counter, nestling it among the pamphlets for the Sierra Villa Farmers Market on Friday afternoons and the Pancake Breakfast at the local fire station on the first Sunday of every month.

"Really?" Clementine asks.

"Really," Trudy answers.

And people sign the petition as they leave with their checked-out books, Trudy is gratified to see. Every time another person signs on the dotted line, Trudy shoots Clemmie a look of triumph, and Clementine rolls her eyes.

TRUDY CONSIDERS THE DAY A SUCCESS as she walks the four blocks home and turns onto her street, Lima Street. The signatures on her petition now take up five whole pages, and she's not done yet. She wants to walk into that city council meeting with a thick wad of petition pages, all signed by irate citizens of Sierra Villa. She flips the sheets, considering the fruits of her indignation as she turns up her brick front path. The fact that her neighbor is zooming up his driveway at the same time in his black BMW convertible with his two sons in their Catholic school uniforms in the backseat barely registers.

But then the yelling starts, even before Trudy can get her key into the front door lock, and she stops and listens. It's that scene-of-a-traffic-accident feeling—dismay and fascination in equal measure.

"Get in the house!" Kevin Doyle is yelling even as the boys walk up the driveway, dragging their overlarge backpacks, and step onto the front porch. For some reason, he never lets them enter the house by the back door, so much of their life is played out on the long driveway. The older boy, maybe seven, is more talkative. The younger one, the one who opened the door for Trudy yesterday, is quieter. Both are blond with the pasty white skin of their father and the small, pinched features of their mother.

The boys enter the house to the accompaniment of their father yelling, "Close the door, close the damn door!" Trudy is sure that something unnatural happens in that house. Why else would he always be admonishing his sons to "get in the house," to "close the door"? He doesn't allow them to play on the front lawn or with the neighborhood children. She stands on her front porch, helpless, feeling that she should be doing something—intervening, protecting the boys—although she has no idea how she would accomplish either, when the Yeller starts his relentless cleaning. He has a power washer, a leaf blower, a car polisher, a chain saw, and various other mechanical devices Trudy can't name. She knows them all by sound though. They all whine or whoosh or shriek.

Today it's the leaf blower. He has a complex about keeping his driveway free of anything associated with nature. The sound! Oh, how Trudy hates that sound! So much uproar for so little result. Why doesn't he take a broom like everyone else and sweep his driveway? With the blower, dirt and twigs and leaves launch up into the air in surprise and then settle back down on *her* driveway, which bothers him not at all and makes her want to scream back at him.

Instead, she quickly opens her front door and slams it shut with as much force as she can muster, a gesture she knows is lost on him. The whoop of the door closing is no match for the roar of the leaf blower.

From her kitchen window Trudy watches him. He's got that disgusting cigar clamped in his protruding teeth and that tiny phone earpiece hooked to his right lobe (she hopes he gets a brain tumor from excessive cell phone use), and he's methodically sweeping the blower across his driveway, right to left, where her driveway resides and where the debris flies over to and settles. Right to left, right to left—dirt and more dirt!

If only she and Brian had had the foresight to build a fence between their two properties as soon as this Kevin Doyle person moved in. A tall, wooden fence so she wouldn't have to see his rodent face. A very high wooden fence so that all the blowing in the world wouldn't yield piles of debris on her driveway.

And then it occurs to her that she can build such a fence now. What's stopping her? Only the habit of discussing every decision with Brian. Only the backbone she received from Brian's calm wisdom. "Well, Brian's not here," she reminds herself. And this time she knows she has spoken aloud in her empty house. Not a good sign for anyone's mental health.

She gets on her computer and finds the Angie's List site. Brian bought himself a lifetime membership when they first posted the site because he was hopeless about home repair and relied on Angie's recommendations when they needed a washing-machine part replaced or a shower floor regrouted. She types in "fence" and up pops a screen full of names; most are handymen or carpenters. She scrolls down and is overwhelmed. There are eight pages of names. This is way more than she bargained for. How does she narrow her search? Does she have to read all the reviews about all these guys? And then her eye catches a familiar name, Fred Murakami, and she sits back in her chair and contemplates it.

On the one hand, she knows who he is. On the other, he's a most unpleasant human being. But then again, he probably won't steal from her or disappear with the fence half done. She can easily track him down across the street.

She reads his reviews. They're all good. He's meticulous, an Old World craftsman. He takes his time, but his finished product is always worth it. She realizes she has to hire him.

There's nothing to do but cross the street and knock on his door again. She waits until Kevin Doyle has finished with the leaf blower and has entered his house with a yell at his trademark high volume, "Get away from the window!"(Why, Trudy wants to know, why? What's wrong with looking out the window?) And then the street returns to its customary quiet. *That's one of the reasons people move up here,* Trudy thinks as she crosses Lima Street, *the quiet, which is now permanently compromised. The luck of the draw,* she laments to herself. Trudy feels like Lady Luck has done an about-face. Until that awful September day last year, she would have considered herself among the luckiest. Now she's afraid it's going to be nothing but a slide through bad luck until the grave.

She heads up the cement path to the beige ranch house, and Fred Murakami watches her come, all the while debating whether to open the door. He doesn't like aggressive women. His wife was no trouble at all, and though she's been dead for close to thirteen years, he still misses her. No, he won't open the door.

Trudy knocks with vigor and without stop. Her experience yesterday tells her that he doesn't like to open his door and therefore, today, she is forewarned and determined. Finally, she wins the contest of wills. He opens the door a few inches, a deep scowl on his face.

"You make a lot of noise," he says.

"Yes, well, it's nothing compared to what he does," and she indicates her neighbor's house with a turn of her chin. "Haven't you noticed the leaf blower and the power washer and the car buffer and the screaming, but of course you can't fix the screaming."

"I don't fix screaming," he says.

"But you could build me a fence along the driveway, couldn't you?"

"Maybe." He wants to say, *No, I can't,* but the recession has hurt his business and he can't be as cavalier about turning away work as he has been in the past.

"How much would that cost?"

"Depends."

Trudy is getting exasperated again. Talking to this man is like wading through a vat of molasses. "On what?"

"The kind of materials, how high."

"High enough so I never have to see the giant rodent." And then Trudy realizes what she's said. She's spoken out loud the name she acknowledges only in the sanctity of her own mind. More fodder for her concern about her sanity.

"Made of what?"

"Wood."

"And how long."

"The whole driveway."

He looks across the street at her driveway. He can't see the far end from where he stands in his own doorway. "How many feet?"

"I don't know," and now exasperation is getting the best of her. "Bring a tape measure and come and see."

He doesn't want to start this, so he doesn't move. She, however, is not going away, "Now, I mean now! Why can't you measure it now?"

He shrugs. He can't think of a reason except for the fact that he doesn't want to engage with this woman.

"All right, come on, I'll give you a tape measure." And she turns and strides across the street, and he finds himself following her rapidly moving back. She walks with as much conviction as she talks.

By the time he gets to her driveway, she's holding out a carpenter's metal tape measure, the square box with the pliable steel coiled up inside, and she places it in his hand. As he gets down and measures the length of her driveway, she stands over him and continues talking, sotto voce. "He screams at his children. Do you hear him?"

"Sometimes."

"Awful. So I want a fence."

"All right."

"How much?" she asks as he finishes measuring and stands up.

He studies the length of the driveway and considers. "Twelve hundred dollars."

Trudy is taken aback. "That's a lot of money."

"Not for this fence. I'm giving you a discount. Nobody will build you a fence for less."

And she believes him. She doesn't know why she does, but she does. "Okay." And then, "You need to start tomorrow."

And again he finds himself saying, "All right."

TRUDY WAKES UP THE NEXT MORNING with a sense of purpose. Today the fence building starts! But when she looks out her kitchen window, out over her driveway, there's nothing to see. There's her empty driveway, looking no different from yesterday, and there's her neighbor yelling at his boys to "get in the car! Why are you ALWAYS late, Aidan?! Every single morning you can't get your butt in gear!"

Trudy sees the two boys scramble into the backseat of the convertible, the younger one, Trudy realizes he's Aidan, tripping over his backpack. Kevin barely waits until they're seated and then zooms out of the driveway, leaving a waft of cigar smoke lingering in the crisp November air. The fence won't do anything about the smell, she knows. What kind of man smokes continually from seven forty-five in the morning, which it currently is, until well after midnight? Every night the west side of her house is assaulted by the putrid odor of cigar. He sits on his front porch whatever the weather, bundled up when it's chilly, stripped to a pair of shorts when it's warm, and smokes. And talks on the phone attached to his ear. In fact, he seems to work very little and sit there far too much, always on the phone. *Who would talk to this man,* Trudy wonders, *unless they had to?*

One night, as she's closing up the house, shutting windows

and thinking about going to bed, she hears him say, "Here's how we'll do it. It's too easy to just fire him. We'll promote him. Well, he'll think it's a promotion." And he chuckles. "He'll come work directly under me and then I won't give him anything to do, not one job, and I won't talk to him." Trudy can hear the glee escalate in his voice, which positively skips along as he says, "We'll freeze him out! He doesn't exist! . . . Then he'll quit. No liability. No paper trail. Hell, he even got a promotion!"

That night, as she heard him plot to humiliate someone, Trudy slammed all her windows shut, but she could tell from his conversation, which didn't miss a beat, that her protest didn't register.

This morning she's waiting impatiently for Fred Murakami to show up. Yesterday, she gave him half his agreed-upon fee so he could go to Home Depot and buy wood. She walks into the living room and cranes her body out to the left to see if his truck is in his driveway. It isn't. Hopefully, that's where he is and when she gets home there will be a stack of freshly cut, sweet-smelling cedar planks piled on the driveway.

That is exactly what she sees when she turns onto Lima Street at five minutes after five, a very imposing pile of raw wood stacked neatly with no Fred Murakami in sight. Trudy searches the backyard, calls his name—nothing—so she marches smartly across the street and drills her knuckles on his door.

Fred watches her come from the barrier of his living room drapes and shakes his head. Sighing, he opens his door.

"I see you got the lumber."

"Yes."

"But nothing's been done with it."

"That's not true. I've set the end posts and stretched the plumb line."

Trudy has no idea what he just said.

"I work seven to four, that's it. When four o'clock comes, I am finished for the day."

"I don't get home until after five."

He shrugs. That's not his problem.

"When will we discuss?" Trudy asks him.

"We've already discussed. A wood fence. Along the driveway. Six feet tall. What is there left to discuss?"

"How 'bout this—I want it eight feet tall so I never have to see even the top of his head. He's a tall man."

"You can't have it."

And he stares at her, not as a challenge but because for him the topic is finished.

"Why not?"

"Building code restrictions. No fence on a property line in Sierra Villa can be higher than six feet."

"Are you sure?"

And now he is getting angry. She's implying he doesn't know his job.

"I have been a handyman for forty-four years. If you don't think I know what I'm doing, hire someone else." And he starts to close his door. This woman is too much trouble, just as he thought.

"I don't want to hire someone else," she says to him, "I want an eight-foot fence."

"Too bad," he says.

"Yes," she says, "it's too bad." Then, "I'll see you at seven tomorrow morning."

He closes the door. She walks quickly across the street. He watches from behind his living room drapes. When she closes her own door, he drops the drape back in place and all is quiet.

. . .

THE FENCE PROGRESSES. At a pace that drives Trudy crazy. The Angie's List reviews were right. He works slowly. When she mentions this to him, as if he didn't know, he simply looks at her and utters the word "meticulous." Is he reading his own reviews?

Trudy knows there's nothing she can do about the pace, but knowing and accepting are two different things. She's sick and tired of accepting things she doesn't like. The biggest, of course, is Brian's death. But then the list includes her horrendous neighbor with his screaming and his power tools and his cigars. And her disapproving son with his dutiful weekly phone calls in which neither of them utters a word worth speaking and neither is satisfied when they hang up. And now she has a handyman who works in slow motion to add to the list!

She tells Clemmie all of this one Wednesday afternoon when things are slow at the library. She enumerates the list for her, ending with her handyman woes.

"Oh, I know Fred," she says.

"You do?" For some reason Trudy is surprised, almost as if she doesn't quite believe Clemmie has a life outside the library, because that's the only place she sees her. *A failure of imagination,* Trudy tells herself.

"My mother always used him, and when David and I wanted to add a deck to the back of our house, I hired Fred."

"How long did it take?"

"Oh, I don't know. . . ." Clemmie thinks about it, then grins. "Forever. He works very slowly."

Trudy throws up her hands—just her luck to have hired the slowest man alive.

"He is definitely an exercise in acceptance," Clementine adds, watching Trudy's face to see how her comment lands. She doubts Trudy has reached the acceptance plateau for any of the items on her list—Brian's death, first and foremost, her son's distance next in line. And immediately Trudy turns away from the younger woman, gathers up a pile of returned books to reshelve, conversation finished. Oh, how thin-skinned she is! Trudy's body language says it all. She felt Clemmie's words as an implicit reprimand. Clementine could kick herself. In an effort to be helpful, Clementine has gone too far. But no, Trudy comes back with empty arms and the need to ask, "But he does good work, right? Everyone on Angie's List said that."

"You will have the world's most beautiful fence," Clemmie assures her. Trudy heaves a sigh of relief and gives her colleague a rare smile.

WHAT TRUDY SEES WHEN SHE GETS HOME that afternoon is a work in progress. All the supporting posts, each exactly six feet from the last, have been cemented into place. Around each post Fred has built a small, sloping mound of concrete to eliminate water pooling at the base of the posts.

"Water rots wood," he tells her the next morning when she asks. "We don't want that." The heads of the posts have been rounded off for the same reason. This way the posts will last longer. She nods; that makes sense to her. She is sure Brian would have approved of this man and his thoughtful work.

"Did you know my husband?" Trudy finds the words jumping out of her mouth before she has time to reconsider.

Fred, in the middle of mixing more cement in a large plastic bucket, looks up at her. The topic of dead relatives is one he doesn't want to even consider. "No," he says, although he remembers that if he happened to be outside his house early in the morning, Brian would wave as he jogged down the street. Fred never waved back. Waving led to conversation the next time around, something to be assiduously avoided. He doesn't tell Trudy now that Brian continued to wave despite his lack of response. He just shakes his head no.

"He died," she continues on despite herself. "One year and two months ago."

"I know," Fred says. It was hard not to know. The man collapsing just blocks from this street. The fire trucks racing in. Their neighbor Peggy, who found him, talking about it for weeks afterward. "My wife is dead almost thirteen years now."

Trudy tries hard to remember his wife and vaguely calls up an image or two of a small Japanese woman who rarely left the house without her husband.

"You know what they say, about it getting easier over time? That's not true," Fred says as if reading Trudy's thoughts.

"How comforting."

He shrugs. Is it his job to be comforting?

For her part, Trudy wonders why she is having this conversation with a man she hired to build a fence. She already feels much worse for it. *Let him build the fence and keep quiet,* Trudy tells herself.

From that morning, she and Fred settle into a routine, something that has always soothed Trudy—the repetition of events. He arrives promptly at seven o'clock, as he told her he would. They "discuss" the fence if she has any questions, and only the fence. Otherwise, she says hello to him on her way out and leaves him to it. Increasingly, she has fewer and fewer questions. At a few minutes after five when she gets home, he is nowhere to be found, already finished for the day as he said he would be, driveway swept up and tools put away. He is as regular in his habits as she. They dance to the same beat and that helps Trudy relax.

Even the Yeller doesn't seem to bother him. Trudy asks him that one morning after she is sure her neighbor has left with the two boys, driving them to the Catholic school several miles west along the 210 Freeway.

Quietly, because the wife may still be home, Trudy asks, "Does it get noisy here in the afternoon?"

Fred has no idea what she means. "No," he says, "just the power saw sometimes when I need to cut the wood."

She shakes her head, glances at the Doyles' house again to make sure the wife isn't outside, getting into her car. "I mean *him.*"

Fred shrugs. "When he brings his sons home, he yells at them to get in the house. Every day. Is that what you mean?"

"Exactly!" Then, "Don't you wonder what goes on inside that house?"

Fred stares at her as if she's insane. In truth, Trudy occasionally worries that on this topic she's veering in that direction.

"It's not my business," Fred says and turns on the saw, conversation finished as far as he's concerned.

But for Trudy the obsession isn't. Now that her mind is no longer focused on the fence building—Fred is in place, the boards are going up—it has more room to ponder the drama next door.

One Saturday afternoon when Fred is not there—he never works on the weekends—Trudy is rinsing out her morning coffee cup when she hears the wife's heels on the driveway. She has a distinct way of clopping along, as if her shoes never quite fit. It's the *rat-tat-tat* of weary feet in low-heeled shoes worn by a heavy woman. She's walking down the driveway to her car, which is parked on the street, her boys with her. She's got a gentle hand on the head of the younger one, Aidan, as he trails along beside her. The older one, Carl, runs ahead.

The wife is just this side of being very fat. She never wears pants or jeans, too fat for that. She wears one long, printed skirt or another every day. And, like her husband, she's always on the phone. But she seems nice. In the year they have lived next door, Trudy has overheard dozens of conversations, and the woman— her name is Brenda—never yells. In fact, she always seems unduly cheerful, telling people all the time that she's "super!" but Trudy supposes that's in counterbalance to her husband's nastiness. And most importantly, she is sweet with her children. She calls them "honey" a lot and praises them often. What Trudy does not understand is how she remains married to the rodent. Doesn't she see how much damage he's doing to the boys?

The children are now pushing each other and shoving as boys do while Brenda clomps along to her car, cell phone to her ear. Trudy hears her saying, "They came back at $769,000.... I know ... I know ... that's not much movement. We could try a counter at $740,000.... Okay, think about it and call me back. Remember, they have an open house tomorrow, so we should make a decision before that.... Right, just call me...."

They have reached the street, and although Brenda has opened the back door of her car for the boys to climb in, they have escalated their roughhousing and are now chasing each other around the car and giggling. She is having a hard time ending her conversation and riding herd on the boys at the same time.

She's gesturing to the kids—*Get in the car*—and saying to her client, "Good ... This is the way it goes.... No, no, it isn't personal.... Take the personal out of it—"

And then Trudy hears the Yeller slam the front door and come onto the porch and yell at his wife, "Brenda! What in holy hell are you doing?!"

All three of them freeze—the wife and the two boys, who are by now in the middle of the street. Hurriedly, Brenda gets off the phone and starts to usher the boys into the car, but that is not enough for Kevin Doyle. He stomps down the driveway and in full view of Trudy, who has moved to the living room window to get a better view, begins to berate his wife.

"What are you doing? What the hell are you doing?! You weren't even looking, were you?! Where were the boys? In the middle of the fucking street! That's where they were!"

"Kevin," she says quietly as she stands by the driver's door, but that does nothing to derail the assault.

"You want them dead, is that it?! You want them run over by a car? Were you even watching?!"

The wife stands there without speaking, her eyes on his ugly face, waiting this out.

"I thought you went to college. I thought you had some brains in your skull." And then he roars, "Those boys are going to be killed and it's going to be on your head!"

He turns and walks back into the house and slams the door, damage done, humiliation complete. There's a stunned silence on the street, like an intake of breath; even the birds have been frozen into muteness.

Brenda closes the back door of her car, makes sure the boys buckle up, gets into the driver's seat, and drives away.

Trudy lowers herself into her armchair and contemplates what she just saw. She's totally unfamiliar with that kind of behavior. Oh, she knows people scream at their wives and children, but she's never experienced that kind of vitriol firsthand. Her parents weren't screamers. Brian almost never raised his voice. The cruelty of Kevin Doyle's words is what undoes her and makes her fear for the boys. Why is he always telling them to "get in the house"? What happens in that house? If he's capable of that kind of anger against his wife in a public place, in full view of the neighborhood, what does he do to those boys once the doors are shut and the curtains pulled? What can she do about it?

She has no answer, but as often happens, Life provides an opening. One day soon after the ugly incident in the street, Trudy decides to come home for lunch, something she hasn't done for the past year. When Brian was alive, they would make dates and meet at the house for lunch and whatever developed after that. Since his death, it's been too hard to be in their empty house at lunchtime, some part of her still waiting to hear Brian's car pull up into the driveway and his eager voice call out as he stepped into the kitchen, "Here I am!" as if he were delivering his person as a present, gift-wrapped expressly for her.

But this day she decides to find some courage and go home. There was a classroom of second graders at the library all morning, and Trudy could use a few minutes of peace and quiet.

As she walks up her brick path, she sees Fred at work on the fence, now close to halfway done, and a brown wrapped package on her front porch. She can't think of a single person who would be sending her something, and when she picks it up she sees that it is, in fact, addressed to the Doyles but deposited on her porch.

She goes to Fred, package in hand. "Did you see who brought this?"

"UPS."

"But it belongs next door."

"No one's home next door. The guy asked me if he could leave it here. I said yes."

"Why did you do that?" she asks him sharply. "Now I have to talk to them."

"No, you don't. Put it on their porch. The UPS guy doesn't care."

"All right."

"I'm going home for lunch," he tells her as he stands up, dusts off his threadbare jeans, worn to white at the knees. "I'll be back in thirty minutes."

Trudy watches him cross the street, open his front door, and enter the house. She stares at the package in her hands. It's innocuous looking, about the size of a cake box, stamped and sent from the post office. *Put it on the front porch and be done with it,* she tells herself. And she makes her way up the Doyles' driveway and onto their porch, where she stands, package in hand, pondering.

Behind the barrier of his living room drapes, Fred scrutinizes her, the need to eat lunch forgotten in his need to watch Trudy. What is this crazy lady going to do now? He watches her ring the doorbell—once, twice, and wait. Didn't he explicitly tell her no one was home? Why doesn't she just put the package down and leave? Ah, now he sees why.

Trudy puts her hand on the Doyles' doorknob. She can't believe she's doing this—is she committing breaking and entering?—but she can't seem to stop herself. The door opens. She bets one of the boys forgot to "lock the damn door!" as the Yeller is always shouting.

She looks quickly behind her, scanning the street. Is she being observed? If anyone asks her, she'll just say she's being neighborly, putting the package inside the front door to keep it safe. That's good. That will work. And then she slips inside the house.

Fred, from the safety of his living room, shakes his head. What a stupid thing for her to do. She could get into a lot of trouble.

Trudy stands with her back against the front door, package in hand, and surveys the living room. Her heart is pounding away in her chest, bombarding her with what she assumes is terror but could also be excitement.

What she sees is a long, narrow room that fits horizontally across the front of the house. There's a fireplace against the street-facing wall and sliding glass doors on the opposite wall out to a U-shaped patio. The furniture is all oversize, as if giants lived there—a huge leather couch that would swallow Trudy up if she deigned to sit in it, her feet not even hitting the floor, and two high-backed armchairs appropriate for a nineteenth-century gentlemen's club. The furniture is grouped to face the fireplace. The rest of the room is empty except for small oil paintings of common scenes—apple picking, sailboats on a choppy sea, a farmhouse—positioned high up on the wall. *Only the giant rodent can see them,* Trudy thinks as her eyes scan the room, a cold and sterile space, no warmth or bright colors or pillows on the sofa, or even rugs on the floor, but nothing out of the ordinary. She's not going to learn anything by standing in this room.

Trudy knows she should back out, put the package down on the front doorstep, and walk quickly back to her house, but she can't. She needs to see the boys' bedrooms. Seeing where they sleep will give her vital information, she's sure of it.

It looks like the bedrooms are off to the left, in their own separate wing. She crosses the living room and makes a right turn into a hallway. Now she's really done it. There is simply no explanation for being so far into the house. If one of them comes home and finds her, she's done for. But that doesn't stop her. She feels her eyesight sharpen. She knows that's impossible, but that's what it feels like. And her hearing gets more acute. Everything feels like it's happening on another planet, one where the elements in the atmosphere combine differently and all objects are more sharp edged and all sounds explode into her ears. There's something thrilling about it.

She opens the first door she finds, and it is definitely one of the boys' rooms. There are bunk beds on the far wall, complete with Spider-Man sheets, and a desk against the window with drawing supplies—Magic Markers and stickers and sheets of faintly brown drawing paper—and the requisite electronic equipment—a laptop, an iPad. There's a wall of cubbyholes stuffed with essential boy paraphernalia (Trudy remembers them all from Carter's childhood): a baseball mitt, a bike helmet, a terrarium that now holds pieces of Legos, a deflated basketball, a board game called Tsuro with an elaborate dragon on the lid, and a whole colony of plastic dinosaurs arranged with infinite care into groupings of like kinds. Trudy remembers Carter's dinosaur phase, which lasted well over a year. Apparently nothing much has changed in that regard. Dinosaurs march in battalions across the wall of cubbies. What she has in front of her is a room any seven-year-old could live in happily. It tells her nothing.

She backs out and tries the room next door. This must be the younger boy's room, Aidan's, because there are more remnants from toddlerhood here—a couple of dirty stuffed animals sitting lopsided on top of a bookcase, a brightly colored plastic dump truck filled with tennis balls, a mural of a rainbow painted on the wall above the bed with a leprechaun at the end who looks a lot like Aidan.

Trudy is disappointed and relieved at the same time, relieved that it all looks so normal, disappointed that she hasn't found any evidence to bolster her belief that something heinous happens in this house. If she's going to do something, if she's going to try to help these boys, she needs evidence. And she realizes as she steps back out of Aidan's room and closes the door that this is exactly why she entered the house in the first place.

There's one more door in the hallway and it's closed. She assumes it's the rodent's bedroom and she's tempted to take a look. She contemplates the door, moves toward it, her hand extended, when she hears, "What are you doing?" and she nearly jumps out of her skin.

Fred stands in the hallway, frowning.

"You scared the bejeezus out of me!" Now Trudy can be furious instead of terrified. It's only Fred.

"You deserve it. What are you doing in here?"

"Something awful happens in this house and I need evidence." This is said as righteously as Trudy can manage.

Fred doesn't even answer her. He takes her by the upper arm—she looks down in astonishment at his hand on her biceps—and leads her out, through the living room, the front door, and onto the porch. Next he takes the package from her

hands and puts it down on the Doyles' doorstep. Then he marches
her smartly and quickly down the driveway, his grip on her arm
tight and insistent.

"There," he says as he deposits her on her own front porch. In
his mind the matter is finished. He turns to the sawhorse he set
up that morning and begins to prepare another slat for the fence.

Trudy is left feeling as if she's been chastised and rescued at
the same time, but, true to form, she allows her anger to flood any
gratitude she might feel.

"If well-meaning people turn their eyes away when they know
something evil is happening, well then . . . then"—she sputters
for a moment and then finds her footing—"then we have the
Holocaust!"

Fred, head down, continues to work. He says nothing, hoping
Trudy will go into her house and leave him alone. No such luck.

"Children need to be saved. Sometimes even from their own
parents."

"The man yells at his kids. It's too bad. But there's nothing you
can do."

And that attitude spins Trudy into overdrive. So cavalier! So
unfeeling! So cowardly!

"Don't you tell me to just sit tight and put up with it!" She's
fairly yelling.

Fred shrugs. He'll be damned if he's going to say another word.
He takes the cedar plank off the sawhorse and begins to nail it to
the supporting crossbars. He hammers longer and harder than
he needs to. Trudy stands at his back, fuming, when, above the
hammering, they both hear the blasting music of a car radio and
turn to see Kevin Doyle speeding up his driveway, the top of his
convertible down as always, the cell phone plugged into his ear, of
course, the cigar clamped in his yellow teeth and its putrid aroma
wafting after him.

Fred turns and eyes Trudy. There is no need for him to say—
Look what I just saved you from. And she doesn't have the good
grace to thank him. She simply turns on her heel and stomps into
her house, angry still.

She paces around the house, stirred up, agitated. Through the
living room, down the hall she goes, then into the small dining
room where she no longer eats, and out the kitchen door. Oh, why
isn't Brian here when she needs him? She'd rail and rant and he'd
listen and she'd figure out this whole mess! She looks around the
heavenly backyard, this place where she feels Brian most fully. It
shelters her and surrounds her and protects her from the rest of
the whole ugly world.

Help me, she says, not sure whether she's spoken out loud and
now not caring. She's calling up something—Brian's spirit or his
love for her or something. *Help me.* And Fred, in the driveway,
measuring another plank, hears her because Trudy has pleaded
aloud.

Here's the issue, Trudy explains to Brian, making sure now that
it's only thoughts she's sending forth and not words, *how can what
I saw inside that house be at such odds with what happens every
day outside of it? Brian, everything inside seemed so ordinary. It
could have been Carter's room when he was a child.*

She paces on the patio, trying to sort this all out on her own.
If you saw those boys' rooms, you'd think nothing was wrong. And
then a thought occurs to her that makes her stop moving and sink
into a patio chair. *Is this a normal family? Could the yelling and
demeaning simply be ordinary life for some people?*

Oh!—and here Trudy sucks in her breath realizing suddenly—
*isn't that worse? That those boys think ordinary life always contains
such ugliness.* Trudy's heart is suddenly breaking. "Oh, Brian," she
voices into the quiet backyard air. "Oh no."

Fred, carrying two more slats of cedar over to the sawhorse, hears the lament. He puts the wood down and stands motionless for a minute, paying quiet attention to the two factions wrestling within him.

Trudy, in the backyard, leaning forward in her chair, forearms on her thighs, her head in her hands, hears, "I talk to my dead wife, too, but she never answers me."

Trudy doesn't move. She knows Fred is standing there and she understands his presence is a compassionate gesture. She just doesn't know whether she can accept it. Finally she says, "Maybe she's had enough of you," without raising her head.

And although Trudy can't see it, Fred begins to grin. His face cracks open into a genuine smile and he lets out a sort of guffaw that could be taken as a laugh. Trudy hopes it is a laugh.

"Maybe so," he agrees.

ON THE FIRST TUESDAY OF DECEMBER, as it nears five o'clock, Trudy tidies up the library. She is always scrupulous about opening and closing the building on time. From the end of the front desk counter, she retrieves the protest petition. There are pages and pages and pages of signatures, hundreds of them, she is very quietly proud to notice.

As Clemmie gently shoos the last people out of the library, Trudy gathers her sweater and petition and keys to lock the library. The two women walk out together, stop on the sidewalk for a moment before Clementine heads to her car and Trudy walks the four blocks home. The sun is almost down now that it's winter and the air is chilly. There may be frost on the lawn tomorrow morning.

"What's going to happen tonight?" Clementine asks.

Trudy shrugs. "I've never been to a city council meeting before, I have no idea. I'll hand over these," she says as she indicates the well-thumbed pages bursting from the clipboard.

"And will you say something? Like a little speech?"

"What for? It's all here." The thought of having to speak in public sends a spike of irritation through Trudy. *Of course not,* she tells herself, *nobody wants to hear me speak. Clemmie doesn't know what she's talking about.* But Trudy, in a rare show of discretion, refrains from telling her so.

"Seven o'clock, then."

"Are you coming?" Trudy is surprised.

"I love the park, too. I thought you knew." Clemmie says this softly, without rancor.

"Well, of course. Who wouldn't love this park?" And the two women look out over the gray green oaks and the winding paths and the gentle hillocks that form the edges of the sunken park.

AT SIX FORTY-FIVE THAT EVENING, Trudy closes and locks the front door of her small house and stands for a moment appreciating the six-foot-tall, meticulously crafted cedar fence along her property line. It is almost finished. And then, as she diagonally crosses Lima Street, she is surprised to see Fred Murakami waiting patiently on the sidewalk in front of his house.

"I thought I would go with you," he says when she nears.

She shrugs. "It's a public meeting."

The two small people fall into step beside each other, their strides matched effortlessly, a serendipity Trudy isn't used to. At six foot three, Brian was over a foot taller than she, and his legs seemed to take up most of that difference. When they walked anywhere together she had to hurry quite a bit and he had to consciously slow down.

"The fence is coming along," Trudy says as they reach the end of their block and cross the street.

"Yes. Almost finished now."

"I feel better—not seeing them."

He knows she means the Doyles, but particularly the giant rodent as he now thinks of the father.

"Ah, that's good then, isn't it? The fence will serve its purpose."

"Exactly!" Trudy is cheered that Fred immediately understands what she means.

WHEN THEY REACH THE Sierra Villa Elementary School auditorium, Fred opens the heavy door for Trudy and they are presented with a room crowded with residents. Someone has set up two long tables, end to end, at the front of the room, below the stage, with a microphone and a name card identifying each of the five city council members, one at each seat. The burgundy upholstered seats, bolted to the floor and worn from generations of proud parents watching their children's plays and graduations, are split into two sections by a narrow aisle. It is there that a podium with a microphone attached to the lip has been placed for residents' comments.

People are milling about, talking to each other, yelling across the rows of seats to neighbors they haven't seen in a while. Children are darting up and down the aisle and across the stage. The hubbub of so many voices bounces off the walls.

Trudy is taken aback. "Is it always like this?" she asks Fred.

He shakes his head. He has no idea. He's never been to one of these meetings in his life. He hates crowds—they make him feel small and mean and anxious—but he's there tonight because Trudy is presenting the petition.

They take seats close to the front and on the aisle so that Trudy can easily reach the podium microphone to present her signed petition pages. But first they have to wait through the reading of last month's minutes and discussion of new business: whether the bike lane should be extended along Foothill Boulevard, whether a building permit should be granted to turn the empty Southern

California Credit Union building into a homeless shelter. There is vigorous debate on both sides of the issues, taking up the better part of an hour.

Trudy tries to be patient, but she finds all this less than compelling. Extend the bike lane, okay, fine, what could be wrong with that? Biking is healthy. Brian would sometimes take out his bike to run an errand or two. He would have liked more bike lanes. And the other issue—of course they should build somewhere for homeless people to sleep. A slam dunk. All those nervous Nellies afraid of people down on their luck should just shut up.

When are they going to get to the park situation? She turns to Fred and whispers the question into his ear. He shrugs and can feel Trudy bristle with irritation. She wanted more than a shrug from him, but too bad. How should he know when the issue of the park will be brought up?

Trudy watches Candace Voltaug, the city council president, shuffle papers as she allows the homeless-people debate to continue. She is just the sort of woman Trudy doesn't like—self-possessed, self-important, and well dressed. She's maybe in her late thirties, Trudy guesses, and her hair is colored a startling shade of blond. She's wearing very high heels, so high they tip her hips forward when she stands. Her finely tailored black suit fits her perfectly and her nails are impeccably manicured. Trudy casts a glance at her own irregularly shaped nails on her small, stubby fingers and looks away quickly—one more thing she never finds time to do: file her nails.

Candace Voltaug has never set foot in the library as far as Trudy knows, and since she almost never misses a day of work, she can be fairly confident in her judgment that this is not a woman who values reading for herself or her children. The longer Trudy sits there and ruminates, the more ironclad the case against the woman becomes in her mind.

Finally, Scott Thurston brings up the issue of the park. And immediately Trudy gets to her feet. She doesn't even wait to be called upon. She marches to the podium, clipboard plastered across her chest like body armor. She can talk to Scott. She knows him. From time to time he and Brian would stand outside their house and talk about baseball—how the Dodgers were doing—or politics. But no, it's Candace who is in charge. It's Candace who won't relinquish the microphone.

"Identify yourself, please," Candace demands as if Trudy were some sort of alien life-form that has to be classified.

"Trudy Dugan. I live on Lima Street and I'm the librarian at the La Cruza branch." Trudy finds it difficult to keep her voice on an even keel—could she be nervous speaking to all these people? *Ridiculous,* she tells herself, *buck up.*

"The Story Lady!" a child's voice rings out from the crowd, and there are a few chuckles from parents.

Trudy ignores all that and continues on. Usually she enjoys being identified as the Story Lady, especially by the children who come to hear her, but now she is on a mission and she won't be sidetracked. She holds up the clipboard. "I have twenty-one pages of a signed petition from the citizens of Sierra Villa who want to preserve the park, who think the idea of a condo development on that land is . . ." and here Trudy pauses and searches for the absolutely correct word, "an abomination!"

Now she must be talking too loudly or too stridently, something, because all at once it's completely quiet in the room—no one rustling about in their seat, no whispering or talking on cell phones.

"What you are proposing is an affront to everything we hold dear in this community!" Trudy is surprised at how angry she is as she stands there. Her legs are shaking.

Candace Voltaug struggles, but she can't keep annoyance off her face. The last thing she wants is to raise the temperature on this debate, and here's this angry, little, badly dressed woman stirring things up even before the city council can present their point of view.

"Mrs. Dugan," she says as calmly as she can manage, "you haven't even heard the very good and cogent reasons for our consideration of the developer's offer."

"There is nothing he can say that would justify destruction of that beautiful park."

"Perhaps there is," Candace says through clenched teeth. "Perhaps you might learn something from listening first."

"Perhaps you would learn something from reading the hundreds of signatures I have here," and Trudy walks swiftly forward and plunks the clipboard on the table in front of the city council president. And now the two women are eye to eye, both far too angry for the content of their conversation.

"Take your seat, Mrs. Dugan." This is said as punitively as Candace Voltaug can muster.

"I'm not finished," Trudy finds herself saying. Where are these words coming from? She has no idea, but she seems to be on some sort of wild ride. She won't back down, and so she skates ahead on the current of anger that is propelling her.

Slowly Trudy turns to face the now-rapt audience. All eyes are on her. She sees Clementine and her kind husband, David, toward the back of the room, watching her with real sympathy in their eyes. There's that nice woman with all the children, Susannah, who signed her petition, and the older couple with the white hair from across the street. She recognizes other faces, too, from the library. All these people watching her, waiting for her to say something brilliant or noteworthy or important. Trudy has no idea what that might be, but she opens her mouth anyway and out come words.

"Why is change always good? Newer this and bigger that.

Why is that better? Why do we need to wipe out what we have in service of something we don't? I love that park." And here Trudy is mortified to find that her eyes may be filling with tears. "And I'm not the only one. If we build those disgusting cement boxes, will anyone say, 'Oh, I love my condo. It's so beautiful. It gives me such pleasure.' Will anyone say that?" And Trudy answers her own question. "Only if there's something seriously wrong with their use of language! People love living things—children, nature . . ." Now her voice falls to a whisper. "Other people . . . ," and she realizes she has to go sit down or she's going to be in trouble. But her legs are refusing to work. She looks out over the crowd and her eyes find Fred's. He's been watching her intently and somehow he knows she's in trouble. She can see it in his face.

Trudy whispers, "Other people" one more time and watches as Fred stands up, a short, graying, tidy man who finds within himself the ability to shout in this packed auditorium, "Yes!" as if he were affirming a preacher's call to arms. "Yes, we need to save the park!"

A couple seated behind Fred stands up quickly and claps. Then another, and a woman in the front row, and then Clemmie and David, and then a whole row of people, and more and more, and through it all Trudy keeps her eyes on Fred, who doesn't turn his eyes away from hers and slowly he smiles at her and slowly she heaves an enormous sigh of relief as she realizes she can now walk back to her seat and stand next to him. The fact that she's getting applause doesn't even register until she's by his side.

 *Wishing*

I LOVED A MAN ONCE. LOVING HIM TOOK ME
by surprise. He wasn't the man I was supposed to love, but he was
the man who swept me away.

I showed up at his front door with no expectations. A friend
had recommended me, that's what Owen had said when he called.
"Michael's two beagles are in love with you."

I had been walking Huey and Dewey for the past year and
Owen, newly returned to the house he owned in L.A., needed
someone to walk his dog. That's what I did to pay the rent back
then. The rest of the time I tried to write.

"I'm afraid it's a big dog," he said in that first phone call.

"I walk big dogs as well."

"A very big dog."

"Maybe I'll charge by the pound, then," I said and he laughed. I
liked that—that he laughed.

I STOOD IN FRONT OF A SMALL Spanish house, most likely built
in the 1920s, with a large arched living room window facing the

street and two or three bedrooms hidden behind in a separate wing. If you had lived in Los Angeles for as long as I had, you knew these houses. They had thick walls and curved doorways, beautiful hardwood floors, and high, pitched ceilings in the public rooms.

I rang the doorbell and immediately heard the manic scatter of a dog's nails on wood and some serious deep-pitched barking. And then Owen opened the door and I was presented with both of them, jockeying for position in the open doorway—the dog, enormous as promised, and the man slender and apologetic.

My immediate thought was that this was absolutely the wrong dog for this man. There was a dissonance about it—large, powerful, willful dog and besieged, boyish owner.

"Bandit, sit!" Owen said firmly. The tone was right. The dog ignored him. "Sit!" was said in a louder voice with the same result. "Excuse me," Owen said to me and closed the door. I heard scuffling and Owen's voice repeating the command to sit and then silence. Slowly the door opened to reveal a now-seated, extremely hairy, huge-headed, eighty-five-pound black dog and a somewhat more composed man in his late thirties facing me. His dark hair was cut short and framed a sharp-featured face that carried a hint of the child he must have been—animated and curious.

"He's a Briard . . ." Owen said, an attempt at an explanation.

"I can see that."

"Do you know the breed?"

"Smart, spirited, devoted," I said.

"Pushy, dominant, stubborn," he countered with.

I nodded. Briards could be all those things. "You didn't know that when you got him?"

"I sort of inherited him. From a friend."

"And you couldn't say, 'No thanks'?"

He shrugged, then grinned at me, somehow amused at the predicament he'd gotten himself into. "Obviously not."

And we both turned and examined the still-seated dog, whose eyes had never left Owen's face.

DURING THOSE FEW YEARS I WALKED DOGS for a living I discovered you could learn an awful lot about a person by walking into their empty house. Most people have no idea how revealing all the detritus of their life is: which magazines they subscribe to, whether they make their bed, what they choose to leave out on their bathroom sink, what they had for breakfast that's still sitting on the kitchen counter. I never snooped. I had a firm rule against opening medicine cabinets and dresser drawers, but what was in plain view was usually enough to give me some substantial clues.

In Owen's house there was practically nothing. A dining room table, round and made of oak, with two mismatched chairs. A living room empty of furniture, the floor covered by a worn but still beautiful old rug in shades of deep blue. One bedroom held a bed, pristine white walls, and nothing else. A second bedroom was completely outfitted as a working office—desk, gray metal filing cabinets, several phone lines, bulging manila folders stacked on a bookcase. On his kitchen counter were several bottles of unopened wine and a box of Cheerios. On the refrigerator there was a snapshot of a little girl, maybe three, at the beach, her blond hair wispy and blown by the wind, squinting into the camera and holding out a starfish by one of its legs. His child? There was no way to know.

THE ARRANGEMENTS WE MADE WERE THESE—I would walk Bandit five days a week, middle of the day, unless I heard from Owen. He gave me a key and said anytime between noon and two would be fine with him and Bandit. There was a dog park not too far from his house, and if I wanted to take Bandit there and let him run around, that would be fine, too.

The first few days I showed up, Owen was at the door to greet me, always polite, always grateful, and somehow rueful that I was doing this task for him, as if he felt he should be walking his own dog. But gradually, as I became a fixture, I saw less and less of him. Most days as I walked up the front path, I would see Bandit through the large living room window dancing with excitement, running back and forward from the window to the front door. As I would let myself in, Owen would yell hello from his office but not emerge.

My relationship began with Bandit and that was fine with me. It was no accident that I was struggling to master a profession that required a single-mindedness of purpose and a self-imposed isolation. I relished the solitary hours each day broken only by conversation with the canines I walked. People were harder. I exhausted myself trying to meet expectations I was sure they had of me—perpetual good humor, constant attentiveness, smart conversation, and never a moment of neediness. All the dogs asked of me is that I show up on time and get them out of the house quickly. That I could do without breaking a sweat.

WALKING BANDIT MADE IT ABUNDANTLY CLEAR that Owen wasn't much good with boundaries. The Briard was affectionate and rambunctious but obviously believed he had as much right to make decisions and lead discussions as I did. He would not turn left when we hit the sidewalk in front of the house, because the dog park loomed several blocks to the right. He would listen to my firm and calm voice telling him to sit at each intersection and then blithely pull me across the street. No one had broken the news to him that he was a dog and, as such, was supposed to take his lead from the humans in his life.

I could tell without ever sharing a personal conversation that Owen valued spontaneity over protocol and exuberance over orderliness and that rules held no sway in his universe. I had found my polar opposite.

For most of my life I felt as though I was in the middle of a military maneuver—doing what was asked of me, never straying outside the lines, and avoiding anything that would garner undue notice. The only time I ever felt free was when I was writing. Maybe because it felt like a secret and slightly subversive activity, I carried no rules over to that realm. And allowed no one else in. I was still at that tentative, terrifying stage where I wanted to be able to write but had no confidence I would be able to master the mystery of it. I carried the kernel of that desire within me at all times. Sometimes it was all that pushed me forward—that incipient desire.

AS I LOOK BACK ON IT NOW, the first strong feeling I had about Owen was envy. When I would let myself into his house and gather Bandit's leash from the front hall closet, I would often hear Owen laughing on the phone, a rolling, infectious sound that ended with hiccups of glee. It was the freedom in that laugh that drew me in. And I would hear it a lot. If only, I thought at times, if only I could be free enough to laugh like that.

I gradually picked up, from overheard snippets of conversation, that he worked in the nonprofit world grant writing or fund-raising, something like that, something that relied on social skills and networking and a passionate belief in the goodness of the cause. I heard the charm and the laughter in his voice and the long periods of listening he did on the phone often punctuated with "Yes, that's exactly right!" making the listener feel he had managed to say something brilliant.

It was his voice, I would have to say, that first drew me toward him, his voice which carried the lilt of his spirit. I would often stop with my hand on Bandit's leash and listen to the rise and fall of Owen's voice and wait for the laugh and the "Yes! Yes!" as he validated whoever was speaking, and then I could snap the leash to Bandit's collar and let him lead me out the front door.

I didn't give all this much thought at the time. I was supremely self-involved, as only beginning writers can be. My few friends from college who would have forced me outside my isolation had scattered after graduation—back to hometowns far from L.A. or to jobs in other big cities—making it only easier to ignore the rest of the world. Only Jennie, my college roommate, was still close by, but she had moved in with a new boyfriend and had very little time right then for our friendship.

I didn't mind. It felt as though all that was essential for my survival happened in those quiet morning hours before the rest of the world was stirring and my obligations began. From the corner of my tiny second-floor bedroom where I had set up my desk, I would watch the sky lighten and the sun spill over the Hollywood Hills in the distance and I would write and despair and write some more and finally despair too much. Had I managed to write an acceptable paragraph in three hours? Should I pare down the opening of my story? What happens next to my characters? What happens?

My head was always full of a completely made-up universe that felt so much more compelling than the mundane world I inhabited. That may be why, one day when I went to return Bandit, I didn't notice glass shards glistening along the driveway like a trail of diamonds.

Owen had been gone when I picked up Bandit. That wasn't unusual. I knew immediately when I let myself in that the house was empty, Owen's absence as great a presence as his actual being. Bandit more than made up for the quiet with barking leaps of

happiness. He jumped as if his legs were made of springs, encircling me with a pent-up energy that directed me straight to the
dog park.

We were gone a little more than an hour. That's usually the
time it took for Bandit to flop down at my feet, long pink tongue
hanging sideways out of his mouth, utterly spent from running
circles around the perimeter of the park and tumbling across the
grass with whichever dog would comply. His prostrate body was
my cue to stand up, attach his leash, and begin the slow walk
home.

I was filling Bandit's water dish in the laundry room when
I heard Owen's car pull up. I lingered. I had to admit to myself
that I lingered so that we would see each other as he came in. Our
conversations were always inconsequential, but something about
them sustained me through the rest of my solitary day. Often he'd
tell me something he'd just done and I would laugh with him. Or
I would give him a report on Bandit's exercise and he would listen
as attentively as if I were divulging national security secrets.

This day, though, he came into the house, worried, his face
dark and his energy tight.

"There's glass on the driveway."

And in the next second his eyes found the broken kitchen window and his face melted with recognition. It was only then that I
also saw the vandalism.

"It must have happened while we were gone. Bandit wouldn't
have let anyone in otherwise."

"Unless it was someone he knew," Owen said as he walked
through the kitchen and into the other rooms of the house. He
didn't invite me but I followed, and when we ended up in his
office I saw that one of the windows in that room had been left
open, the screen pushed out, as if someone had exited the house
that way.

Owen scanned his files, the paperwork on his desk, double-checking that it was all there.

"Is anything missing?"

"No."

And then his eyes settled on the bookshelf where the bottles of wine from the kitchen had been arranged on the top in the shape of an arrow pointing to the open window. "This was meant as a message."

"Telling you what?"

"Just announcing his presence."

"You know some strange people."

"I used to."

And then, because there was a moment of awkward silence— I didn't know what to say and he wasn't about to elaborate—he asked me, "Would you like a cup of tea?"

I said yes although I never drank tea. I said yes because he still seemed upset. I said yes because I didn't want to leave.

We sat at his round dining room table in the two mismatched chairs. Bandit slept at Owen's feet, snoring slightly from time to time. The tea Owen made us was some kind of herbal concoction and I didn't like it, but I sipped it anyway.

"What do you do with the rest of your time?" Owen asked me.

"I walk other people's dogs."

"And when you're not doing that?"

I hesitated. My morning hours at my desk were so sequestered from the rest of my life I wasn't sure I wanted to tell him, and so I was slow to answer.

"Is it illegal?"

And that made me laugh. "No, just fragile," I said.

And he nodded as if he understood. "Just being born?"

"Yes."

"And each day, you're not sure it won't all collapse and there you will be, back where you started without anything to show for all your effort."

I just looked at him without answering—how did he get inside my head?

"Can you tell me what it is?"

He was looking directly at me as he spoke, his brown eyes never left my face. He was wearing a blue shirt, I remember, bright blue with the cuffs rolled up on strong forearms. His body leaned forward over the table and his naked hands cupped his mug of tea. He was waiting with infinite patience. The rest of the world receded to the periphery of my consciousness and in that moment there was only the two of us sitting in this high-ceilinged room looking at each other. It unnerved me—the intensity of his interest, the answering pull within me that I suddenly recognized. What was happening here?

I stood up quickly, took my mug of tea to the kitchen sink, and only then managed to say, without looking at him, trying to keep my voice light, "Oh, I'm messing about trying to write some short stories."

He followed me into the kitchen. "Exciting, isn't it?"

"Sometimes . . . when I get it right." Then the truth: "Yes, it is." And we smiled at each other.

THAT DAY SHIFTED OUR ROUTINE, imperceptibly, but definitely. After that, oftentimes if he wasn't on the phone, we would sit at Owen's oak table and drink tea, and then coffee when I finally confessed that caffeine was my lifeline, and we would talk. He seemed to be home more often, and I made sure I had no dogs waiting for me in the early afternoon.

What did we talk about? At first it was our work lives. I learned about the nonprofit, Art into Life, that convinced him to come back to California and fund-raise for them. Their mission was to pair working artists—writers, painters, poets, architects, photographers—with afterschool programs in the city schools. It was a way for kids who had never been to a museum or read a book that wasn't assigned in school to see, learn, and try out their creative wings. The organization was in its third year of operation, long enough to convince the community that they were viable, but not yet at the stage to make the kind of impact they envisioned. That's where Owen came in.

Living and working in New York, Owen had been employed by a small family foundation that gave out yearly grants to carefully chosen artists, three or four at a time. The last awards had gone to a weaver who created wall hangings from used denim, a glass artist who constructed Tiffany-style lamps, and a conceptual artist who used found sites—an abandoned gas station, a crumbling factory—to stage his work. All very well and good, Owen said, supporting an individual artist's work, but when this job came to him he decided reaching kids at an early age was an even better idea, and he came back to L.A. where he had lived before, and reclaimed the house he had been renting out.

I wondered if the person who had broken into the house had been his renter, communicating something like *You made me leave* with those wine bottles arranged in an arrow and pointing out the window. Whoever did it was angry, that much was clear.

But I didn't ask. There seemed to be an implicit etiquette to those early conversations. Each of us spoke about what we wanted the other to know. And each of us listened and accepted and didn't probe. It worked. A sense of shelter grew, a sense of being heard but not challenged.

When we sat in that quiet dining room in the early afternoon, the sun coming in through the westward-facing windows, I felt safe enough to talk about the work I had done that morning at my desk or even the struggle I'd put up with nothing to show for it. Owen was the only person in my life then who knew about my writing.

My parents, who lived in Pleasanton, in Northern California, would call dutifully every Sunday night and, from time to time, carefully raise the question of what I was planning on doing with my life. It was my mother who would always preface her inquiry with "I know the first few years after graduation are for figuring out what you want to do," and then my father, on the extension, would jump in and remind me of how expensive my UCLA education had been. There was no way I could ameliorate the fact that their college-educated daughter was spending her days taking dogs for a walk and picking up poop without telling them about the writing. And I wasn't ready to do that. My father, who was a scientist and worked at the neighboring Lawrence Livermore National Laboratory doing something with national defense contracts that he couldn't ever completely explain to us, would have dismissed a literary career as a pipe dream. My mother, who had spent her career as a middle-school counselor in the Alameda County School System, would have worried about the amount of rejection I would have to suffer.

But with Owen, the words rushed out of my mouth. "I had a good morning!" I would say as we sat down. And he would put the two mugs of coffee on the table, sit down across from me, and say, "Tell me," as if he hadn't anywhere else to be or anything else to do. "Tell me everything"—as if my progress made him personally happy, as if he had a stake in it. And so I would. I have never had a traditional mentor in my life, but those early afternoons with Owen were as close as I ever got.

That's where things rested for months. I walked Bandit five days a week. Owen and I had our midday coffee in his dining room when he was home. He listened eagerly and because I was so hungry to share my early morning secret, I was the one who talked and talked. Over those months I learned very little about his life until late one Thursday night, after midnight, when my phone rang, startling me awake. Owen sounded frantic.

"Bandit's gone" were his first words. I wasn't fully awake. I didn't quite understand.

"Gone where?"

"I just got home and he's not here and the backyard gate is open."

"I'm sure I didn't—" I started to say.

"No, of course not," he cut me off, "I didn't mean to imply. I just picked up the phone without thinking." I heard him take a deep breath and then another. "I woke you," he said, sounding only minimally calmer. "I'm sorry, Anna. What can you do? Please, go back to sleep."

"I'll be there in ten minutes."

WHEN I PULLED UP TO OWEN'S HOUSE, the kitchen and dining room lights were blazing. I could see him pacing as I let myself in through the back door.

"I walked the streets calling him but it's dark and he's black and . . ." He sat down at the table. "Nothing."

"Has he done this before? Gotten out?"

"Never."

"Let's try again. We'll take the car. You drive and I'll look—we can cover more area that way."

Slowly Owen drove the dark streets of his neighborhood. The streetlights were dim and far apart, yielding only modest pools of amber light here and there. Most of the small houses were dark by now as well. It was close to one in the morning.

"Try the dog park," I said, and Owen turned left and then left again and there was the shuttered gate of the park, padlocked for the night.

We got out of the car and walked the perimeter, calling the dog's name into the empty air. He would have come if he had heard us. I knew that. He wasn't there.

"I'm so sorry," Owen said.

I shook my head.

"This is my problem and I woke you up. I don't know what I thought. . . ."

We were back at his car, our eyes still searching the blackness with the hope of somehow seeing a large black dog come loping out of the gloom toward us.

"I love this dog, too," I told him, and it was true. This furry, ill-trained, exuberant dog had gathered in a piece of my heart. I put my hand on Owen's arm and he took my hand in his without looking at me.

"I don't know what I'll do if he's gone for good," he said. "I didn't want him, that's the truth, and I certainly didn't want to love him, but here we are."

"Let's drive the streets again."

And we did, only this time Owen drove with one hand and held my hand with his other. I scanned the sidewalks and front yards for a hint of motion, any motion, and called Bandit's name as Owen inched the car down street after street. And then, when we were very close to his house, I saw a man—he seemed quite young, maybe early twenties—standing under one of the street-lights, his long blond hair bright against the darkness. Bandit sat by his side, calmly, a leash attached to his collar. It looked like they were waiting to be found.

Owen was looking to his left, his eyes scanning the opposite side of the street, so he didn't see the man smile and then spread his arms out as if to say, *Here I am.* His blond hair fell over his shoulders and shimmered in the light. He looked like an angel.

"Owen, look!"

I was watching the man and Bandit, so I didn't see Owen's face when he saw the pair, but I felt the car jolt to a stop and heard him swear, "Of all the fucking idiotic—"

The blond man ambled over to Owen's window and looked in. His eyes did a swift sweep of me before smiling at Owen.

"I found your dog," he said.

"None of this is the least bit amusing, you know."

The man shrugged and then grinned. He was beautiful. He knew he was beautiful.

"Put the dog in the car," Owen said without a trace of civility in his voice.

The man opened the back door and Bandit happily leapt in, but the man wasn't done. He kept his hand on Owen's door through the open window.

"Very nice, Owen," he said, looking at me.

"Go home, Tony." And the man stepped back, raised his hands in surrender.

For the two blocks it took to get Bandit home, Owen said nothing and his eyes never left the road. I watched his profile, waiting for him to speak, willing him to explain—who was this Tony?—but I said nothing. I remember feeling, as we drove home, that Owen's anger put up an impenetrable shield. It's what I told myself at the time.

BOTH OF US STOOD IN OWEN'S KITCHEN and watched Bandit drink from his water bowl as if he had just returned from a forced march through the Sahara—loud slurping noises and water spraying half the laundry room floor.

"I really thought he was gone," Owen said.

We stood close together. I nodded. I was afraid of that, too.

"Did that man, that Tony, find him, do you think?"

"No," Owen said, "he took him."

"And broke into your house," I suddenly knew.

"Yes."

"Not the best friend to have."

Owen turned and looked at me then. He took my hand again. "I'm trying, Anna," he said and then put his other hand on the side of my face.

When he leaned in to kiss me, the certainty leapt up within me that I had been waiting since the day I met him to move into his arms, to feel his body against mine. We stood in the brightly lit kitchen kissing softly until Owen turned off the light and led me into his bedroom, the one that contained a single bed. That night it was all that we needed.

Feeling Owen's naked body against mine was a revelation. There was none of the awkwardness of the first time, that fumbling discovery of a new body that feels, at first, like a foreign country. Not with Owen. Our bodies knew each other—that's the only way I can describe it. Touching Owen, moving with Owen, looking up into his face—it felt like coming home.

"Finally," Owen whispered into the darkness as we lay beside each other afterward.

I turned to face him. I'd had sex with enough men to know that something else entirely had happened here. "Owen, what is this?"

"Shhh . . ." he said and he pulled the sheet over us and drew me so close to him that I no longer knew where my skin ended and his began.

I woke just as the sky was lightening through his uncurtained windows. Owen slept on his stomach, sprawled across the bed with the same unself-conscious abandon I associated with his laugh.

In the morning light I distrusted my own sense of what had

happened the night before. I needed to be back in my apartment, at my desk, anchored to my small and tidy life, not swept away into this confusing territory. Who was this man? What was I doing? There was something tugging at a corner of my consciousness that told me to step back. I wasn't sure if it was my natural caution or something more. *I should leave,* I told myself, *while he's sleeping.* I got up and put my clothes on quietly.

But I couldn't go without touching him. It was impossible. I leaned down and kissed him lightly on the side of his face. He smiled without opening his eyes. "You going?"

"Work," I said.

"Mmmm, so glad I'm your work," he said, "I get to see you later."

And then I couldn't leave at all. I sat down next to him and he gathered me into his arms. "Stay," he said. And I did.

WHEN WE WERE ALONE IN HIS HOUSE or sometimes in my tiny apartment, we were both happy. Of that I am sure. And for a while, that was all we needed. The two of us, with time carved out of the rest of our lives, filled to the brim with the other's presence. Owen would joke that we should find some small but fertile island somewhere in the Pacific or Caribbean and make a break for it. We could live out the rest of our days there, he said, supremely happy with each other.

"You are the love of my life," he told me one day while we were preparing dinner together at his house. Owen had put some music on, the jazz he liked that I was struggling to understand, and had poured us each a glass of wine. For some reason I remember that on his refrigerator door along with the picture of his niece holding the starfish was a picture he had snapped of me running with a joyful Bandit across the grass of the dog park. I remember thinking that we were beginning to invade each other's lives just a little.

While I chopped and he sautéed the vegetables for the soup we were making, he was telling me about a workshop he'd observed that afternoon. A young poet, female, black, was working with a group of fourth graders who'd never read a poem in their lives.

"Every time she got to the end of a line, this one kid would pipe up, 'That don't make no sense.' Then she'd read the next line and he'd say the same thing. 'That one don't make no sense, either.'"

Owen was laughing as he told me the story and I began to laugh with him. We got the giggles in his kitchen as he mimicked the child's voice and then the poet's stern "Wait a minute . . ." whenever the child interrupted.

I was leaning against the kitchen counter, knife still in hand, wiping tears of laughter from the corners of my eyes when Owen just fell silent, mid-story, and the silence hung between us.

"What?" I said.

And that's when he said it. "You are the love of my life, Anna."

I heard my intake of breath in the quiet kitchen. I was staggered. I couldn't say a word.

He grinned at me. "That's a good thing."

"I know," I said, overwhelmed with the wonder that we had found each other. Owen, understanding without another word being said, gathered me into his arms.

I LOOK BACK NOW AND THINK, *If only, if only we had been able to keep the world at bay.* But that's the dream of any woman newly in love. We all have pasts. We all have secrets waiting for the right time to tell. There is no way for the now not to be contaminated by the lives we'd lived before.

. . .

WE WERE VERY CAREFUL AT FIRST. I continued to write in the early morning hours, even if it meant leaving Owen's bed at first light. I continued to walk Bandit and Huey and Dewey and my other clients' dogs. Most days Owen was home when I got there to pick up Bandit but not always. We made dates. We didn't willy-nilly overrun each other's life within days or even weeks of sleeping together. Neither of us, it seemed, wanted to rush things. I understood my natural reticence to plunge headlong into any new thing. I wasn't sure why Owen felt the same way, "reticent" not being an adjective I would ever associate with him. At the time I thought he was respecting my pace, not pushing for more time, more of me, because he understood I would have been uncomfortable.

And then we had the opportunity to go public. The head of Owen's nonprofit, Christina Johar, was hosting a party to welcome two new photographers into the fold. "We should go," Owen said one day as we sat in his dining room, having our mid-afternoon coffee, Bandit snoring at our feet, and I readily agreed. I was more than curious about this other world of Owen's, his professional life. I was hungry for more of him.

We drove into the Hollywood Hills, east of Vine Street, "Old Hollywood" as it was known because when the film industry was in its infancy, this was where all the talent lived. As we climbed higher and higher on streets that narrowed and bent in hairpin turns around themselves, Owen told me a little about his boss. She was married to an Indian doctor, hence the "Johar," but had grown up outside Atlanta on a sort of plantation. "Minus the slaves, of course," he added and I shook my head, smiling, as he knew I would.

She had impeccable manners coupled with a steely sense of purpose and therefore managed to accomplish a myriad of things while retaining the affection of almost everyone she dealt with. Owen adored her.

When the iconic Hollywood sign—enormous white letters
blazingly lit and spread across a hillside—popped into view, Owen
pulled the car over to the curb and let one of the parking valets
whisk it away. In front of us was a long and very steep set of stairs
that led, presumably, to the house.

We climbed hand in hand, our breath becoming more ragged
the higher we got until finally we crested on a flat pad of land that
held the house. The view was spectacular. We could see the few
tall buildings that made up the downtown skyline. This was 1976
and the major downtown building boom of the 1990s was fifteen
years away. When we turned west, we could see straight to the
setting sun, pink and orange tendrils gripping the horizon line at
the Pacific Ocean. A 180-degree vista.

And then there was the house. I'm sure it had been designed
by some mid-century architect, although I couldn't have told
you who. But someone had had an idiosyncratic vision and
built a structure that seemed to float on air, out over the hillside,
anchored by massive steel beams plunged into the rock. Through
the floor-to-ceiling panels of glass that stood in for the front walls,
we could see groups of people holding drinks and milling about.
Floating out of the house was the forced laughter and busy chatter
of cocktail party talk.

Instantly I regretted my decision to come. I was never much
good at small talk or glib conversation, and the scene in front of
us seemed like an obstacle course I was ill prepared to navigate. I
said nothing, but that didn't stop Owen from answering me anyway. "We don't have to stay long."

I rested my chin on his shoulder and we both took in the
brightly colored scene in front of us. "Is there a safe harbor in
there?"

"I'll find you one."

And we walked in.

Christina greeted us at the door. She was a woman somewhere

around forty, I guessed, who looked like she spent a great deal
of her life making sure she was beautiful. Even I, who wallowed
comfortably most days in sweats, could tell how expensive her
clothes and jewelry were and marvel at the amazing cut of her
blond hair, which swung with every movement of her head and
settled right back into place.

She embraced Owen briefly and then turned her considerable
scrutiny on me. "Anna," she said, "we must talk," and grabbed my
hand and led me through the crowded living room and out the
enormous glass doors onto the terrace. Looking backward as we
traversed the living room, I mouthed to Owen, "Safe harbor?" and
he shrugged, as if to say, *Maybe, maybe not.*

"I've wanted to meet you for months," she said as she led me to
a corner of the terrace where the view was even more spectacular.

"Really?" I was genuinely surprised. Owen had talked about
me at work?

"Well, we're all mad about Owen, you know. I've known him
for years and years. Did he tell you that?"

I shook my head. He hadn't.

"From his days in New York. When I was single and he was
single, of course, and we . . ." She trailed off.

"Had a relationship?"

"Oh no, no," and she laughed. "I was going to say when we
helped each other through, but that makes it sound like we
were in trouble when really we were in that section of life when
nothing makes sense. The beginning of your twenties—oh, so
confusing."

I nodded. I was in the beginning of my twenties and she was
confusing me. My eyes sought out Owen through the open terrace doors, and as Christina continued on about how she had met
Owen—at a gallery opening—and how coincidental it was that
they lived within three blocks of each other, and how they'd meet

at a restaurant halfway between their apartments at least twice a
week, I saw him standing in front of a wall of bookshelves talking to a man who, even from this distance, seemed intense and
brooding. The other man was doing all the talking, gesturing as he
spoke, touching Owen's chest to make a point. There was something about what I was witnessing that made me uncomfortable,
but I couldn't have named it then.

At a certain point Owen looked up and saw me watching, and
the expression that flashed across his face made no sense to me. It
looked like grief. I shook my head at him and instantly he smiled,
said something to the man, and moved across the living room
toward me.

Christina watched him come, stopped herself mid-story, and
said quietly to me, "He's crazy about you. Remember that."

We left soon after and on the way home, I did all the talking.
Owen answered if I asked a question, but that was all. We pulled
into his driveway, got out of the car, and started walking to the
back door.

"It's still early," I said. "Do you feel like dinner? I really didn't
eat anything there."

He took my hand, shook his head, and led me into the house,
into the bedroom. He kissed me with an urgency that felt like a
test—did I feel the same way? He undressed me quickly and took
me to bed with a single-mindedness that unnerved me. Afterward,
he gathered me against his body, my head on his chest, and said
nothing as he stroked my hair. His heartbeat raced beneath my
ear. I listened for a long time till it gradually slowed enough for
me to drift off to sleep.

THE NEXT MORNING I WOKE TO AN empty bed and a sense that
something had shifted. Owen wasn't in the house, but I found

him sitting on the patio where we often had our morning coffee. Unlike the sparsely furnished house, someone had spent hours and hours in the garden making it lush and beautiful. Now, at the beginning of the summer, there were lavender and butterfly bushes in shades of purple, coral astromeria on long, thin stems, and one whole wall of iceberg roses against a side fence, cups of white petals splattered against the dark green foliage.

Owen sat at the glass-topped table, his gaze out over the lawn to the property-line fence, where scarlet bougainvillea made a waterfall of blossoms and a green-throated hummingbird pinwheeled from flower to flower. His right thumb drummed against the handle of his coffee cup in a rhythm he wasn't even aware of.

"Owen," I said softly as I slipped into the chair next to him, "talk to me."

And so he did. "Did you see the man I was talking to last night when you were with Christina?"

"Yes. He seemed so intense. Like he was trying to win an argument."

Owen nodded. "Always."

"You've known him for a while?"

"Not well, but yes, for years."

I was sure I didn't want to hear the answer to my next question, but I asked it anyway. "What was he trying to convince you of?"

"To go home with him."

And I knew what he meant.

Finally, Owen looked at me. "If you hadn't been there, I would have. Do you understand what I'm saying?"

And I did. In that moment I knew I had understood all along. It was what had kept me from asking too many questions. It was the worry tugging just outside my consciousness.

"You would have had sex with him."

"Yes."

"Then what are you doing with me?"

"I love you."

I shook my head. None of this made any sense to me. I was still too young and too inexperienced to understand how a man could love me and our lovemaking but still have a more elemental pull within him that trumped it all.

"I thought . . ." Owen stopped and then began again. "Anna, I hoped . . . No," he said more firmly, "I was starting to believe that all the rest of it would fall away."

"But it hasn't."

There was a long moment of silence before Owen answered my question, which really wasn't a question at all. "No."

We didn't look away from each other. We studied the other's face and that made the whole conversation infinitely harder.

"Are you telling me this because you want to stop seeing me?"

"I'm telling you this because it happened."

He waited for me to say something. The only thing I could manage was the truth. "I don't know if I can simply get up and walk out of here."

I saw relief flood his face and I grabbed onto it as validation that I should stay, that he wanted me to stay. But in the end what he wanted or I wanted didn't matter. It took me a while to understand that, and so we continued on in a relationship that was vastly altered and yet, in its heart, remained unchanged.

For a while we were held aloft by our belief that transformation was possible, or that it might be. Then one or the other of us would falter and lose hope, but never at the same time. We went forward hobbled and hurting, and so we clung more desperately to each other. It was during one of those times, when the way forward seemed impossible and the way out seemed more so, that I finally understood Owen as I had to.

IT WAS AN ORDINARY MONDAY, the middle of the day, and I had
come to pick up Bandit for our walk. As I let myself in through
the front door, I heard voices in the backyard. Angry, yelling
voices. One was Owen's and it shocked me. Over all the months
we had spent together I had never heard him raise his voice. But
these voices were shouting over each other, not listening, spewing
forth emotion without any censor.

I remember I had Bandit's leash in my hand and that the dog
was skating with anticipation in circles around me, but I didn't
snap on the leash and leave with him. Those desperate male
voices pulled me through the house and out the back door to the
patio, where just the day before Owen and I had had breakfast
and talked about a weekend trip to Laguna to let Bandit run on
the beach, to get away together.

It was the wholesale destruction that hit me first. All the
beautiful plants uprooted, the butterfly bushes and lavender flung
across the lawn, the daylilies and impatiens trampled underfoot,
their leaves mashed into a green pulp. There was something so
raw and naked about the damage, such a statement of annihila-
tion. The patio was littered with tender white rose petals, the
bushes strewn across the bricks like debris. It felt like madness
had been let loose in the yard.

And there was Tony ripping the remaining plants from the
soil, screaming at Owen that his work wasn't appreciated, that
Owen didn't deserve such beauty, that Owen was selfish and self-
deluding and treacherous.

And there was Owen screaming back at Tony that he didn't
want this kind of craziness, that he had the right to decide what
kind of life he lived. And then Tony whirled around and for a
moment the two men faced each other, no more than two feet
between them, both breathing hard, and then Tony spat out,

"Coward!" and turned and continued to destroy all the beautiful work he had done.

I didn't move. I couldn't. What I was witnessing was ugly and vindictive, something no one in their right mind would want to experience, and yet . . . and yet . . . the very air in that small backyard seemed charged with portent, the way the atmosphere feels before a storm, ions scattering and reassembling with restless speed. And the angry words, the screaming voices were the lightning strikes across the sky—sizzling, burning, and crackling with energy.

As much as I believed Owen as he screamed—"I don't want this. Get out! Get out of my life!"—I knew without a doubt that what I saw before me went to the core of who Owen was. Not the angry words, nor even the craziness of it all. Not the ugliness. No, I knew Owen well enough to be sure of that.

But it was the intensity of the connection, that's what I finally understood. Owen was tied to this beautiful, provocative person in a way he would never be to me.

I turned, went into the house, and put Bandit's leash down on the dining room table where I knew Owen would find it and know that I had been there. Then I got down on my knees and buried my face in the bountiful fur of the dog's neck and whispered over and over, "I'm sorry. . . . I'm so sorry," until finally I could stand and let myself out through the front door for the last time.

OVER THE YEARS, I HEARD THAT OWEN had moved back to New York, then Texas, for some reason. I went back to school and got a master's in creative writing. The discipline of those two years helped me finish my short story collection, and the master's helped me land a teaching job at a California State University campus where many of my students were bilingual.

I met my husband there. He was teaching political science and we both stood up at the same time during a faculty meeting to protest the plan to slash the Chicano studies department's budget. This was in the early 1980s when the cultural expansiveness of the sixties and seventies had run its course.

Soon after we married, our daughter was born, and my life was so busy—new baby, new marriage, a full teaching load—that each day felt like a mountain to scale. But I was happy. I had married the right man. I was besotted with Grace, our daughter. When I thought of Owen, it was hard for me to remember the young girl who walked dogs for a living and loved a charming, graceful man who wanted to love her back.

And then he called me. My daughter was just turning four, and we were having a discussion about whether she could wear her party dress to preschool when the phone rang. I was distracted when I picked it up. We were late, the discussion had gone on too long, and I was just about ready to give in—what difference did it make if she wore her party dress to sit in the sandbox?

"Anna?" is all he said and I found myself reaching for a chair, my legs giving out under me.

"Owen."

He laughed. "That was quick," and immediately I thought, *I've missed that laugh.*

"Would you be able to have lunch with me?" he asked. "I'm in town."

"Yes."

ON THE DAY WE HAD ARRANGED I made sure Gracie had a playdate after preschool, and I drove to the restaurant in West Hollywood with a certain amount of trepidation. More than ten years had passed. We were at the end of the 1980s. The country had changed. My life had changed radically. I was bound to two people I cherished beyond measure—my husband, Alex, and our daughter. I had no idea how Owen had spent the past decade and what changes those experiences had wrought within him. Would we even have anything to say to each other?

I parked my car—a young mother's car, a safe, sturdy Volvo—on a side street and walked down Santa Monica Boulevard to Crespi's and then stood outside trying to gather some calm into my racing heart. The restaurant was a small place with a dark green awning and the sleek lines of a modern café. I knew the person at the reservation desk was going to be young and thin and wearing black and would show me to our table with a slight swagger. As it turned out, I didn't even notice who that was because when I walked into the restaurant, Owen was already there, head down, reading the menu.

Oh, how much older he looks was my first thought. He was thinner. His face was gaunt, but when he looked up and saw me, his smile transformed his face and I saw the Owen I remembered.

I walked toward him with my heart hammering again, but when he stood and opened his arms and gathered me in, all the ten years of absence evaporated. My body still knew his body and something within me instantly settled.

"Beautiful still," he said with his arms encircling me.

I shook my head as I pulled away and we both sat down. It was something I never believed about myself except for those months with Owen.

At first all we did was look at each other, without a word, just looking to take in the other's face, to make sure we could find the person we used to know so intimately in a face changed by a decade of living. Without the smile, the face I examined looked vastly changed. I wondered if he felt the same way about me.

We didn't make small talk. We ordered to get the waiter out of our hair and then we put our hands on the table and began.

"Did you bring pictures?" Owen asked. Somehow he knew I

had married and had a daughter. Maybe through Michael, whose dogs first brought us together and who subsequently became a friend. I didn't know. It didn't matter.

I had brought snapshots of Grace and handed them over. "She looks like her father."

"Oh," he said, "I'd never get tired of looking at this sweet face."

"I know," I said, so grateful he saw what I did in Gracie.

And then over lunch I told him one Gracie story after another. How she insisted on cutting her own hair when she was two. How she wouldn't go to her best friend's birthday party because the little girl had "said a mean thing" to her. How she spent an entire year wearing only pink, even her shoes had to be pink. He listened in that absorbed way he had listened to my recitation of Bandit's outings, with complete interest, his eyes never leaving my face.

I felt like I was rattling on too long, so I finished with the unnecessary declaration that my daughter was strong willed and sure of herself and that she has been teaching her mother to be a bit more flexible and mellow.

Owen raised his eyebrows in disbelief and I knew instantly what he was saying—*Anna, flexible? In what universe?*—and I laughed even though he hadn't said a word and told him I had qualified the statement with "a bit."

"Now you," I said, "tell me."

And he did. Years back in New York working as a dean at the NYU Tisch School of the Arts, a second house in Texas because the state has no income tax.

"Really?" I said. "There's more to the story than that."

And he grinned, pleased, it seemed, that I had caught him up, but he didn't elaborate.

"Are you happy, Anna?" he asked me over coffee. And I could honestly tell him I was.

"I married a good man," I said, and he nodded as if that fact gave him tremendous comfort.

"You know," he started, then stopped for a second but pushed on. "I still feel guilty—"

"No," I cut him off.

"Because I should have told you sooner."

"It wouldn't have made any difference." I said this unequivocally.

"I think about that a lot. I should have, but I don't know if I could have. I wanted—"

"The same thing I wanted. To love you."

He nodded. "Yes. To love you."

And there it was, out on the table. I didn't blame him. I had no regrets. I loved him still and he saw it. He saw it all. It was easy for me to ask then, "Are you with someone?"

"Yes. Matt. For several years now. He's from Texas," and Owen grinned at me.

"Aha, the Texas connection. And is he good to you?"

"Yes."

"With no drama?"

He looked at me quizzically.

"The last time I saw you Tony was ripping plants out of your garden."

He shook his head remembering, then smiled gently at me. "Much less drama, but, Anna, there's something else." And that's when his eyes left my face and fell to the table, where his beautiful hands played with the silverware. I waited. He kept shaking his head as if he couldn't or shouldn't say what he had come to say.

He took my hand finally and looked up. "Matt is very sick. . . ."

Oh no, I thought, *please don't . . .*

"And I needed to tell you. . . . He wasn't when I met him. . . .

At least we didn't know enough six years ago to know. . . . And because we've been together . . . I'm sick as well, Anna. . . ."

He's going to die. In those early days of the AIDS epidemic there was no hope. He was going to die.

"No!" I heard myself say. It was a groan and I put my hands over my face and began to sob. I had no control over the sounds that came from me. Something split apart and a cataract of grief I had yet to know in my young and sheltered life rose up and poured out of me.

"Please, Anna," he said, but I couldn't stop. I had a husband I loved and a daughter who was the world to me, but at that moment the fact that Owen was dying overwhelmed it all.

"Anna," he said, "don't. We've been so lucky."

And I looked up at him finally, at this person who was as dear to me as anyone I had ever known, and knew in my soul what Owen had given me. Only Owen would say we were lucky. Only Owen would be so grateful in the face of what was to come.

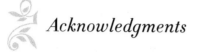 *Acknowledgments*

Without the encouragement and wisdom of my two first readers, Karin Costello and the mysterious Jenny Wolkind, these stories would never have been written. They know they have all my love and profound gratitude.

Lynn Pleshette has supported my writing for over thirty years, and Marly Rusoff grabbed hold with no lifeline and had the courage to go forth. Thank you both for believing in my work against all odds.

And Nan Talese opened her heart to me and my stories and made this book a reality. There is no way to convey my overwhelming appreciation.

A NOTE ABOUT THE AUTHOR

Deena Goldstone is a screenwriter who has worked in feature films and television movies. She lives in Pasadena, California, with her family.

A NOTE ABOUT THE TYPE

This book was set in Celeste, a typeface created in 1994 by the designer Chris Burke. He describes it as a modern, humanistic face having less contrast between thick and thin strokes than other modern types such as Bodoni, Didot, and Walbaum. Tempered by some old-style traits and with a contemporary, slightly modular letterspacing, Celeste is highly readable and especially adapted for current digital printing processes which render an increasingly exacting letterform.